THE
BEDROOM
WINDOW

BOOKS BY K.L. SLATER

Safe With Me

Blink

Liar

The Mistake

The Visitor

The Secret

Closer

Finding Grace

The Silent Ones

Single

Little Whispers

The Girl She Wanted

The Marriage

The Evidence

The Widow

Missing

The Girlfriend

The Narrator

THE BEDROOM WINDOW

K.L. SLATER

bookouture

Published by Bookouture in 2023

An imprint of Storyfire Ltd.
Carmelite House
50 Victoria Embankment
London EC4Y 0DZ

www.bookouture.com

ISBN: 978-1-83790-409-9
eBook ISBN: 978-1-83790-408-2

horror that cannot be faked and it's going to take a great deal of elbow grease to remove every speck.

She's left the most taxing job until last. The master bedroom is the worst affected and it takes her over an hour to thoroughly clean it and change the bedding. Finally, she bags up all the stained and spoiled items and throws open the windows, allowing herself a moment to stand on the balcony and inhale the fresh, salty tang of sea air.

She strips off her soiled clothes and adds them to the disposal bag before heading for the rainforest shower in the family bathroom with its gold taps and immaculate marble surfaces. The scalding rush of water blasts all the filth from her skin and hair and she relishes the cleansing sight of it disappearing down the plughole. A fluffy bath sheet dries her skin quickly and she dresses in the freshly laundered clothes she brought with her.

The lounge and its panoramic glass wall showcase the North Sea in all its glory. She steps out onto the south-facing balcony and watches as the waves whip the sheer rock face, spewing forth in a flurry of hissing white spray.

She turns her face into a cutting gust of wind that blows straight in from the ocean. She relishes the sting, a balm to her devastating loss.

She'd always known something was wrong, here at Seaspray House. She'd known, almost from the very moment they'd arrived, that the day would come when everyone finally saw the truth. The day the terrible secret was revealed. She'd felt it building like a knotted rope slowly tightening around her neck. So in some ways, what happened was no surprise.

Still, never, not in a million years, had she expected it all to end like this.

PROLOGUE

She squeezes the rust-coloured liquid from the mop and steps back from the bucket to survey her work. The floor shines beautifully under the weak rays of sunlight that arrow in through the expanse of glass in the ceiling atrium, illuminating the entire entrance hallway like a divine light. Glossy porcelain tiles like this are stunning but every smear shows, and they are a devil to clean. Especially today.

She empties the dirty water down the sink and refills the bucket with fresh lemon suds. It helps mask the metallic smell, although it's impossible to eliminate it completely on a first clean. She carries the mop and full bucket through to the master bedroom and looks around at all the blood.

A symphony of claret patterns the arctic walls and floor. Initially, there seems to be a pleasing rhythm to it – like an abstract art installation – but, on closer inspection, the awful authenticity of the blood spray becomes all too apparent.

It's those coagulated knots that stand proud of the smooth, white plaster. The jelly-like consistency that allows the viscous body fluid to cling to the vertical surfaces like glue. This is a

ONE MONTH EARLIER

ONE

LOTTIE

The old red Fiat's engine strains as it trundles up the hill and I wind down the window to let a little cool sea air into the stuffy interior.

'It's freezing, Mum,' Albie instantly complains. He still looks pale after a recent chest infection and so I roll it back up a couple of inches.

Neil twists round in the passenger seat, shivering for effect. 'You'd better get used to the cold, buddy. Doesn't look as if the wind and drizzle keep many people in around here.'

Albie stares down the hillside at the people milling around on Whitsend beach, a wide and long expanse of sand just a couple of miles from the more popular resort of Whitby, a seaside town situated at the mouth of the River Esk. I have memories of visiting there as a little girl from our modest little house about an hour's drive inland from here.

'Looks quite chilly today to say it's the middle of May,' Neil adds, eyeing the dog walkers wrapped up against the biting wind. Like a lot of people, we'd always fostered a dream of living at the coast. It was always sunny and warm in our imagination when we talked about it, though, in that way you made your dream life the best it could be.

Neil used to be someone who enjoyed being outside whatever the weather. Even after twelve-hour days in the summer, he'd get home and say, 'It feels like I'm getting paid for doing something I love.' Soon as he got a bit of spare time, he'd be off-road cycling around the woods and tracks surrounding our home.

It's almost two years since Neil had a serious accident at work. An accident that changed the direction of our lives.

Neil had instantly lost the use of his legs and his left arm. Doctors had told him to prepare for the fact there was a real possibility there might be permanent paralysis. The shock had ricocheted through our small family unit. I'd allowed my temporary contract as part-time admin assistant to lapse at the local school. We'd decided to tell Albie the truth about his dad's injuries to try and prepare him for the challenging, life-changing possibilities that might come our way.

When he'd started his recovery, Neil had spent a lot of time pottering around in the house looking for things to fix. He'd developed a penchant for restoration-type shows.

He had a slight limp for a while and the grip of his left hand is still weaker than it was, but if you didn't know it, it's not that obvious. He's still a ruggedly handsome man who has the power to get my heart racing.

Everything we've been through in the last couple of years channels through my mind. Neil's depression, the hopeless trapped feeling I often woke up to in the early hours. Not to mention our mounting debt. It's all thankfully behind us now.

Yes, there are people back in Nottingham we'll miss. I have a couple of friends I'll be sorry to let go, but it's been a long time since we've met up socially anyway because of Neil's long period of recuperation.

Albie has had lots of problems at school during this past year and frankly, I'm relieved he's got the chance of starting a new school.

'According to Google, we're almost there.' Neil frowns at his phone screen and then the narrow road in front of us.

'Can't see a turning yet,' I murmur. 'Are you sure you put the right postcode in?'

Neil places the phone on his lap. 'Yes, Lottie, I put the correct postcode in. Do I win a prize?'

I don't dignify his easy sarcasm with an answer. He never used to be like this; it's something I've noticed since the accident. I do worry sometimes about the effect it may have on Albie, who has witnessed the undercurrent of Neil's frustration on a daily basis.

As we climb higher still, I grip the wheel and glance back down towards the swathe of pale sand with its scattering of dog walkers, runners and families. All of them undeterred by the weather and larking around in the surf. I can remember the feel of salt on my skin and the sand scratching between my toes after a day trip to the beach: a flashback of my mum peeling off a cold, damp cossie and roughly rubbing my skinny damp body with a towel before the long journey on the bus back home.

Just when I think the sputtering car is finally going to give up the ghost, the hillside mercifully flattens out and Neil silently directs me to turn left, onto an unmade road.

The track bends to the right and, suddenly, a small, dark building looms up out of nowhere. Here it is: the estate cottage, the accommodation that comes with the job. The stone is damp and dark, the windows small and crooked. It looks... different than in the advert where it had appeared cosier, more welcoming.

'*That's* the cottage?' Albie pipes up in the back, clearly unimpressed. I'd shown him the photograph of the exterior and we'd imagined how his bedroom might look. Our vision was tidier and much brighter than the reality.

Albie has got a point. The cottage doesn't look much bigger than one of those old-fashioned outdoor coal houses, but then as I manoeuvre the car out wider and come to a stop in front of it, I can see it's actually a reasonable size.

I glance at Neil and turn off the engine, unclicking my seatbelt. He's out of the car before I can ask him what his first impression is.

'Can you let me out, Mum?' Albie says, straining to see which direction his dad is walking off in.

I open the car door to release the broken child lock that's permanently stuck on and Albie is out in an instant. 'You're going to need your jacket on,' I call, but my cautionary words are carried away by the wind as he runs off at full pelt to join Neil.

As I get closer to our new home, my heart sinks. The once-white plaster on the walls is grubby and, in places, flaking off, exposing the brickwork beneath. The roof is coated with a layer of spongy, dark-green moss, several clumps of which have fallen off in messy splodges on the cracked, uneven path. The photos Neil had shown me had obviously been taken some years ago when the property was in better shape.

'There was work being carried out on the cottage, so I didn't get to see inside,' he'd told me after his visit to Seaspray for a face-to-face interview. 'But it looks great from a distance.'

I shove my hands into the pockets of my fleece and keep my head down against the wind. I don't want to look at Neil. I can well imagine his internal dialogue right now, questioning why he'd ever thought this was a good idea. Why I'd encouraged him to go for a job he'd thought was too good for him.

After spending several months seeking work in Nottingham with no luck at all, I'd sensed Neil was fast losing faith that he was ever going to get a position. He'd run his own successful building business for years, but that didn't translate to the kind of experience most people wanted in an employee. He posted his CV on various job sites and one day when he'd been especially grumpy and low, an agency that specialised in premium-end landscaping and gardening jobs in the North had spotted his details. They'd contacted him and told him they only recruited for qualified and highly experienced staff. Both boxes Neil ticked many times over.

When they'd told him about the rare opportunity that had become available at the Seaspray Estate in North Yorkshire, although there was no address given, the photograph of its stunning clifftop position soon gave its location away. Neil couldn't believe his luck. If successful, he would have a full complement of staff and his role would be largely management duties.

I'd googled Seaspray Estate the day the agency approached Neil. The website had launched with sweeping drone footage of the extensive grounds. There didn't look to be a blade of grass out of place and I'd felt a sense of pride that Neil would work tirelessly to keep the grounds looking fabulous.

I'd clicked through the various pages on the website including 'About us'. The photographs showed some of the dazzling array of flowers in the summertime but, disappointingly, no photographs of people. Finally on the 'Contact us' page, I'd spotted a small, non-expandable photograph of an older man standing in the middle of a flower bed leaning on a spade. He wore a flat cap and held a mug of tea aloft as if he were saying 'Cheers!' I'd instinctively known this must be Tom, the retired head gardener Neil had been told about.

Neil had already said that Neeta and Ted, the owners of Seaspray House, seemed very private people, but I was surprised they didn't appear at all on the website.

I'd googled 'Ted and Neeta Williams' and there were plenty of links to articles mentioning their charitable donations in the town. When I'd clicked on images, only a couple of photos came up. One was tagged as 'Neeta and Ted Williams of Whitsend Bay'. In both, Neeta was looking down slightly with just a small smile on her face, and Ted had covered half his face with his hand. In one he pinched the top of his nose; in the other, coughing and covering his mouth at the exact moment the camera had clicked. It had seemed odd and yet... maybe it wasn't odd. Maybe they just didn't like their pictures being taken, which was fair enough.

Neil had applied and within days had secured an initial interview via Zoom with a recruitment consultant. It had given him a real boost of confidence. The interview had gone well, and, within a week, the consultant had called him back. 'They want you to go up to Seaspray for a face-to-face interview, Neil,' she'd told him. 'Is that doable?'

Following a train journey to York where Neil had met with Ted Williams and been taken to the estate for his interview and tour, the job was offered to him. In the space of a week, he'd gone from little or no job prospects to landing the position of his dreams.

And now, here we are.

I can hear Albie talking excitably. My son looks over at me and beams and I'm gratified his pale face seems to have gained a little colour.

'Dad says he'll put up a basketball net for me at the side of the house, Mum!'

'First impressions, I think the cottage could be really special.' Neil sweeps an arm around. 'Look at these views! With a bit of time and effort, I reckon I could transform this place. It's the chance I've been waiting for.' When Albie runs to the bottom of the small garden, Neil moves closer to me, tucking a wisp of escaped hair behind my ear. His fingers linger there, tracing the soft skin beneath my jaw. His touch sends a little frisson of pleasure down my neck. It's been so, so long since we've enjoyed the physical closeness I used to take for granted.

Another consequence of his accident. 'I feel like we can rebuild our lives here, Lottie. Do you feel it, too?'

I swallow and nod, my eyes pinned to his. It feels like such a mountain to climb, to get back what we had but... in this moment, it seems to me that Neil believes we can achieve it.

He pulls me closer to him, the warmth of his body enveloping mine. I glance over his shoulder at the cottage, taking in the cracked windowpanes, the missing roof tiles and the broken handle on the front door. I know Neil is very capable when it comes to DIY, there's no doubt about that.

'Wow, look!' Albie's shrill voice cuts through the air from the bottom of the garden and we pull apart to see. He's peering through a sparse screen of conifers at the end of the garden, parting the ferny leaves to reveal an enormous property perched a little higher up on top of the hill. 'That's a really cool place, like in a movie or something.'

'There she is,' Neil murmurs, as they walk down to Albie. 'Seaspray House.'

It looks so much more imposing in real life than on the Google searches I've done. I place my hands on my son's shoulders from behind and take in the vast swathe of glass and metal that forms the property. It perches on the top of the hillside, brilliant, white and majestic. The front and upstairs of the house are sheer glass. The light is reflecting on it, obscuring our view. But I think it must look magnificent when it's lit up at night.

'That's where your dad is going to be working,' I tell Albie. 'Impressive, eh?'

I see movement at an upstairs window. 'Ooh look, there's someone up there watching us.' I point.

Neil squints. 'I can't see anyone.'

'I definitely saw someone... I thought I did. Or a shadow of someone...' We stand and watch for a moment.

'Nope. Nothing there,' Neil says, looking away.

'Must be a trick of the light,' I murmur, squinting my eyes.

'It's a cool place,' Albie says. 'Wish we were going to live in that house instead of this one.'

Neil ruffles his hair. 'The cottage is part of our fresh start, buddy. We're coastal folks now, remember.'

We all laugh. It's a good answer, a great attitude.

TWO

After a bit of a tussle with the awkward lock, Neil manages to open the cottage door. Albie ducks under his arm and is first inside and Neil ushers me through before him.

Inside the cottage, I brace myself for a musty odour and a draughty interior, fully expecting the damp stonework to have seeped through into the bones of the house. But the hallway is clean and dry. It looks like the original terracotta floor tiles under my feet, and cream walls set the warm colour off perfectly. Further inside, I'm delighted to find a log burner in the small lounge with its low ceiling and adorable wonky beams. I can just imagine how cosy this room will be in winter with a roaring fire and the three of us snuggled up against the weather.

'It's so quaint in here,' I murmur, taking in the charmingly mismatched three-piece suite. A chunky woven blanket is draped artfully over the arm of the chair and the shelving in the two slim alcoves either side of the burner are full of well-used books.

Albie darts forward and snatches up what looks like a homemade chocolate cookie. 'Are these for us, Mum? I'm starving!' His eyes pop when he spots a PlayStation and several games. 'Cool!' He bounds over to inspect them, leaving a trail of biscuit crumbs in his wake.

Someone has gone to great lengths to ensure a welcoming scene on our arrival and I feel touched and pleased. If this is anything to go by, Ted and Neeta Williams will be dream employers and neighbours.

I slip back out into the hallway and into the kitchen. As I'd expected, it's small, but the space has been well-used with pale-lemon compact handmade cabinets, a fold-down table and lots of open shelving. Copper saucepans and other classic culinary equipment hang from hooks in the ceiling and the leaf-green painted walls, giving the room a slightly cluttered but homely appeal.

I spot canisters containing small amounts of teabags, coffee and sugar. 'How thoughtful.'

'There's milk, orange juice and bottled water, too,' Neil says approvingly, as he closes the refrigerator door. He opens a cupboard. 'A wholemeal loaf in here as well.'

'Wow!' Albie gasps when I pull up the blind. We all stand stock still for a few moments, taking in the stunning view framed by the kitsch curtains. The idyllic scene stretches right down the hillside to the beach and sea beyond.

'OK, so I won't be complaining when I'm peeling spuds at *this* sink,' Neil says. 'We don't get this good a view when we pay for one on holiday!'

I feel a pinch of regret that we haven't been away since before the accident.

'Can we see my room now?' Albie springs out of the door, charging upstairs. 'I hope it's bigger than my crummy old one,' he calls back.

It's true. The rooms in our terraced house in Nottingham were all a bit cramped. Albie has always dreamed of having a gaming chair in his bedroom but there wasn't any space for that.

'I don't think there's that much Albie will miss about our last house.' Neil grins as we follow him up the narrow flight of stairs that hugs the wall from the hallway up to a tiny landing with four doors leading off. Neil opens the door closest to him. 'Hot water tank,' he says before closing it again.

'Can this be my room?' Albie calls from the next door down and I hope he hasn't wandered into the master bedroom by mistake.

I needn't have worried. This is Albie's bedroom with its neat single bed with a new, plastic-wrapped mattress, a small wooden wardrobe, and a mahogany chest of drawers. I look out of the small window and see he's got a fabulous view of the beach and sea – probably an even better view than the kitchen. I punch my hands onto my hips. 'Hey, how come you get the best bedroom view?'

He giggles in delight. 'You can come in and look at the sea from my room any time you like, Mum!' he says, magnanimous in his excitement.

We all troop into the master bedroom next. It's about twice the size of Albie's room, but certainly not enormous. The wardrobes have been built in to utilise the space under the eaves, the attractively panelled wooden doors in keeping with the rest of the traditional cottage interior.

We discover there's only one small bathroom in the whole cottage, but it's clean with modern, white hardware – including both a bath and overhead shower – and sparkling tiles.

'Looks like this has recently been fitted,' Neil murmurs approvingly, running his hand over the edge of the ceramic sink and peering behind the pedestal at the pipework. 'Someone made a good job of it, too.'

I place my hands on the narrow windowsill and take in the view from our bedroom. It overlooks the small garden and I can see the partial rooftop of Seaspray House over the top of the line of conifers that marks out the boundary of the land.

Back on the landing, I open the final door to find a box room so tiny I know we'll struggle to get even a single bed in there. The slatted blind is pulled down and the coffee-coloured walls make the space look even more dim and closed in.

'Oh well, it'll come in handy for storage,' I say, closing the door again. 'I love it downstairs but I hope they'll let us decorate up here if we want to.'

'I'm sure they'll be fine about that sort of thing,' Neil says easily. 'The Williamses seem quite laid back. Ted, anyway. You'll see what I mean when you get to meet him.'

'I'll make us our first cuppa in the new kitchen,' I say when we get back downstairs. Before I can walk away, Neil grabs me and plants a kiss on my lips. It's been so long since he's shown me any impulsive affection like that, it takes me back a bit.

'What?' He laughs at my shocked expression.

'You just surprised me, that's all. I'm not complaining.'

'In that case...' He grabs me again and plants another smacker on my lips. 'There's another for good measure!'

I laugh and pull away. 'That kettle's not going to boil itself, Romeo.' As I walk into the kitchen, my heart lifts a little. I hardly dare hope, but this is what I've prayed for. That Neil and I will get closer again and finally put the difficult times behind us.

Despite having a thousand and one other jobs to do, I fill the kettle and stand for a few moments, staring out of the window and down the hillside. I haven't got twenty-twenty vision, but I can still clearly see the grey waves whipping up with the breeze and a few kids darting in and out of the water.

There's movement beyond the gate and I catch sight of a short woman with a dark ponytail and a child with a head of bright-red hair walking past. The woman glances at the cottage as she passes.

I start at the sound of the front door opening and an unfamiliar male voice calls out, 'Hello? Anybody home?'

I hover cautiously behind the kitchen door until Neil appears in the hallway, smiling widely. 'Ted, hi!'

Ted Williams is a fit-looking, broad-shouldered man who I'd guess is probably in his early sixties. He's clean-shaven with salt and pepper hair worn long in the neck and slicked back from his face. There aren't many people who can make my husband look on the short side but Ted stands about six-foot-four next to Neil's six foot. They lock hands, grasping arms at the same time. Neil turns to me. 'Ted, this is Lottie, my wife. Lottie, this is Ted Williams, my new boss.'

I offer my hand. 'Hello, Ted, it's so nice to meet you. Neil's told me a lot about you.'

'Really? All good I hope!' He throws back his head and gives a hearty laugh before apologising for a short coughing fit. He's quite well groomed for a man of his age with smooth skin and good teeth.

'And this young man—' Neil ruffles our son's dark-blond hair '—is my son, Albie.'

Ted's voice softens. 'Hello there.'

'Hello,' Albie says.

'Looking forward to starting your new school?'

He gives Ted a guarded nod. 'Yes.'

Albie hasn't been sleeping well for the last couple of weeks and he's wet the bed twice. I'm convinced he's nervous about starting his new school although he hasn't said as much.

Ted turns back to me.

'So, how's it going, Lottie? Settling in alright?'

'We've only really got around to checking out the cottage and putting the kettle on,' I say. 'Next on the list is emptying the car boot and then removals are coming on Monday.'

Ted looks around approvingly.

'Oh, and thanks for leaving a few provisions,' I add. 'Albie's very impressed with the PlayStation. That was really kind of you.'

Ted waves our thanks away. 'No worries. My wife wanted to make sure it was comfortable for your arrival. How was the journey?'

'Very good,' Neil says. 'No problems.'

I hear the kettle click loudly behind me in the kitchen. 'I'm making a hot drink, Ted,' I say. 'Will you stay for a cup of tea?'

He checks his watch, murmuring to himself. 'Let's see... I've got a topsoil delivery coming in about thirty minutes so yes, I should be able to fit in a quick cuppa.'

Once made, we take our drinks into the lounge and Ted looks around approvingly. 'Cosy in here. I've always liked it. Tom – our last gardener – and his wife, Mary, were getting on a bit and so they didn't do much with the place in the last few years, but I'm sure you'll make it your own.' He takes a sip of his tea. 'Don't feel you've got to ask before decorating or anything. So long as you're not knocking down walls, you've pretty much got carte blanche to do as you like with the interior.'

Neil shoots me an 'I told you so' look and I give him a little smile in return.

'Do they still live in the area?' I ask, sipping my tea. 'Tom and Mary, I mean?'

Ted hesitates and places his mug on the wooden coffee table before answering. 'Can I ask you both to do me a big favour?' he says, looking from me to Neil.

'Course,' Neil says quickly. 'What is it?'

'This may sound odd, but can I ask you not to mention Tom and Mary Gooding again? And particularly not in the earshot of my wife?'

I stare at him. I can't believe he's just said that. He used the word 'ask' but it sounds more like an order to me.

'Oh, sorry,' I say lightly, but my curiosity is piqued. Neil told me the old gardener had been here for years, so I can't help wondering why his wife is so sensitive to any mention of them.

'No, no, you mustn't feel bad, Lottie. It was silly of me to bring them up, but it's really nothing to worry about. It's just that...' He sighs. 'Let's just say there was a disagreement of sorts before the Goodings left the cottage. I don't want to go into details, but it really upset Neeta and she's only just getting over it. So I'm really hoping not to have to hear their names now the problem is over.'

'Say no more, Ted,' Neil remarks solemnly. 'We understand completely. Sorry for the mix-up.'

Even though he brought their names up in the first place...

Ted holds his hand up to stave off more apologies. 'Thanks for your understanding. Much appreciated.' He turns to Albie. 'Now then, buddy, what do you think to this PlayStation I had set up just for you?'

THREE

NEIL

SUNDAY

He's been awake since 6 a.m. They didn't get to sleep until midnight because of Lottie's non-stop speculation about why Tom and Mary Gooding might have left. This is the last thing he needs to happen: Lottie getting obsessive and her imagination running wild. He'd thought all that was behind them.

When he hears Albie get up, he takes him downstairs, makes him a bowl of cereal and swiftly gives in to his request for a breakfast PlayStation session while he's still in his pyjamas. Then he makes tea, which he takes up to Lottie in bed.

'Gosh, I slept late... what time is it?' She half-sits up in bed, raking her fingers through her hair and reaching blearily for her phone on the bedside table. 'Seven-thirty! Is Albie up?'

'He's fine, happy downstairs on his PlayStation,' Neil says, reaching for his trackie bottoms. 'You've got Ted to thank for your lie-in.'

She'd usually have something to say about the early-morning gaming session, but she clearly still has something else on her mind. 'You know, something occurred to me in the night.

Do you think that fallout was the reason Tom and Mary Gooding left Seaspray Cottage, or do you think they were retiring anyway and just—'

'Not this again, please.' Neil rakes his fingers through his hair. 'You were still going on about it at nearly midnight.'

'It was eleven-thirty when I put the lamp out,' Lottie says defensively. 'Anyway, why aren't you interested? Don't you want to know what happened? You're going to be working for these people so it might be sensible to be a bit more curious.'

'As I said last night, I can't believe I've landed this amazing job. I'm so bloody grateful to be given this chance, and the last thing I want to do is start ruffling any feathers.'

'I don't mean I'm going to quiz Ted directly, silly. I'll soon get to know the people who live around here and someone is bound to know what happened.'

'Lottie, no!' He frowns at her and shrugs off his dressing gown. 'Please don't mention this to anyone. I don't want to get on the wrong side of Ted before I start.'

Lottie lets out an exaggerated sigh. She allows her eyes to blatantly travel over his torso and arms as he stands there in his boxer shorts. 'Why don't you come back to bed for a bit?' she says huskily.

'Tempting, but I've already promised to watch Albie play the next level of his game. Besides, you deserve a bit of time to yourself and we've plenty of time for cuddles later.' He winks and grins at her as he pulls on a T-shirt. He loves Lottie and still finds her very attractive. He often feels aroused when they cuddle, when her nails might trace a wavy path from his neck down his upper back, just the way he likes it. But whenever she tries to move things on a step beyond that, it feels like a shutter comes down in his head and he's effectively physically disconnected.

It had never been like that before the accident and the doctors had confirmed there didn't appear to be any obvious nerve damage or physical reason for his very personal difficulties.

'These things can take time,' his consultant had told him. 'Give yourself a break, Neil. Your recovery has been remarkable and hopefully, in time, you'll find most things will return to some normality.'

Easy for him to say. Using words like *hopefully* and *normal* weren't especially helpful when you were experiencing a rising panic that your mojo had evaporated before you'd even turned forty. He'd noticed that Lottie had been far more attentive and affectionate than usual this morning, which was nice but added to the pressure. Last night, the two of them had enjoyed a cuddle after turning the lamps out. Sadly, the effect of this was to bring Neil's worries about his waning abilities in the bedroom sharper into focus than ever. He felt like he was letting her down at every turn.

Lottie's voice breaks into his thoughts: 'I'm going to cook us a nice meal tomorrow night after your first day at work. How does creamy chicken and bacon pasta sound?' It's one of his favourite dishes. 'I might even open a bottle of Sauvignon if you play your cards right.'

'What, on a school night?' he jokes, referencing their recent decision to try not to drink alcohol during the week. It's what Lottie might be expecting to happen after the food that worries him.

'It's a *special* school night, so yes.' Lottie is on a roll now, cradling her mug in both hands and staring into space with a dreamy look on her face. 'Albie is bound to be tired after his first day at his new school, so he might be in bed a bit earlier and we can... well, you know, catch up on a bit of "us" time. God knows we need it.'

Neil swallows and reaches for his socks. 'Have you seen my watch?'

'On top of the dresser.' Lottie puts down her mug and pats down the quilt before folding her hands together on top of it.

'You chill for a bit while I keep Albie entertained, and then shall we all go down for a walk on the beach?' Neil suggests. 'It's going to be nice and warm today according to the weather forecast and I'd like us to get down to the beach together every day, if we can. Even for a short time.'

Sometimes Neil wonders if she didn't prefer him mooching around the house every day, watching television and relying on her for everything. He knows she has serious abandonment issues thanks to her mother leaving when she was young and, as a result, can be possessive and overbearing if she feels threatened in any way. Those traits had disappeared when he was effectively housebound. Back then, what Lottie said went without question. But he didn't feel resentful – quite the opposite.

He'd been so grateful for her support and encouragement when his confidence had been rock-bottom, but now it's time for him to fly again. He can feel a drive and enthusiasm rising in him like the swell of the tide. He will put himself back together, piece by tiny piece and make the most of this amazing opportunity.

They get down to the beach for eleven o'clock and it's already busy with people, dogs and, further up the coast, a gathering of people at the edge of the water.

'I think they're learning how to surf, Dad,' Albie says, his eyes wide with wonder. 'Can I go and see?'

'Sure, we'll walk up and you can run ahead,' Neil replies and when Albie shoots off, he turns to Lottie. 'How amazing is it to see him like this?'

'I thought he could only get enthusiastic about gaming these days,' Lottie agrees.

'I love watching the sea thrashing around even though it's a nice day.' Neil stops walking and regards the bluey-grey waves crashing in, pushing a thick lip of foam closer to their feet. 'It's got such character.'

Lottie smiles and stares dreamily at the horizon. 'The North Sea never seems calm and flat. It always seems so... I don't know, *angry*.'

Neil reaches for her hand and squeezes it. 'I hope the bad memories don't start coming back now you're nearer your childhood home.'

She nods. 'I think I'll be fine. I want to put everything that happened behind me and think about our future.'

He feels nervous when she says things like that – stuff that's come straight from the mouth of her therapist although she hasn't attended a session for ages. When he had the accident, they could no longer meet the cost of it. Neil is afraid of the 'everything' that Lottie refers to because he doesn't know exactly the detail of what happened to her back then. All she's ever told him is that she woke up one day and her mother had gone. She left and never contacted her daughter, never returned. As a father himself now, Neil can't comprehend how a parent who did that could possibly live with themselves.

'Mum! Dad! Come and see!' Albie is racing back towards them again, his face ruddy and etched with pure excitement. 'Those guys up there are from the Seal Surf Academy. They do beginner lessons for kids. Can I try? Can I?'

Lottie laughs. 'Can we check it out before we say yes?'

Ten minutes later, Albie is signed up to a block booking of six junior surf sessions, the first lesson being next Sunday at ten.

While Lottie waits for the paperwork, Neil stands looking at the sea. The way it always looks the same and yet, in reality, is slightly different every time. He feels ten foot tall being able to fund this activity without a second thought now he's in full-time employment and they've got rid of a good chunk of their debt.

He turns to watch his wife and his son, both happy, both enjoying life again and that's when the guilt cramps hard in his gut.

Why can't he just forgive himself and accept the chance to start again without the ever-present shadow he's carried with him for the last two years?

Lottie must never find out the truth.

She must never know what really happened the day of the accident, or why he was so keen to move away and make a fresh start.

FOUR

The next day, Neil is awake early again. He makes Lottie's tea and brings it upstairs.

'I know you want to make a good impression, but just take it easy today,' Lottie says, shielding a yawn with a hand. 'No use going mad and wearing yourself out.'

'I will.' He begins to thread a belt through the waistband loops of his jeans. 'I'll be fine, no need to fret about me.'

'I mean it, Neil. You must pace yourself; it's a long time since you've done a full day's work.'

He looks at her as he buckles the belt. 'I'm fine, Lottie. I've been signed off as being medically fit for work and now I'm raring to go.'

'Have you told Ted you won't be climbing any ladders? Your balance isn't what it was; it would only take a tiny slip and—'

He clenches his jaw. 'I'm trying to stay positive here. I'm going to be fine, OK?'

He kisses his wife and escapes out of the bedroom. He looks

in on Albie, who's just stirring. 'Hope today goes really well, champ. Big first day for us both.'

'Thanks, Dad. Bet you'll do brilliant,' Albie says sleepily.

'Bet you'll do better, son. Love you.' Neil kisses him on his forehead and goes downstairs.

Any luck, he should be back no later than five tonight, so there'll be plenty of time to catch up with Albie then and find out about his day. There is a lot of lost time to make up with his son. All those weeks that turned into months when he was so low, he didn't know whether Albie was at home, school or what the heck he was doing.

Neil closes the door behind him and walks around the side of the house to the cottage's small front garden. He feels more nervous than ever about the new job. Lottie means well, of course she does, but being reminded of one's shortcomings and limitations at key moments like today... it takes its toll.

A short distance beyond the neat garden gate lie acres of tracks, fields and the slope of the hillside. So, even though the cottage garden is tiny, the feeling of space and enjoyment of the land is wonderful.

Neil stands for a moment, regarding the view. Apparently, people get used to living in a place like this and hardly notice their surroundings after a while. He can't imagine ever being that blinkered. He makes himself a promise there and then: no matter how long he lives here, he'll take a few moments each morning to appreciate what he has.

He has plenty of time to get over to Seaspray for his first day. There is nobody around. It's way too early for the school run and, although he can see dog walkers on the beach, none of them have made their way up the hill yet.

He can hear the sea: a distant *whoosh* that has a rhythm all of its own. It's too early to feel really warm yet. The sun hasn't yet broken through a sky that is heavily shot through with cloud. But shards of dazzling blue are flashing through in places with the promise of excellent weather on its way, mid to late morning.

Neil draws the fresh, salty air into his lungs and holds it there for a few moments before releasing it in a long, slow outbreath. It feels so good to feel that life is getting back to something like normal again. There had been a time, not too long ago, when he'd felt overwhelmed by the mountain he knew he must climb if he was to claw back even a low level of independence for himself again. It was at this stage Lottie was still helping him with the most personal of tasks that no man would ever choose to have his wife do for him.

To give her credit, the often short-tempered and slightly scatty Lottie had more than risen to the challenge. Overnight, she had somehow seamlessly transformed into a most bewilderingly organised woman. She'd never come to him with a problem without offering a solution as well. When he'd had trouble getting up out of his armchair, Lottie had found a piece of equipment that had made things a lot easier. She was a wonder.

She'd given up the school job she'd loved without hesitation and become his full-time carer. The benefit payment hadn't come close to covering Lottie's lost wages, nor the lucrative business contracts he'd been forced to leave behind. Their finances had paled into insignificance against the logistical problems of just surviving and, as a result, things had got worse without them really noticing. They'd got worse very quickly.

Lottie had come to him one day to say the oven had just stopped working, the boiler was on the blink and the credit card was maxed out. The money from the secured loan they'd taken out on the house was gone. They literally had nothing.

Neil shakes his head to dispel the memories. He has to stop revisiting the bad times; they are all behind him now. *Look to the future*, that's what's important now.

They're living in the estate cottage for a peppercorn rent.

Granted, it's small, but it's also cosy and plenty big for the three of them. His starting salary is just under forty-five thousand pounds a year, which is a hell of a lot more than the meagre amount they've been forced to scrape by on while they got back on their feet. They've been able to clear the credit cards and the secured loan they used to consolidate debts when they sold the house. It's left them with no money once again, but so what? Being healthy and almost free of debt is better than any amount of savings in the bank. They just have to make sure they pay off that last chunk of debt over the next year or so.

If Lottie doesn't want to work yet then there is no need. So far as Neil is concerned, she's more than earned herself a rest after supporting him day-in, day-out for so long. However, he knows his wife isn't the sort to sit around all day. Before long, she'll probably find something local and part-time and, when the time comes, he will support her the best he can.

Neil feels physically and mentally stronger than he's done for years. Their money problems are almost behind them and today is the first morning of his new job. It feels like he's been given another chance at life and he's going to take it with both hands.

When he reaches the imposing entrance of Seaspray House, with its ten-foot wrought-iron electric gates and high stone wall that traverses the entire perimeter of the property, Neil ignores it as instructed. He carries on walking to the less obvious entrance to the grounds at the side.

He swipes the digitised security lanyard across the keypad sensor and waits as the wide, wooden gate begins to slide slowly open. The gardens beyond are magnificent. There is no other word for it. They are highly manicured and require heavy and sustained maintenance to keep them looking perfect. When he'd travelled to Seaspray for his interview, Ted had taken him on an extensive tour of the estate and had given him a good overview of what it will take to keep the gardens in good order.

'The topiary trees and bushes need trimming regularly. You can tickle them up with a pair of shears, but we have a company that comes in to sort out all the heavy and inaccessible tree work. Likewise, the ponds are cleaned by our external specialist twice a year.'

Neil had felt instantly relieved that a lot of the major physical tasks were taken care of. Still, now he's here, the whispers in his head are getting louder.

Are you good enough? Have you taken on too much?

'We employ mainly local students for the general labouring work. Obviously it's seasonal, but you'll be in charge of your own budget and you've got flexibility in how you use your staff.' Ted had patted him lightly on the back as if he'd sensed his uncertainty. 'I've seen your CV, Neil. You can do this stuff standing on your head.'

When Ted had made that particular comment, Neil had felt a swell of pride and can-do attitude inside. Ted was right, he *could* do this. He had fought for and got the job, fair and square.

Once the gate has opened wide enough, he slips through and begins to walk up the path where he can see the garden outhouses on the other side of the expanse of pristine lawn.

As the estate manager, Neil is to have his own space in a building not unlike a posh garden office. On his interview visit, Ted had showed him the sturdy, large rectangular structure built from good quality wood and glass. It has a desk, a fridge and a kettle, even a couple of easy chairs together with a private loo and wash basin. From Neil's new base he'll have panoramic views of the gardens and a bird's-eye view of the super-modern glass and steel Seaspray House that stands proudly at the head position as if it's surveying the land. There's another similar structure a little further down from his own that provides the casual staff with seating, plus a small kitchen and bathroom facilities for use on their breaks. It's perfect. All of it.

As he nears his office, Ted appears from one of the greenhouses. He pulls off a heavy-duty glove and raises his hand as Neil approaches.

'Morning! Welcome to Seaspray,' he calls out. The two men shake hands when they come together. 'The start of a winning team, I'm sure.'

'I'm really looking forward to it,' Neil says and means it. 'I can't wait to get started. Do you work in the grounds yourself?'

'I like to do a bit here and there. Like you, I had my own company for years. I built this house, in fact.'

Neil looks back at the house and gives a low whistle. 'That must've been some project. You've done an amazing job.'

'Cheers. It was a project and a half, for sure. Miss my building days sometimes, but I still keep up with the networking meetings, boozy conferences and the like. All the good bits. Doesn't always go down with the boss.' He grins and winks. 'Speaking of the boss, Neeta's going to one of her charity meetings this morning, but she's going to pop down to say hello before she leaves. In the meantime, let's get a brew on and have a quick chat.'

Inside the garden office, Ted puts the kettle on and Neil glimpses a heavy gold Rolex on his wrist. He points out where various items are stored. 'Anything else you need, just buy it and claim a reimbursement.'

His breath seems to catch in his throat and he starts to cough.

'You OK?' Neil asks him, concerned, but Ted waves him away.

'I'm fine. Probably just the fibres settling in here.'

'Yes, this place looks and smells brand new,' Neil says, regarding the fittings and pristine walls of the garden office.

'That's because it was constructed just for you.' Ted beams.

'Old Tom was rather set in his ways. He wouldn't entertain anything but the ramshackle shed he'd worked in during his time here. Neeta insisted we pulled it down when he retired.' Ted looks over Neil's shoulder. 'Ahh, speaking of, here she is. My lovely wife.'

The sliding glass door opens behind him and Neil turns around. Ted is watching him and he forces his expression to remain neutral as a woman – probably a good seven or eight years older than him – approaches.

There's no doubt about it, Neeta Williams is stunning. With her short, feathered glossy black hair and flawless brown skin, she is impeccably groomed in tailored jeans, patent heels and a formal cream tweed jacket with fancy gold buttons.

'Hello, you two.' She steps inside, instantly filling the office with a light floral scent. She offers a slim, elegant hand to Neil. 'I'm so pleased to meet you. I'm Neeta; how are you getting on?'

'Hi, I... I'm good, thank you. I'm Neil.'

'Yes, I guessed as much!' She grins, showing perfectly straight white teeth, framed by precisely applied, pillar-box red lipstick. When she fixes her brown, amber-flecked eyes on his, Neil feels nervous as a schoolboy. 'Your wife – her name's Lottie, isn't it? And your son... how are they finding the cottage?'

Yes, it's Lottie and Albie, Mrs Williams. They're—'

'Mrs Williams? Gosh, that makes me sound a hundred! Please, Neil, call me Neeta.'

'Thank you. Lottie and Albie are loving the cottage. We can't believe the great views of the sea and beach.'

'Yes, we're certainly all very lucky to have such a great vantage point up here. I hope you'll bring your boy up here sometimes; the grounds are perfect for children to let off steam and get them away from the PlayStation.' She glances at her husband.

'Absolutely,' Ted agrees. 'It's an education, too. We'll find him a few jobs to do and he can learn about the land.'

'That's very generous of you both, thank you. I'm sure Albie will love that.'

'Well, don't let me hold you up,' Neeta says brightly. 'I'll leave you two boys to it. Lovely to meet you, Neil. I hope you and your family will come for dinner soon? It would be so nice to catch up and to get to know you all better.'

'Thank you, that sounds lovely,' he says, thinking how pleased Lottie will be to get a good look inside Seaspray House itself.

'I'll pop down to the cottage then, at some point, to introduce myself to Lottie. We can sort out the details for dinner between us.'

Still all smiles, she turns from Neil and, in the blink of an eye, he catches the look she throws Ted. If he didn't know better, he'd swear she's just regarded her husband with a pure, unadulterated hatred.

FIVE

The two girls walked along the freezing cold street, swapping sweets from their pink and white candy-striped bags of pick 'n' mix. Claire didn't like the jelly snakes and Charlie couldn't stand the sherbet flying saucers.

Claire had paid for the sweets from her pocket money. Charlie hardly ever got any, so it was only fair. As they walked, the girls chatted about school and their favourite shows on TV. Charlie was three years older than Claire and went to the senior school just down the road from the primary school. When they reached the narrow private road that wound up the hillside to the big house where she lived with her parents, Claire stopped talking and inspected her remaining sweets. 'See you tomorrow, Charlie,' she said, her mouth full of half-chewed candies.

It was four o'clock and the bitter wind cut effortlessly through Charlie's cheap anorak. Claire had on a thick coat, fur-lined boots and a woolly scarf. She didn't seem in the least bit bothered by the cold. Charlie thought about the freezing house and empty cupboards waiting for her ten minutes away from here at the small, rundown house she shared with her mum, Kay, on the Bellingham council estate situated at the edge of town.

'Can I come to your house for a bit?' Charlie mumbled. 'My mum's working until late, so I might as well stay here, with you.'

Claire shifted her weight from one foot to the other. 'I think my mum might be too busy today. She won't want us getting under her feet.'

'We'll go up to your bedroom!' Charlie said brightly. 'I'll show you how to make a paper fortune teller.'

'I thought you'd said you couldn't tell me because it was a big secret.' Claire frowned, plunging her hand into the sweet bag again.

'I know, but I changed my mind.'

'How come you changed your mind?'

'Because we're best friends, aren't we?'

Claire hesitated, her eyes narrowing. 'I'll have to ask Mummy if it's OK for you to—'

'She won't mind, will she?' Charlie blurted out. 'I used to come to your house loads and now I hardly ever do.'

'My mum said... she said I shouldn't ask you back to the house as much.'

Charlie's stomach cramped. 'Why, though? What does she mean?'

Claire's cheeks reddened. 'She just said you can't keep coming here every day.'

Charlie watched as Claire chewed lazily and open-mouthed. The brightly coloured candy was now a slick, murky ball rolling around her tongue.

Fury burned in Charlie's chest. She knew now what this was all about. It must be that damage to Claire's new hand-carved Disney bed that her parents had surprised her with for her last birthday. It wasn't as if Charlie had meant to chip Ariel's pretty snub nose! The lamp base had clonked the edge of it when she'd swung it back, pretending it was a magic sword.

'I'll be careful not to break anything this time,' Charlie offered, feeling increasingly desperate as the fury receded as quickly as it came. She pulled the useless thin anorak closer to her as it started to rain. She thought about how cold her house would be if she went home. The gas had been cut off last week because her mum couldn't afford to pay the bill until the end of the month when she got her salary from the cleaning agency where she worked two jobs. Every morning when she opened her eyes, Charlie felt sure that the mould in the corner of her bedroom had crept another millimetre further towards her pillow. Just lately, she'd kept waking up in the middle of the night, coughing and spluttering. Sometimes, she couldn't get back to sleep because of the cold.

She really didn't want to go back to the house on her own today.

'OK then, I'll ask my mum,' Claire said reluctantly. 'But if she says you can't stay, you'll have to go home.'

Relief flooded Charlie's chest. Mrs Fuller would be pleased to see her, she felt sure of that. Charlie's mum said she was a nosy cow because she liked to ask Charlie personal questions about her mum's job and why her dad left. Charlie thought she'd probably saved lots of things up to ask with not seeing her for a while.

Charlie linked her arm through Claire's as together they turned in to the private road. She could almost taste the lovely ham and cheese sandwiches and hot chocolate Mrs Fuller would make for tea while they sat in the fancy big living room with its real fire and the biggest television she had ever seen in a house.

At the end of the gravelled driveway, she stopped walking, entranced for a moment. The house seemed to have grown taller and wider than ever since she'd last been here. Warm lamps glowed inside, illuminating the windows. The emerald lawns looked so pretty and neat, unlike her home with its own small patch of overgrown grass and weeds that Charlie's mum insisted on calling 'the garden'.

When they reached the tall gates, Claire turned to her. 'You'd better wait here,' she said, looking worried. 'I'll have to ask Mummy if you can come in first.'

So Charlie waited, alternately scraping the toes of her well-worn shoes on the gravel. A few minutes later, Claire's mum came to the door.

'Hello, Mrs Fuller,' Charlie said, in as confident a tone as she could muster.

Yasmin Fuller's flinty eyes settled on hers. 'Hello, Charlie.'

'Claire asked me to come for tea because she wanted me to show her how to make a paper fortune teller and I'll be very careful not to break anything,' Charlie said in one long breath.

Mrs Fuller's face darkened. 'Unfortunately, Claire is too busy to play tonight.' Her voice pinged like the guitar string Charlie had over-tightened on purpose in Mr Byron's music lesson.

'I can watch television while Claire is busy,' Charlie said.

'That won't be possible, I'm afraid.' Mrs Fuller's mouth puckered tightly like a knot.

Suddenly, Charlie's bravery deserted her and she felt like crying. Her fingers burned with cold, despite her pulling them up into the sleeves of her anorak. When she took a step forward to plead further, Mrs Fuller pushed the front door closed another inch so half of her face fell into shadow.

'Please, Mrs Fuller,' Charlie said tearfully, hugging the thin material closer to her, 'my mum's not home for ages yet and I—'

Mrs Fuller opened the door wider again and Charlie stopped speaking, believing that at last she was to be invited in. But Yasmin Fuller's eyes remained cold when she fixed her glare on her.

'I'm sorry, Charlie, but the answer is no. And... well, I think it's best if you stop waiting for Claire after school. She can walk up on her own from now on.'

Then, before Charlie could answer, Mrs Fuller closed the door, leaving her standing there, staring at the glossy dark wood with its shiny lion's head knocker. She began to shiver with the cold and the humiliation.

The part of her that had pleaded with Claire's mother suddenly felt frozen. She turned and began to walk off down the drive. It felt like she was standing back and watching herself as she bent down and picked up a large smooth stone from the driveway. She brought her arm back and hurled it, hard as she could, directly at the enormous bay window that housed the pretty lamps.

When she heard the glass crack and shatter, Charlie was already running. She no longer felt cold or humiliated. She felt free and avenged.

She'd made her mind up there and then that, however long it took, she'd make Claire Fuller and her bitch of a mother sorry that they'd ever treated her like this.

SIX

LOTTIE

When Neil has left for his first day at Seaspray House, I help Albie get ready for his first day at the new school. Later, when I get back home, I'll oversee the removals company who are due to deliver a few sparse sticks of furniture and the rest of our belongings early afternoon.

Neil has already called ahead and explained the track leading to the cottage isn't suitable for a large removals lorry. The cottage comes furnished, so we sold or gave away most of our already well-used furniture. But there is still a lot of clothing, personal items, bicycles... stuff like that, to come.

Beck Primary School is about a ten-minute walk inland from the cottage or just a few minutes' drive if you have to go by road, which is the long way around. Ted told Neil the way from the cottage and he's showed me the simple route on Google Maps. This morning, the wind has dropped away and left blue skies and fluffy white clouds, so we opt for the walk.

'Will I walk to school on my own soon?' Albie says.

'We'll see. There's no rush.'

'I don't mind if you want to walk with me every day, Mum.'

That's when I realise just how nervous he is. Since he

turned nine, he's been pushing for his independence in lots of different ways. One of those is walking to school on his own. We've had countless exchanges about it. But this morning, he doesn't argue. He doesn't walk ahead or talk about gaming. He's quieter than usual and sticks to my side like glue.

'It's going to be OK, you know,' I say. 'You'll soon make friends. All that trouble is behind you now, sweetie. You've got a fresh start.'

'Hope so, Mum,' he says.

We walk through a leafy, gravelled lane with tall hedgerows where Albie points out wildflowers. We stop a couple of times to listen to the symphony of birdsong and he uses an app on my phone to identify the different whistles.

'I like this walk,' Albie says, stopping to inspect a small yellow flower. 'I think I'll be fine walking on my own soon. I don't want the other kids to think I'm a baby.'

I squeeze his hand and admit to myself this walk is a very different journey to his last school. Much to Albie's annoyance, I'd insisted on driving him there and back right up until his very last day. There had been two busy roads to negotiate and part of the walk skirted the roughest part of the sprawling housing estate with its shadowy alleyways and boarded-up houses that attracted some dubious-looking individuals.

This walk is pretty and pleasant, a million miles away from what we've had to put up with before. But, as we walk, I think about the cottage. I realise that, despite the feeling of being close to people and activity on the beach thanks to the great views, it's fairly isolated. We don't see another soul on the hillside on the first half of the journey.

'It's going to be fine, you know,' I say, ruffling his hair lightly. 'You'll soon make friends and your new teacher, Miss Cavendish, seems lovely.'

'Yeah,' he says. We had a Zoom call with her at the beginning of the summer term.

'I think you'll be so much happier here, Albie. I bet lots of kids in your class will surf and do stuff down at the beach at weekends.'

He perks up a bit. 'That will be cool!' Then, 'I hope there are no bullies here.'

My heart squeezes. 'Me too. But any problems, you need to tell Miss Cavendish right away. You know that, right?'

He nods.

'She knows all about the problems you had at your old school and she said it's a really nice class you're joining here. So I honestly think it's going to be fine.'

'Hope so, Mum.' He suddenly presses closer to me and says in a hoarse whisper, 'Uh-oh, are they coming over here?'

It's the woman and young girl with the red hair again, climbing up the other side of the hill. The girl smiles and waves.

'Let's slow down and say hello,' I say and, to my surprise, Albie doesn't complain. The woman is short and lean with dark hair in a ponytail and she speeds up when she sees we're waiting for them. When they reach us, I see she has wisps of purple in her fringe and at the ends of her ponytail. 'Hi,' I say. 'I'm Lottie Carter and this is Albie. It's his first day at school today.'

I nudge a silent Albie.

'Hello,' he says, looking at the floor.

'Hi, Lottie, hi, Albie! I'm Keris and this is Edie.'

'Hi,' Edie says confidently. 'Whose class are you in?'

Albie's cheeks burn. 'Ermm... Miss Cavendish's.'

'Me too!' Edie's face lights up. 'Hey, want to see something secret hardly anyone knows about around here?'

Albie looks up, gives a single nod and wanders off behind her.

I raise an eyebrow. 'Looks like those two have hit it off already,' I say.

'Edie will talk his ears off... about fossils. That's what she's going to show him now. If he's the slightest bit interested, she'll want to make him her best friend.'

I make a sound of relief. 'Well, Albie's usually really slow in making friends, so it's brilliant he'll already know someone.'

'Edie can be a bit of a loner, too,' Keris agrees. 'She's more confident with adults than with other kids her age. It's unusual for her to take to someone so quickly.' We start to walk slowly along the path while the kids begin to poke at something in the ground with sticks. 'I hear you've moved into the little cottage on the Seaspray Estate?' She gives a nod back towards our home.

'Yes. My husband, Neil, is the new estate manager.'

'Hmm, that's what the local grapevine reported.' She turns and gives me an impish grin. Her sensible walking boots kick up dust in front of me as she strides confidently ahead on the narrow path.

'The grapevine? Sounds like it might be a reliable source of information,' I say drily, looking down at my feet. I've got flat black ankle boots on with a smooth sole that are far too slippy for the rough ground.

'Don't worry about it; soon be someone else's turn to get talked about. I've been there, so I speak from experience.'

'You're not Whitsend Bay born and bred then?'

'God, no. We've only been in the bay for about six months. My arrival was a bit scandalous. I don't think they'd seen a single mum before, especially one with purple hair... or green, as it was back then.'

She looks over her shoulder and laughs at my expression. 'I'm only teasing. They're not too bad around here really, just a bit set in their ways. People were friendly enough once they got used to seeing me around. You're linked to Whitsend royalty anyway, so you'll have no problems fitting in.'

'Royalty?'

'The Williamses. They're right at the top of the unofficial

hierarchy of this town. They're very visible... well, their money is. Not forgetting their house and fancy cars.' She hesitates. 'Sorry, I don't mean to sound mean.'

'Do you know them well?'

'Me? No. Never met them personally. But I know the school benefits from regular donations from the Williamses, so it's a name we hear a lot of around here. I knew the couple who worked for them before, Mary and Tom Gooding. They were lovely people, but then one day they'd just gone... lock, stock and barrel. People raised an eyebrow at that.'

'Oh really?' I think about Ted referring to a falling-out, the items they left behind and Neil's instruction to keep my mouth shut. 'Did you know the Goodings well?'

'Not really. We'd pass the time of day if we bumped into each other and I sometimes saw Mary down at the allotments so we'd have a cuppa and a chat. She was nice, but the old guy, Tom, he was a bit of a grumpy old sod. If she was with him, she acted like a different person. Hardly said a word.' She wiped her brow as she walked with the back of her hand before adding, 'I suspected he might be quite controlling with her.'

The kids thunder by us, laughing and calling out to each other. My heart warms to see Albie so carefree. We walk in silence for a minute or so, and when we near the end of the track, Albie runs back to me, holding out his hand to display what looks like a flat grey piece of slate. 'Look, Mum, it's a fossil. Edie says it's millions of years old!'

Keris peers down at it. 'Looks like alum shale. That's probably the remains of a small reptile you can see pressed into the rock there.'

'Cool!' Albie's eyes shine as Keris's fingernail traces what might be a small, segmented tail. Edie calls him and he runs off again.

'Friendly warning, Lottie: soon his bedroom will be full of fossils just like Edie's,' she says, smiling. 'I put some shelves up for her to display them but now they're chock-a-block and the fossils cover half the floor, the top of her drawers, the windowsill... everywhere!'

I laugh. 'Thanks for the tip. I'll prepare myself.'

We start the descent towards the single-storey, brick primary school nestling against the bottom of the hillside. The path is wide enough here for us to walk side by side.

'So, what do you plan on doing with yourself while Albie's at school and your husband is up at the estate?' Keris asks.

'I'm going to look for a part-time job once we've settled in a bit. What about you, do you work?'

'Oh yes. I work too many hours but at least it's from home and I enjoy my job. I'm a virtual PA, providing a service to lots of small companies. Call handling, admin duties, diary management... the list goes on.'

'Oh that sounds interesting.'

'It's varied, I'll say that.'

We're now at the bottom of the hill where the lane meets a side road. Suddenly, there are lots of parents and kids around, all converging at the gates. Several parents catch my eye and give a nod of curious acknowledgement. Everyone knows each other here and they clearly recognise we're newbies.

'Listen, I've got to shoot off this morning, but if you fancy meeting up for a coffee at the beach then just let me know,' Keris says.

'Thanks,' I say. 'I'd like that.'

'Perfect!' She digs in her pocket and pulls out a phone. 'I'll send you a text now, so we have each other's numbers.'

Not bad, I think, as I save her details into my phone as a new contact. Third day here and it looks like I've already found myself a friend.

SEVEN

When I get back home, it's more unpacking and putting stuff away for me. I ferry stuff back and forth between rooms upstairs and take a peek outside between the slats of the blind in the spare room.

My heart leaps when I see Neil briefly walking down a path with a wheelbarrow before he disappears. It's just a glimpse but he looks tall and handsome... and happy. He looks *really* happy. When he moves out of sight, there's further movement and a slim woman in oversized sunglasses and a bikini top with white shorts picks up a book from a table and takes it somewhere out of sight. I had no idea I could see so much of the grounds from here.

Thanks to the lack of photographs of the Williamses online, I don't know what I expected Neeta Williams to look like but it wasn't quite as slim and attractive as this. I stand there a few more seconds but there's no further movement.

My good mood dissipates and suddenly I feel a bit low and de-energised. I decide it must be the cloying heat in here and move away from the window and out of the room, closing the door behind me.

. . .

There's a rap at the door mid-morning and a middle-aged man stands there wearing navy overalls with 'Dave's Removals' emblazoned on the pocket. They're early.

'No way we can get the wagon up to the door, love. Sorry.'

My heart sinks. 'The day we got here, we saw the track was bad. My husband called your office and left a message on your answerphone,' I say, my heart rate working up to a steady gallop. 'Nobody got back to us so we assumed it would be OK.'

The man pulls the corners of his mouth down. 'Message didn't get through to us at the cutting edge, love. That track out there is full of potholes and we can't carry the big items over it. Health and safety regulations, see.'

'So... what do you suggest?'

He blows out air and runs a hand through his short salt and pepper hair. 'I mean, we can carry the bags and wheel the bikes down, I suppose, but some of the boxes are too big to see where we're going.'

I know when I'm beaten. 'Just bring what you can then,' I say, irritated. 'You'll have to leave the rest at the end of the track.'

'Right you are, love,' he says cheerfully before turning to leave and then looking back and giving her an exaggerated wink. 'Don't suppose there's any chance of a cuppa, is there?'

'You must be—'

'Everything OK here, Lottie?' a voice calls out. My spirits lift at the sight of Ted approaching down the path. He's wearing loose jeans, tan Caterpillar boots and a lumberjack-style checked shirt over a white T-shirt.

'Oh, hi, Ted! This is the removals guy. He says they can't get the truck up to the cottage.'

'I'm pretty sure anyone with an ounce of driving skill could get a double-decker bus up here.' Ted smirks.

It's not the right approach and Dave instantly digs in his heels. 'We're not insured for surfaces like this and I'm not prepared to put my job on the line to break the rules.'

Ted straightens up and the mirth melts from his face, replaced by a hardened expression. 'You'd better empty the van at the end of the track then.' His voice drops low and dangerous. 'A couple of my strapping lads will get the stuff to the cottage, no bother. We wouldn't want you straining your back.'

'Ted, I can't expect you to do that, it's not—'

He holds up a hand. 'It's no problem at all, Lottie. The lads will sort it.' He shoots Dave a withering look. 'What's the world coming to, eh? A so-called removals team scared of a few potholes. Maybe it's a young man's game.'

'Now hang on a minute, guv—'

'Like I said, just leave the gear at the end of the track.' Ted turns his back as the tubby removals guy stomps off, chuntering. Ted had seemed so amiable when he'd popped down to the cottage on Saturday, I'm surprised to witness this sudden, tough edge. I feel my eyes gravitate to his wide shoulders and muscular forearms and avert my gaze. He coughs, bending over slightly as if he's got something stuck in his throat.

'Can I make you a cuppa, Ted?' I offer. 'I can't tell you how grateful I am.'

'Thanks, but I need to get back up to the estate. Expect the lads down in the next ten minutes. They'll take the stuff wherever you need it, upstairs, downstairs, no problem.' He turns to leave and then hesitates. Looks back at me. 'By the way, Neeta said she's going to pop down to say hi when she's got a moment. Thanks for your understanding about not mentioning the last tenants.'

'No worries at all,' I say brightly, surprised he's felt the need to stress his message yet again.

'Neeta seems like a confident woman but... well, she can get quite low at times. She worries about other people too much, that's her problem. Allows stuff to play on her mind, if you know what I mean?'

'I know exactly what you mean,' I say. 'The sort of stuff that won't let you get back to sleep at three a.m., I expect?'

'Spot on,' Ted agrees. 'Sounds like you've been there. Neeta could do with a friend like you, who gets it. Anyway, I'll send the lads down.'

Thirty seconds later, he's out of sight.

True to Ted's word, a couple of eager young men appear at the cottage door within ten minutes and make numerous trips back and forth, their arms full of boxes and bin bags. They refuse my offer of refreshments and hoist furniture onto their shoulders as if the heavy wooden pieces are light as a feather, insisting on placing everything in the rooms in which the items will be needed.

Thirty minutes later, they've left and the cottage feels full to bursting with ever more of our belongings. I can't believe Ted made it so easy for me, though. That could have been a real nightmare.

I glance at the wall clock in the kitchen. Eleven-thirty. I give myself an hour to unpack as much stuff as possible before stopping for lunch. I'll start with the bedroom and call at the general store for the ingredients for dinner later. I want the room to look inviting later when Neil and I get cosy after our meal and bottle of wine.

I open a box full of clothes. Lots of socks, underwear, belts and scarves in this one. I quickly empty Neil's balled socks, filling one of the small, top drawers in the vintage mahogany chest that came with the furnished cottage. Underneath the soft items, I find some small binoculars Neil must have tossed in his sock drawer. He took up birdwatching at one point during his recovery. He'd sit for hours in the garden with his notebook, marking down various observations. That only lasted about a month before he moved on to architectural modelmaking and woodcarving on YouTube after that.

Previously, Neil had been a man who'd had little time for new hobbies. He'd built up his small gardening company from scratch. He'd had about a year where he'd suffered from chronic back pain, but after visiting his GP and a chiropractor, the pain had finally eased and the business started to really flourish. Then he won a lucrative landscaping contract to maintain the grounds of a high-end apartment build close to where we lived in Nottingham. It had felt like a real step up in growth and Neil had been adamant we should celebrate the high note with a family trip to London. Albie – then seven – had been thrilled to eat at the Hard Rock Café before we'd all enjoyed a night at the theatre to see *Matilda the Musical* where Neil had surprised us by booking seats just a few rows from the stage. For the first time, we'd had the money to spend on a few frivolous items without losing sleep that it would compromise the bills. It had felt like we'd finally turned a corner from always having to count the pennies.

But within days of us getting back from London, Neil found himself suddenly short-staffed on the new project from a variety of causes including illness, family problems and pre-booked holidays. Without a second thought, he'd rolled up his shirt-sleeves to help out. As a team, they'd been limping along, just about managing to satisfy the minimum requirements to prevent the contract from falling behind.

One day, Neil had to supervise the early delivery of a large, wrought-iron fountain complete with an Aphrodite statue before his labourers arrived on site. When the delivery had taken place, instead of leaving it in situ, Neil had tried to move it so he could begin removing the swathes of cellophane wrapping. The lifting equipment he'd been using had slipped and fallen, pinning him to the ground. It was ten minutes before the staff had begun to arrive and found him injured. Another fifteen minutes before an ambulance and fire crew had arrived to cut him loose.

I sigh and put the binoculars aside to take back into the spare room. Now's not the time to revisit those difficult times and I resolve to keep my mind on the here and now.

When I open a drawer, I see the floral drawer liner is folded and buckled. I remove it to readjust the fit and find a single, folded sheet of paper underneath and a photograph of an old house. I study the faded image of the dark old building on top of the hill where Seaspray House stands now. White sheeting covers something at the side of it, maybe building work. At the edge of the photo, I spot the stone corner of the cottage and the slope of its tiled roof. It looks like it was much further away from the main residence back then, but then the new house is probably three times the size of the old one, so it makes sense we're now living in closer proximity.

When I unfold the paper, I see it's a short handwritten letter. It doesn't take long for me to read it.

I read it a second time and then I read it yet again and the back of my neck prickles.

Later, I get a short text from Neil.

> *Sorry, I'll be late. Ted wants to go through some paperwork for an hour or so.*

So much for the romantic meal we're supposed to be having to mark his first day! I'll cook something simple so it won't spoil if he's back later than expected.

When Neil finally returns from Seaspray House, it's six-thirty. He's upbeat and doesn't even mention the planned meal.

'How did it go today?' I say.

He sits down and starts to unlace one of his heavy work boots before leaning his elbows on his knees and looking up at me. For a second I think he's going to say the job is not what he'd hoped.

'Lottie, what can I say?' He looks at me and laughs suddenly. 'The job is bloody brilliant! I have a great boss, a great team to manage and I've got *you* to thank for giving me the confidence to go for it.'

I smile and pick up the kettle. It feels strange, seeing him striking out on his own again. He's even got a bit of his old confidence back. During the time he'd been effectively housebound, I'd gotten used to him relying on me for every last thing. Asking my advice on the simplest decisions, like what to wear for a hospital visit, or what he might eat for lunch. I'd known where he was every minute of every day and I had felt utterly content.

For the first time in my life I'd known without a shred of doubt that Neil could not, would not, leave me.

'Neeta and Ted have already made me feel so welcome. Their life's like something out of a magazine. You should see Ted's Rolex and he says they have a cinema room in the house. Albie's going to lose his mind when he sees that!'

'Sounds wonderful. I... there's something I wanted to show you, Neil.'

'Oh yeah, what's that then?'

'I found something upstairs that's a bit worrying.'

'Oh?' He stops unlacing his boot and looks up, concerned.

'I found an old photograph and I also found a letter.'

'Doesn't sound that worrying, to be fair.' He goes back to attending to his boot.

I take the piece of paper out of my pocket and unfold it before handing it to him. 'Looks like somebody started to write it but maybe got interrupted. Have a read.'

Neil frowns and starts reading out loud.

To whom it may concern.

If anyone finds this and something has happened to us then please don't believe everything you're told. I've tried to find out exactly what has been happening up there but... they're good at covering their tracks and

'It kind of... just stops,' Neil says, turning the paper back and forth in his hand.

'That's the point, though,' I say sharply. 'A bit worrying, wouldn't you say? *What's happening up there...* that's obviously Seaspray she's talking about.'

He puts the letter on the floor and pulls off his boot. 'She? It's not signed off. Could mean anything, if you ask me.'

'It looks like a woman's handwriting,' I remark. 'If Mary Gooding wrote this then what she says in the letter has actually come to pass, hasn't it?'

'Huh?' He moves over to the table and picks up a free local newspaper that was pushed through the letterbox earlier.

'Well, something *has* happened to them.'

'Yes, they've retired,' Neil says drolly. 'Nothing remotely sinister about that.'

'Ted *said* they'd retired, but what if—'

'Oh Lottie!' He stands up and walks over to me in his socked feet, wrapping his arms around me. He smells of the outside, of earth and the spicy aftershave I bought him last Christmas. 'You're reading too many true crime books in bed at night.'

'It's not a laughing matter, Neil.' I push him gently away. 'I think it's odd.'

He sighs, his eyebrows beetling. 'Mary Gooding was getting on a bit, right? Ted said she'd been unwell and that there'd been some kind of a fallout. Ted was completely upfront about all that.'

'She was in her late sixties, I think. That's hardly ancient. What if that letter—'

'Hardly a letter. It's just a few lines, the ramblings of a confused person.'

I almost wish I hadn't mentioned it to him. It's too late now, but I hadn't expected him to be so instantly defensive of the Williamses.

'You met Neeta today?' I fill the kettle and flick on the switch before turning to look at him.

'Yeah, she came to say hi before going out. She was all dressed up and...' He hesitates. 'She said she's really looking forward to meeting you and Albie.'

'That's nice. What's she like then? How was she dressed?'

He hesitates and I turn to look at him. Is it my imagination, or are his cheeks turning pink?

'She seems lovely. Very friendly.'

'I mean, what does she look like, silly?'

'Well, she's tall and slim... I think you'd have liked her outfit. She seems really nice.'

'What's the house like?'

'The house?'

I look at him. 'Seaspray House? The big glass mansion on the edge of the cliff?'

'Oh yeah, right. Got you.' He pushes his boots aside and stands. 'The house looks really impressive, from the outside at least. Immaculate, big airy rooms and glass walls... but I didn't go in.'

I frown. 'Why not?'

He shrugs. 'They didn't invite me in. I mean, why would they? When it comes down to it, I'm just the hired help.' He laughs. 'I'm hardly going to ask for a nosy around. Neeta said she's going to pop down and say hi at some point.'

I reach for the photograph and place it down in front of him on the scratched wooden table. 'I found this, too.'

He picks up the photograph and studies it.

'That's obviously the house that used to be up there. They must have torn it down to build Seaspray,' I say. 'I don't know what the white sheeting at the side was for.'

'Can't say as I blame them. It looks a bit like Dracula's old gaff.'

'It's Gothic architecture, Neil. A good example of it, too, I'd say. I'm surprised it wasn't a listed building. They'd never have been allowed to knock it down then.'

'Personal taste, I suppose, but Ted made a damn good job of the new house. There's nothing that guy can't do.' Neil takes a last look at the picture before putting it down. 'He was telling me he's thinking of buying a Ferrari. Can you believe it? God, what I'd give for a drive in that!'

'Very flash,' I say. 'Where's all their money come from?'

'Not something you can really ask; I'm guessing Ted sold his successful building company or something. Right, I'm going up for a shower.' He starts to walk away before turning back and adding, 'Oh, and just a thought. If Neeta calls down, it's probably best you don't mention finding that note. You don't want to remind her of their disagreement and upset her.'

I can't wait to meet this woman who's got grown men running around fixing stuff so she doesn't get upset.

EIGHT

TUESDAY

The next morning, we get to the playground just as the school bell rings. We were late leaving the house thanks to Albie misplacing his reading folder and so didn't see Keris and Edie on the way in, either.

The classroom doors open and the kids pile inside. Miss Cavendish, Albie's teacher, makes a point of giving me a wave.

'How's it going? Still unpacking?' She smiles as she approaches, her youthful skin luminous in the early light.

'We're settling in fine, but it still feels like I'll be unpacking for the rest of the year!'

'I can imagine. I just wanted to let you know Albie had a good day yesterday. He was a little quiet as you'd expect being new, but he's made a friend already in Edie Travers.'

'Thank you so much. He met Edie on his first morning's walk to school!'

'Well, I rotate the kids' seats regularly, so he'll get to know the others in no time at all.'

I breathe out. I wasn't able to get much out of Albie last

night but didn't want to press him too much. 'I'm happy he's made a friend already. It usually takes him ages to pluck up the courage to speak to people.'

The teacher smiles. 'Edie's a lovely girl and very confident. She hasn't been at the school that long herself, so she knows how it feels to be the newbie. She's just what Albie needs to help bring him out of his shell.'

I thank her and she heads back to the classroom. I'm grateful for the time she's taken to reassure me. This school is tiny compared to Albie's sprawling primary back in Nottingham. There were three times the number of kids on roll there and although the staff tried their best with limited resources, I always felt like Albie – being a quiet boy up until the last few months – sometimes got forgotten about in the melee of bad behaviour and high rate of staff absences.

I join the throng of parents exiting the playground but turn off into reception rather than heading to the school gates. There are a few parents waiting at the hatch. Someone wants to pay for a child's school trip, and another owes money for his daughter's school meals. I take out my phone and see I have a text notification from Neil.

'Hi, can I help?' a voice calls from the hatch and I realise I'm now the only parent waiting. I push my phone back into my bag and step forward to speak to the middle-aged receptionist who's peering over cat's eye spectacles at me with a face of full make-up and her hair pinned very firmly into a neat French pleat.

'I'm Lottie Carter. I think I have some new-starter forms to fill in for my son, Albie.'

The receptionist glances down at her desk, sighing as she flicks through slips of paper and files before finding the appointment book. 'You would not believe the deluge of paper we get in here each and every day.'

'I do know how it feels,' I offer. 'I used to work in a school office back in Nottingham. I used to keep a filing tray at the side to dump all the stuff in I got given at the hatch!'

The woman looks at me, blinking her astonishingly bright-blue eyelids as though she's suddenly seeing me in a different light. 'What a good idea! Tell you what, I'll buzz you through and you can sit at the spare desk to complete the admin. No sense in you trying to balance it on your knee out there.'

When the double door buzzes, I walk through into the office.

'I'm Gloria, known as Mrs Stafford to the children.' We shake hands. 'Pleased to meet you, Lottie.'

As I fill in the various contact forms, photographic permission and trip parental authority letters – all of which I'm very familiar with from my old job – we pass the time of day.

Then Gloria takes a phone call and I open the text message from Neil.

Sorry, be a bit later home tonight. Ted needs help with a job off-site. Text when I'm on my way home.

My throat tightens. It's not just the irritation of him agreeing to help Ted when I'm supposed to be making us a nice dinner again; it's the deeper ruminations that make me nervous. The feeling he's somehow already started to move away from us.

When Gloria comes off the phone, I pass her the completed contact form. The receptionist scans over it and her eyes widen over the top of her bifocals again.

'Oh, your husband works up at the Seaspray Estate?'

'Yes, he's the new estate manager there.'

'The Williamses are *such* nice people. Did you know they donated the funding for our floodlight football pitch?' Gloria points to the window, indicating the field at the rear of the school. 'Before that, the kids had to travel miles on a hired coach just to practise after school.' She looks back down at the form and smiles fondly to herself. 'Yes, we're big fans of Mr and Mrs Williams here at Beck Primary, as you can imagine.' She checks the form. 'How's your husband finding it up there?'

'It's very early days but yes, I think it's going well.'

'Mrs Williams, Neeta – she's a stunningly attractive woman. Dripping with diamond jewellery and designer labels and yet she's got absolutely no ego.'

I think about Neil's text letting me know he'll be later home than planned again. I've already postponed our supposedly romantic dinner from last night to this. Now it feels like I might as well give up altogether.

For as long as I've known Neil, prior to the accident, he's been the kind of man who works very hard but, at the end of each day, it's always been tools down and home. I find it extraordinary he's willingly volunteered to help Ted Williams for a second consecutive day.

'How lucky, getting to live in the Seaspray cottage, too.' Gloria's voice interrupts my thoughts.

Against my better judgement, I hear myself broaching the exact subject I've been warned off. 'Mr and Mrs Gooding lived there before us, I believe? We're so lucky their retirement created an opening for Neil.'

As I'd hoped, Gloria is not a woman to mince words. 'The less said about those two, the better.' She presses her lips together and shuffles the paperwork in front of her. 'How they got away with what they did, I do not know. They were very lucky the Williamses didn't press charges.'

I try and fail to keep the surprise from my face. 'That sounds quite serious. What happened?'

She swallows and picks up the phone. 'I shouldn't have really said anything.'

'I won't repeat anything you tell me, Gloria.' I stare as the woman punches in a number and presses the receiver to her ear.

'I'm not one to listen to idle gossip and I'd rather hear what happened from someone I can trust.' I see Gloria falter as the flattery hits its target.

The older woman sighs and puts down the phone. 'You haven't heard this from me, OK?'

'You have my word.' I'm almost bursting with anticipation.

'There's no easy way of saying this. Tom Gooding, he... he assaulted Neeta Williams. It was terrible really but it's not for me to go into the details. Suffice to say he was fired on the spot.'

'Goodness! Were the police involved?'

'No. I think... it was dealt with quickly and privately. As always, the Williamses, despite being unjustly treated, sought to do the right thing. I heard Mary Gooding had been in a bad way for some time, suffering from some kind paranoia or anxiety. Police involvement would have probably pushed her over the edge. As I say, please don't repeat anything I've said,' Gloria adds hastily.

'Do other people know what happened up at Seaspray?' I ask, feeling breathless.

'They do not!' Gloria looks horrified. 'There are just a handful of us who know the truth. People who know Mr and Mrs Williams well, of which I consider myself one. On their many visits to the school I always make sure they're taken care of, and Mrs Williams is always interested in how my Bengal cats are doing. I've only spoken to a handful of people I trust. And now that includes you.'

It doesn't take me long to figure out that if Gloria has so willingly spilled her guts to me, a complete newcomer to the bay, then chances are she's told a good few other people, too.

I wonder how the very private and very generous couple would feel about *that*.

NINE

I'm getting tired of the unpacking and cleaning now. My back is aching, reminding me of the broken promise I made to myself in the new year to start exercising again. Just like the year before, I'd had good intentions but being the only person who could do anything in the house during Neil's recovery meant I felt constantly exhausted. When push came to shove, I couldn't face a brisk walk, never mind a run.

This unpacking has to be done, though, and I keep thinking how nice it will be to have everywhere neat and organised. I can't wait until the place really feels like home.

I also want make a start on cooking a batch of meals for the freezer. Just simple one-pot stuff like chilli con carne, curry and shepherd's pie for the times Neil is late home, which seem to be becoming the norm. But I'm trying not to think about that.

Last night, when Neil went up to shower, there was a problem with the boiler. Now, there's no hot water so my hair is a greasy mop that I've pulled back from my face with a frayed old floral scarf.

Neil, not wanting to bother Ted, has ordered a new timer from Amazon, which will be delivered today. 'It was the last one in stock, so it would be great if you can be in when it comes,' he told me this morning. 'We need that part, or it'll be cold showers all weekend.'

Albie was grumpy this morning, insisting he could walk to school on his own, that several of the kids in his class already do so. 'There are no drug dealers around here, Mum. It's different to where we lived before.'

It was a fair point but I don't feel comfortable with him walking alone so soon. 'That might be so, but I prefer to take you in anyway,' I told my disgruntled son. 'We can look at it again when you're ten.'

When I'd insisted on him washing his face and hands with cold water this morning, I'd cemented my 'Unreasonable Mother of the Year' award.

I glance in the hall mirror when I pass. I'd made a slice of toast and jam when I'd got back from the school run and had managed to spill a dollop of raspberry jam down my top. Rather than change, I wipe it off, leaving a dark, sticky mark, and get on with the last of the unpacking.

When the doorbell sounds just as I'm about to make a coffee, I'm expecting Neil's parcel. When I open the door, the tall, willowy woman I saw in the garden stands there. Close up, I can see she's in her late forties with short black hair and smooth skin and she is very attractive. She looks immaculate, dressed simply in dark navy jeans, a fine grey wool sweater and white trainers with a distinctive green and red Gucci stripe.

For a moment I can't speak; I just freeze for some unfathomable reason.

'Hello, you must be Lottie! I'm Neeta Williams.' She holds out a hand. 'It's so lovely to meet you at last!'

I force myself to snap out of it and shake her hand.

'Neeta... hello! Please, come in.' I step back from the

doorway and out of the cloud of my visitor's strong floral perfume.

I feel a wave of dread at being caught out looking so scruffy... and her looking so ravishing, too! Hopelessly, I attempt to smooth back wisps of hair and wipe a finger under each eye to remove any smudged eyeliner.

'Are you alright?' Neeta says, concerned. 'You look a bit hassled. Have I called at a bad time?'

'No, I'm fine. I just feel such a mess! Please, come in.' I do feel a bit out of sorts all of a sudden, but I usher her over the step into the kitchen. 'Neil mentioned you might pop down. I'm so sorry about the clutter.'

'No need to apologise, you've just moved in. And you look absolutely fine, by the way!'

It's kind of her to reassure me, even though we both know she's lying through her teeth.

I point to the worktops, stacked with stuff I've taken out of the cupboards. 'I was just wiping the shelves before I put the last bits away.'

Neeta looks concerned. 'Oh dear, I hope the kitchen wasn't dirty...'

'Not at all! The place is spotless. I just gave it a quick wipe.'

'Oh, that's a relief! I booked an end-of-tenancy clean from a local cleaning company. I wanted everything looking spick and span for when you moved in but Ted found a few bits they'd missed when he checked.' I think about the letter and photograph concealed under the drawer liner. He'd obviously missed those items, too. 'When the last tenants moved out, we found they'd been living in a bit of a mess.'

When they'd 'moved out'. It is interesting phrasing after my conversation at the school.

'Well, it was very clean, so thank you for doing that.' I know I'm babbling. I try to force myself to relax. I'm assuming Neeta will judge me but she actually seems very nice and not like that at all. 'Can I get you a tea or coffee? Or perhaps a glass of water?'

She checks her fancy watch. 'Go on then, a quick coffee would be nice. Thank you!'

While I fiddle around with coffee pods and the milk steamer, Neeta looks approvingly around the room. 'You've already got it looking so much homelier in here,' she says. Diamond rings glitter on her slender fingers as she flicks idly through a Gordon Ramsay cookbook on the worktop before moving over to the window. 'I've always thought this is a great view. It's very cosy in here.'

Neeta watches me pour milk into a stainless-steel jug and pop it under the milk steamer pipe. She's standing close enough to me that I can smell every last note of her sweet, floral perfume. It's a little sickly, so I walk over to the fridge to escape it and Neeta steps back, turning her attention to the coffee machine. 'Gosh, aren't you clever? Ted has one like this at home, possibly even more complicated. I haven't got a clue how to use the thing.'

I finish the coffees and hand her one. 'It's just practice really.' I hesitate before adding, 'I could pop up and show you how, if you'd like.'

'Oh no... I'll leave that to Ted!' She follows me through to the lounge.

'More mess in here, I'm afraid.' I cringe at the overflowing boxes of cushions, books and mismatched blankets we had in our old lounge.

'I'm sure it'll look lovely when you've finished. Neil mentioned Albie's started at his new school. I've seen him when you both walk to school. He seems quite a happy boy, pointing out plants and birds.'

'Yes, we're hoping he'll be very happy here,' I say. It's baffling that Neeta has managed to see so much detail from the main house, which stands a good way back from the hillside path. Still, it's nice of her to say such things.

'And he's a handsome little chappie... just like his daddy!' Her comment rankles, but I push it away. She picks up a framed photograph of Neil with Albie on his shoulders when he was much younger. 'Ted's going to find Albie a few jobs to do at Seaspray, if he wants to come up. How old is he?'

'He's nine,' I say. 'Nine going on nineteen! He's pushing against boundaries and feeling his feet a bit. What about you, Neeta, do you have children?'

I'm alarmed to see her physically stiffen. After a few moments of awkward silence, she answers me stoically. 'No. Ted and I couldn't have children. Sad really, but we made peace with it years ago.'

Silence rings in my ears. 'Sorry. I didn't mean to be intrusive.'

'No, it's a fair question. We would have liked little ones but... I suppose what's meant to be is meant to be.' She stares into the middle distance and after a few moments I feel moved to fill the space.

'I completely get that. Time moves on so quickly and—'

'You're so right, Lottie. Time moves on and you try to forget about the lack and get used to the freedom being childless affords.' Neeta's voice sounds almost monotone now, like she's falling back into a well-rehearsed defence. 'We've always loved our holidays abroad although we haven't been for a while.' I watch as Neeta's mouth stretches into a semblance of a smile. 'We're really very lucky. We've nothing to complain about.'

'That's good.' I shift in my seat as the feeling of discomfort grows inside me. There seems to be a big disparity between what she's saying and how she looks. Her dull eyes, the corners of her mouth turning down... I'd like nothing more than to change the subject but suddenly, I can't think of a single thing to say.

Neeta looks straight at me, her demeanour perking up. 'Anyway, I'm so looking forward to meeting your boy. Albie. If you and Neil fancy a night out when you're settled in, then please don't hesitate. We're available for babysitting!'

I think about Albie and the way he can be a little shy when meeting new people. That's why I'd been so surprised when he'd felt at ease with Keris and Edie. It always takes him a long time to develop trust with new people. A bit like me. There's no way he'd want to stay with the Williamses if Neil and I fancy a night out. Not for the foreseeable future, anyway. But things might change if he visits Seaspray a few times.

'Thanks so much for the offer,' I say. 'I'm sure Albie will want to get to know you both. He's a bit nervous after—'

I bite down on my tongue. I don't want to get into any negative stuff in this, our first meeting. But Neeta is instantly astute. 'After what?'

'Albie had a bit of trouble at his last school with some of the other boys. I began to think it might really affect his education and... well, let's just say it was a difficult time. He sort of went back in his shell after that.'

It had happened after our circumstances changed. Neil went from being an attentive, loving husband and father to an emotionally distant shadow of his former self following the accident. He was forced to close the business. I had no choice but to watch my confident, capable husband sink rapidly into a bleak hopelessness from where he seemed to find it impossible to imagine any future worth having. He often lashed out verbally in frustration, becoming snappy and snide, even with his son.

I'd sat down with Albie and explained that Daddy wasn't cross with him. 'He's upset he can't work any more or go out on his bike. He's not angry at *you*, even though it sometimes feels that way. Do you understand?'

Albie had nodded but then he went quiet on me, too.

School summoned me after he started having problems with

the other kids. The few friends he'd had disappeared, and he became more insular. Somehow, he then began attracting the attention of bullies in the year above him who started spoiling for a fight every break and lunchtime with Albie always coming off worse.

Neeta's brow furrows with concern. 'Gosh, I can imagine it must have been hard, especially on top of everything else you've been through. Poor Albie, having to deal with bullies at such a young age.'

I don't elaborate. I have no intention of telling Neeta all the gory details of what we went through as a family back then. But it hasn't escaped my notice that Neeta said, *On top of everything else you've been through.*

What did she mean by that? I think she must be referencing Neil's accident. He'd given them very little detail about that period on his application, he'd said, although obviously he'd had to explain why he hadn't been working for the last two years. Neil is a private man, always the sort to underplay any challenges. I'm fairly sure he wouldn't have gone into any real detail.

'It must be a big relief, getting Albie away from such toxic surroundings. And at his school, of all places,' Neeta says.

'Yes, it was one of our main reasons for relocating.' I realise, too late, how that must sound. 'I... didn't mean that was the *only* reason we moved. Our main reason was Neil's job. We couldn't have done it at all without that.'

'Don't worry, I know what you mean.' Neeta smiles, taking a sip of coffee. 'I think there usually have to be a few reasons for making a big move, don't there? It's a big decision and lots of things have to align to make it possible, not all of them good,' she says generously. 'I expect if you were completely happy back in Nottingham, Neil wouldn't have even applied for the job. So I'm glad the opportunity to move here came at the right time.'

'Thank you,' I say, feeling my shoulders finally relaxing a

little. 'We were very grateful at the chance you and Ted gave Neil... and gave to us as a family.'

'Ted and I, we believe in giving people second chances. We all need them sometimes, don't we?'

Neeta turns her face slightly away as she smiles and something about her profile looks almost familiar. But when she turns back, the impression fades.

'I think Neil said you worked in a school before he had the accident.'

In the short time since he's worked at Seaspray, Neil seems to have given Neeta a pretty good potted history.

'It was just part-time, working in the local school's office doing some bookkeeping and admin, but I was sad when I had to give it up.'

Neeta raises her eyebrows. 'Are you hoping to get a job locally?'

'I'd like to, but it's a case of finding something that fits in with school hours.'

She thinks for a moment. 'I'm sure we can sort something out to help with that. Perhaps Neil could pop out to do the school run and bring Albie back to Seaspray until you finish work.'

'Oh, that's really kind, thank you!' I instantly imagine Albie freaking out because he has to spend time with people he doesn't know. 'But hopefully I can get something that doesn't put you out like that.'

'Really, it would be no trouble and we'd like having a youngster around the place. Such a shame you had to finish work to become Neil's carer,' Neeta says easily. 'He said you were wonderful – said he didn't know how he'd have got through the dark times without you.'

I drink my coffee to help cover my expression. I can't imagine Neil being so open with someone he's only just met.

He'd barely told his friends back in Nottingham anything about what he went through during his recovery.

'Depression is a terrible thing. It sounds like you both went through a very tough time,' Neeta adds.

'Neil spoke to you about that?' I say faintly.

'He did.' Neeta's tone is empathetic and, somehow, it makes things so much worse. 'I think it was a relief for him to talk to someone else about it, you know? That's often the case, isn't it? Those closest to you can be the hardest people of all to talk to.'

I put down my coffee cup, my throat too tight to speak. The clink on the wooden table sounds like a thunderclap in the silence of the small space.

Neeta is oblivious. 'Now, I came down here to suggest a bit of a get-together in the near future. Perhaps a meal one evening, in a couple of weeks or so? I thought it would act as an ice-breaker of sorts, seeing as we'll be living in such close proximity.'

'That's... kind of you,' I say, immediately wondering about Albie. Neeta hasn't offered for him to come but she obviously knows we'll need a sitter. And then I think about Keris and how she's already suggested a sleepover for the kids, so it might not be a problem.

'That's fine. I'm sure I'll be able to arrange a sleepover for Albie at his new schoolfriend's house.'

'No need for that, Albie's invited too!'

'That's kind of you but if it's an evening meal, it will be quite a late night, so I think it's best if—'

'Surely it won't hurt just the once? I mean, it's not like he's a toddler, is it?' She smiles.

'Well, no, but...'

'One more seat is no problem, so please don't worry about that. We can sort out a date soon, I'll let you know.'

I'm not worrying about *that*. I'm worried about Albie being bored out of his skull spending the whole evening with four adults. He doesn't miss a trick, either, so Neil and I won't be able to completely relax with him listening in.

It's only one night, I suppose, but I don't appreciate being railroaded into making a decision about my son.

'When we sort out a date I'll book Luigi's; it's Ted's favourite restaurant in the next town.'

'Oh! I... sorry, I thought you meant we'd be coming over to the house.'

'To Seaspray?' She gives me a faint smile. 'I'm afraid we're not big entertainers. We prefer to eat out. No mess!' She leans towards me and says in a stage whisper, 'If truth be known I'm a terrible cook. I'd be so intimidated being judged by an experienced homemaker like you, Lottie. Neil's told me all about your delicious Sunday roasts.'

I laugh at that. 'Just regular meat and two veg... a few roast potatoes and gravy. Nothing special, I assure you.' I feel secretly pleased at Neil's compliment.

'Sounds delicious! Maybe you can give me a couple of cooking lessons. Ted will be overjoyed if I serve him something other than readymade lasagne.'

I glance at her willowy figure and glowing skin. There's not much evidence of a diet of ready meals... more like salad, salad and more salad. Without dressing.

'I'd be very happy to help. Just say the word.' I'm not certain if she's being serious.

She looks at me. 'You know, I'm really looking forward to getting to know you, Lottie. It'll make such a nice change having a new friend so close by and I sense you're an interesting person with hidden depths.'

I don't quite know how to respond to that. Particularly as she's hit the nail on the head. My depths go so deep, I've almost forgotten what's lurking down there myself. After a moment or two, I say lightly, 'Well, I don't know about hidden depths, but it will be nice to get to know you too, Neeta!'

I remember she has already gleaned stuff from Neil that has made me nervous and uncomfortable. I don't know what he must have been thinking.

Neeta hesitates, then says, 'I don't want to sound unkind, but the population of Whitsend Bay is getting older. People never seem to move away from here so there's hardly any fresh blood.'

Neeta stands up, brushing down her immaculate jeans when I remember. 'Oh, by the way, I found a photograph upstairs.'

'Photograph?' Neeta repeats. Her face pales. 'I thought Ted had ensured the cottage had been completely cleared prior to your arrival.'

'Neil says it's a picture of the house that was there before you built Seaspray. I found it in a drawer in the bedroom,' I say, omitting to tell her about the letter, too. 'I'll get it for you.'

'No, no. Just tell Neil to give the photograph to Ted, will you? I must get going now. I've stayed too long.'

She rushes then, to the door, pulling it open and stepping outside. Her calm demeanour is disturbed and she clearly can't wait to get away. I call out goodbye and she raises a hand without looking back.

Looks like that old photograph unnerved Neeta for some reason and I find myself wondering exactly why on earth that might be.

TEN

A full ten minutes after Neeta leaves the cottage, I'm still thinking about the stuff she knew about Neil, about us.

I run the tap until the water is nice and cold and then I fill a glass and drink it straight down, my mind a blur of sounds and colours. I try to talk myself down. Neeta has shown me nothing but concern and kindness. Yes, she's made the odd comment about Neil's appearance but only in a complimentary, jokey kind of way.

I'd been so unnerved when Neeta recited personal information that Neil had told her. Information I never thought he'd discuss outside of our home. Sometimes, people act out of character and he's been stressed about the move, the new job. When people are nervous, they can speak out of turn. It doesn't mean he's been untrustworthy, but it is a shock he's spilled his guts in such a short time of meeting her.

What was it my therapist had said a few years ago? *Try to avoid going from zero to one hundred miles an hour on the strength of a look, a comment or mere suspicion.*

I know Neil loves me. He loves Albie, too. I've never found out that he's lied to me. Deep down, even when I get nervous and insecure, I know my husband would never do anything to hurt our little family unit.

When Neil gets home, he fills the cottage with a raw energy. His cheeks are ruddy, the effects of working outdoors in the sun already giving him a healthy glow. Even the golden glints in his mid-brown hair seem brighter.

It's a world away from the pale, lacklustre shell he was left with after the accident.

'How's your day been?' I hand him a glass of water when he sits opposite me at the rustic wooden table.

He drains half of it in one gulp. 'Thanks, I needed that. It's been a scorcher.' He sets his glass down. 'It's been a great day, though. The hours have raced by. I'm loving it. What have you been up to?'

'Neeta dropped by this morning,' I say lightly. 'She wants the three of us to go for a meal soon. To get to know each other better, she said.'

'That's nice,' he murmurs, looking at his phone.

'When we've agreed a date, she's going to book a restaurant in the next town. She insisted Albie come with us, but I'm worried it might be too late for him. The meal's not going to be at the house, which is a bit weird I think, don't you?' I say, watching him.

He taps the phone screen and the trace of a smile plays over his lips.

'Sorry, what?' He looks up briefly.

'The meal. It's at a restaurant, not up at the house. You'd think with a place like that at their disposal, they'd be used to entertaining but Neeta claims she doesn't do much cooking. Perhaps I should have suggested we just get a takeaway or something, keep it simple. Have you been inside the house yet?'

'Inside?'

'Yes, inside! Like, have you popped to the loo or anything, or followed Ted in while you were talking?'

'No, but I have my own facilities in the garden office. So there's no need to—'

'I get that. I just thought they might've asked you in for a cuppa or something.'

He shrugs. 'I have tea-making facilities in my—'

'Yes, I know. In your office. Must just be me, but I'd have thought you'd at least have stepped inside, had the chance for a quick recce.'

'Nope. Sorry to disappoint you.' He grins. 'If you're so desperate to see the place, why don't you just ask her?'

'Oh yes, like I'm going to do that. Not.'

'Well, whatever. Neeta would be very happy to show you around, I'm sure. Anything nice for tea?'

'I was a bit concerned that Neeta knew some personal stuff about us. About "our problems" as she referred to it.'

He puts his phone face down on the table and gives me his full attention. 'Oh?'

'Yes. She mentioned depression and what a devoted carer I'd been. Sounds like you've given her quite a detailed history of what happened.'

He sits up a bit straighter. 'I told her how amazing you've been throughout my recovery, if that's what you mean.'

'And the depression?'

'I just told her I'd got very low and I don't remember using that exact word.' He frowns. 'What's this about, Lottie? You know I wouldn't discuss our personal circumstances in detail like that. Especially not with someone I just met – and my employer, at that. I don't want her thinking I'm not fit to work.'

'I know... at least that's what I thought. But she seemed to know stuff. Like that I have a history of depression, too.'

'What? Did she say that?'

'No, but... it was the way she looked at me, the way she said it. I just felt like she knew.'

Neil lets out a long breath and picks up his phone again.

'Well, she doesn't know, Lottie. She can't know that and I certainly haven't told her.'

He looks disappointed he's had to defend himself, frowning now as he taps his phone screen. But I don't regret asking him; I had to, for my own peace of mind. Although even now, I don't feel completely reassured.

I read a couple of chapters of *Demon Dentist* with Albie and broach the subject of whether he wants to go up to Seaspray House to see where his dad works.

'I'm not sure,' he murmurs, keeping his eyes on the book.

'You'll be with your dad the whole time and you'll get to meet Neeta and Ted, too. They really want to get to know you, and think of it this way.' I nudge him playfully. 'You might even have fun!'

'Maybe.' He shifts against his pillow.

'You only have to go once and if you don't like it up there, that'll be the end of it. Deal?'

'OK,' he sighs moodily.

I don't usually push him out of his comfort zone, but I think he really needs to embrace our new home and get to know the people around us.

It's certainly something I need to do for myself.

ELEVEN

The next few days go by really quickly but they're not without problems.

I'm trying to get the cottage in order the best I can but it's getting more difficult as the week progresses because I'm not sleeping well. We usually go to bed around 10.30 to 11 p.m. and I drop straight to sleep. Then around two o'clock in the morning, I've been waking with a start, throwing off the quilt with my heart pounding and my body sweating.

Every time I've had a nightmare but I can't remember the detail. Only the feeling of panic and sadness almost exactly as I felt it the day I came home and it became apparent Mum had left.

A couple of days after my conversation with Neeta, Neil arranges with Ted to pick Albie up from school one day and take him up to Seaspray. Albie is a bit nervous at the prospect of this, but finally agrees because I think he really wants to see where his dad works.

I decide to walk up there just before Neil's finishing time so

I can walk back with them. Ted and Neeta are outside and they all stand together in a group, chatting.

'I was just telling Ted and Neeta about the jobs you've been looking at,' Neil says, pleased with himself.

'Oh, there's nothing definite. I've only just started having a little look around.'

'Found anything good?' Ted says.

'There are a couple of part-time positions with decent pay, but they don't fit in with school hours.'

'I meant it when I said Neil could pick Albie up from school on the days you have to work,' Neeta says immediately. 'If these jobs are decent then we could try it at least.'

'Thanks, Neeta. It's really kind of you to offer, but I—'

'If it doesn't work out then what have we lost? I'm sure he'll enjoy some time up at Seaspray.'

'Albie's done a great job today. Me and his dad could do with him helping us out a bit more. Might be a bit of pocket money in it for him even,' Ted adds. 'Right, Neil?'

'Sure.' Neil beams. 'What do you say, son?'

'Yesss!' Albie punches the air. 'Can I, Mum? Can I stay up here if you get a job?'

I feel a sharp twinge in my chest. I'm starting to feel a bit like an outsider here with these three so pally together. But I won't feel pressured into making a decision before I feel ready.

'We shouldn't put Lottie on the spot like this,' Neeta says and smiles at me when I give her a relieved look. 'Take as much time as you like to decide. The offer is there for as long as you want it.'

'Well, I think it's a great idea, for what it's worth,' Neil chips in, unhelpfully. 'What do you say, Lottie?'

Ted, Neeta, Neil and Albie all look at me with the same eager expression on their faces. A knot of heat throbs in my throat.

'Thanks, Neeta,' I say, ignoring Neil. 'I'll have a good think and we can talk about it as a family. But whatever we decide, I do appreciate your offer.'

Neil clamps his mouth closed at last and folds his arms across his chest.

He isn't quite ready to leave, so I walk back down to the cottage with Albie to get tea ready.

'It's brilliant at Seaspray, Mum. Do you know there's even a little wood in the grounds? Ted took me there to show me the old tree-house. I'm gonna help him repair it and then it's mine.'

'Yours?'

'Yep!' His face shines with happiness. 'We're going to repair some of the broken wood bits and repaint it and then it's mine. Ted says nobody else can go in it without my permission!'

'That sounds amazing, Albie,' I say, smiling at his enthusiasm. 'How come they have a tree-house up there when they have no kids?'

'I don't know, but you should see it. It's really cool!'

I feel a bit uncomfortable Albie is so full of visiting Seaspray House. I suppose, if I admit it, it stems from hidden insecurities. A feeling that other people can unduly influence the people you love and maybe even take them away from you.

The constant and exhausting 'watching for signs', the certainty in my belly that something bad was about to happen... it had started when Mum first left. On the last morning I saw her, everything had seemed completely normal. Nothing out of the ordinary at all. Over the years, I've revisited every second of every minute of those final few hours I was with her and I can confidentially say there was nothing. No sign of what was about to happen.

Mum was in a good place at that point. She'd kicked the heavy drinking habits ages before that, got her life together.

We'd had a cereal and toast breakfast together and I remember she had seemed relaxed. But over time I've often wondered if that in itself had been some kind of a sign? The fact she went to the trouble of making me a hot chocolate before school was unusual... did she know that would be the last time she'd see me?

From that point forwards, my watching out for signs became a bit manic. If I felt the churning in my stomach, the butterflies in my guts, I could easily become paralysed with fear. It was almost impossible to function then because I'd feel a terrible compulsion to start checking things again and again. Wash my hands, check my school bag, brush my hair. Wash my hands, check my school bag, brush my hair...

I don't like thinking back to those days. They're not happy memories. But it's not just that. It's everything else that happened back then.

Stuff I haven't thought about for a long time. Stuff I wish I could forget all about.

I see Keris a few mornings on the walk to school and we meet up at the beach shack where we drink good coffee and enjoy a freshly baked croissant after we drop the kids off at school.

'I've been looking at part-time jobs,' I say. 'There are a couple of decent openings, both admin and local, but it's hell trying to get hours to fit in with school.'

'Tell me about it,' she says. 'That's why I ended up working for an agency. Easier to choose your own hours.'

'I don't suppose the agency you work for has any positions to fill? I've got general admin experience as well as some book-keeping.'

She shakes her head. 'Sorry, no,' she says regretfully. 'Open-ings are like gold dust because the work's so flexible. But I will ask for you anyway, you never know. What will you do if nothing comes up with school hours?'

I take a sip of my latte and sigh. 'Thing is, Neeta Williams has said Albie can stay up at Seaspray on the days I have to work. They're happy for Neil to nip out and pick him up after school.'

She looks surprised. 'Now there's an offer!'

'I know. It's just... I feel like I'm neglecting him, you know? With everything still being so new and all, he's bound to still feel a bit unsettled.'

'Tell me about it. I'm the authority on mother guilt. I look at Edie and can't understand how on earth she can be growing into a kind, intelligent and well-adjusted kid having me as a role model.'

I laugh. 'Give over, you're a great mum! But I know what you mean. I guess we all beat ourselves up over our kids.'

'What does Albie think about it?'

'He's all for it. Neil too. I thought there was no way Albie would want to go anywhere else after school, but I can't believe how he's come out of his shell since we've moved.'

'He's playing for the school football team now, Edie says?'

I nod. 'He's like a different boy, Keris. You wouldn't believe it. Also, he already loves going up to Seaspray.'

'Have you had a tour around the house yet?'

I shake my head. 'Not yet.'

Keris's mouth falls open. 'What are you waiting for? I'd be straight in there having a nosey round, if I was you.'

'It's not through lack of wanting. I'm waiting for an invite. Seems like Albie and Neil are on the guest list but I've got to wait my turn.'

'Neil and Albie have had a look around?'

'Not yet. But Ted's told Neil about the cinema room they have and stuff so I guess it won't be long before Albie wants to watch a movie in there.'

'Nice they're taking an interest in Albie, I suppose, and making it easier for you to find a job.'

'True and I have to admit, Ted and Neeta are brilliant with him. He's excited to start earning a bit of pocket money doing some jobs up there for them with his dad and Ted's going to do up an old tree-house for him.'

Keris dabs a couple of croissant crumbs onto her fingertip. 'Then what are you waiting for? If I were you, I'd snap their hands off before they change their mind.'

TWELVE

Duncan appeared in their lives one night after Charlie's mum had been out 'on the razzle', as she called it. Kay had already been threatened by the agency for her poor timekeeping and warned she could lose both cleaning jobs if it didn't improve. This happened about the same time Charlie had noticed the bottles and cans of alcohol building up at the side of the dustbin in stark contrast to the empty food cupboards in the kitchen.

Charlie had been in bed fast asleep when shouting had disturbed her from downstairs. Already fully dressed and assuming her mum had knocked back one brandy too many, she'd rolled out of bed, ready to help Kay upstairs, as she'd had to do several times this month. But she froze in her tracks at the top of the stairs when she heard a man's voice cursing loudly.

'Stand up then, you silly bitch!'

Her mother made a small mew of pain and Charlie imagined the aggressive man squeezing her arm hard. She sprang back to life and ran downstairs.

The two adults stood in the hallway. Her mum was slumped against the wall and the man was holding her upright with an unkind, pincer-like grip on her upper arms.

'Leave her alone!' Charlie snapped, springing forward. The man let go and Kay slumped to the floor. 'Mum... Mum! Are you OK?'

'Oi, oi, who's this little firecracker then?' The stranger pushed his flabby whiskered face close to Charlie's and she caught the same unmistakeable whiff of alcohol on his breath that her mum often smelt of when Charlie got home after school.

Kay mumbled incoherently and Charlie felt worried her mum might not just be drunk but be really ill. 'I think Mum might need to see the doctor,' she said. The man stayed quiet and just kept staring at Charlie.

'Kay didn't tell me she had a kid,' he murmured finally, his mouth curling up on one side in an unpleasant sneer.

Charlie tried to haul her mother to her feet, but she could not seem to rouse herself. She fell into a deep snoring sleep and so Charlie got a blanket from the sofa and draped it over her where she lay.

When she stepped back, she saw the man still watching her. 'You're a good girl. I can see that.'

'You'd better go now because Mum is asleep.'

His eyes flickered over her chest and legs. Charlie looked down at her top and trousers to see if she had something on her clothes, but there was nothing. She wished the man would hurry up and leave so it was just her and her mum again. Then he said, 'Your mum said I could stay over tonight.'

'She was drunk, so she didn't mean it,' Charlie said simply. 'You can't stay here.'

'Why's that?'

'Because... my dad will be home soon.'

The man laughed. 'Good try, love. Kay told me your old man was a waster who left her when you were still a nipper. It's pretty obvious there's no man around.' He made a point of looking around at the flaking paintwork, the chipped door-frames. From where she stood, Charlie could see the two kitchen units that looked like gaps in a row of teeth where the doors had fallen off. There was nobody to do any jobs in the house and her mum couldn't afford to pay anyone to help out.

Even though her heart pounded harder still, Charlie tilted her chin and looked him in the eyes. 'My mum doesn't know you very well, so you can't stay here.'

'She wants to get to know me, though. She made that very clear.' He winked.

Her heart started to hammer. It was the middle of the night, so Charlie couldn't run and wake Mrs Cornell, who lived on the next street. She didn't know any of the other neighbours well and her mum had said one of them had reported her to the council for anti-social behaviour. But Charlie didn't like this man at all. He didn't seem like a good person.

Just as she started to feel a bit light-headed, he moved away from her.

'I know where I'm not wanted, so I'll get off. But I promise you this, lovely—' he turned and looked at her, his eyes hard and cold '—I'll be back. You can rely on that.'

Two days later, Charlie and Claire were walking back from school, each one either side of the path. Charlie had ignored Claire's mother's instruction not to wait for her at the end of the day.

'As long as I don't come to the house, she won't know we're still friends,' Charlie reassured her.

The girls tossed a ball to each other across the path, laughing when the other dropped it.

As the space narrowed, with tall bushes either side shielding them from open view, a tall, broad figure stepped out directly in front of them.

'Hello again, Charlie.'

Charlie whispered, 'It's that man I told you about, Duncan. He's the one who came to the house.' Claire stared at him with wide eyes.

'What do you want?' Charlie challenged him boldly.

'You're a pretty little thing.' He ignored Charlie and walked over to Claire. 'What's your name, then?'

Claire didn't answer and Charlie took a step forward.

'She doesn't want to speak to you and I don't either. We're not supposed to talk to strange men.'

He laughed. 'Strange? I'm your mum's fella, your new uncle.'

Charlie thought about her mum. The day after she'd collapsed in the hall, she'd been quiet and miserable. 'Why did you send him away?' she'd demanded. 'He helped me home and I didn't even get his phone number.'

Charlie stared at him.

'I've been at your house all day and I'm going back there later. So you'd better start showing me some respect.' Then he turned to Claire. 'Now, I can tell this young lady has far better manners. What's your name, lovely?'

'Claire,' she said in a small voice.

'Don't talk to him,' Charlie hissed.

The man took a five-pound note out of his pocket and held it out to Claire. 'You get yourself something nice, love. And when I next see you, we can have a chat. You can sit on my knee and tell me all about it.'

Claire took the money and thanked him. He patted the top of her head and left his hand there, allowing it to slide smoothly down her hair and settle on the skin of her neck.

'Lovely,' he crooned, his eyes staring into the middle

distance. He removed his hand and smelled it. 'Really lovely,' he whispered again, a strange look on his face.

THIRTEEN

LOTTIE

For the third night in a row, Albie gets home and changes out of his school uniform before dashing up to Seaspray. I can't believe he seems to have lost all interest in gaming so quickly. I usually have to prise the controls out of his hands just to get him to eat and do his homework.

It's great he's getting fresh air and spending more time with his dad, but I didn't quite expect his visits to Seaspray to be as frequent. I don't think he'd even notice I was absent some afternoons if I did get a job.

'Tell Dad tea will be ready in an hour!' I call to his disappearing back. Neil should finish at five and Albie will come back with him. There again, Neil never seems to be home on time.

I text my husband:

Albie on his way up.

I made a cottage pie yesterday, which I'll warm up with some vegetables for tea, so I have a bit of quiet time. Talking to Keris and also seeing how enthusiastic Albie is to go up to the house has inspired me to reconsider getting a job. Also, Neeta has walked down with Albie and Neil on a couple of days to say hello and I've realised she's just trying to be friendly and helpful. I still feel uncomfortable at the thought of her and Neil having more cosy chats about our personal life but that's probably just all in my head.

I fire up the laptop and pull up the job website where I'd spotted the vacancies.

One of the openings is an admin clerk at a sportswear manufacturing company at an industrial estate on the outskirts of Whitby. The other is a purchasing officer at a specialist manufacturer of swimming pool covers and chemicals together with other pool-related items. That one is a slightly better hourly rate but is around a thirty-minute drive inland.

On balance, I'd prefer the sportswear company. It's local and according to the job description, staff qualify for a generous discount on clothing, which will be brilliant for keeping Albie looking smart for less during his growth spurts.

I tweak my current CV and thirty minutes later, I've applied for both positions.

Later, in the spare room, I move over to the window and lift one of the slats of the blind just enough to see out. Seaspray House sits there grandly in front of me, transparent and tempting. I'd love to get inside and see how the other half lives. I can imagine sitting there with Neeta regularly and enjoying a cool drink in the lovely grounds.

There's no surprise I can't see Neil anywhere. There's lots of the estate I can't see from here, some of it the other side of the hill. I caught sight of him the other day but that was just pure luck. He's told me he spends a lot of time in his office. 'I'm looking through all the plans of the land and the planting schedules the previous head gardener worked from. Add into that the ordering that has to be done ahead of when we need it and you can imagine the extent of the paperwork.'

A movement catches my eye inside the house. Neeta appears out of a doorway and walks across the glass landing that runs the whole of the upstairs. I pick up the binoculars I found while unpacking and fiddle with the focus wheel until I have perfect magnified vision. She's wearing a pair of shorts, hot pink this time, and a short top that shows her trim midriff. She enters another room and then, after a few minutes, comes back again carrying a small stack of what looks like folded clothes.

Something about the angle of this particular window means I get a partial view of one side of the house. I know Neil would disapprove.

Neeta disappears into the first room again, which I think must be her and Ted's bedroom. I can see the side of a headboard and further down, the crumpled sheets hanging from the bed. That room must have amazing views of the ocean and it has a private balcony on the side. There's a grey raffia lounger out there with a thick, luxurious cushion and a matching table and couple of padded recliners. Living there must feel like being inside a double-page glossy feature of *Ideal Homes*.

I imagine Neeta sitting there on the balcony, drinking her morning coffee while browsing on her iPad or leafing through a magazine. How must it feel to wake up to that amazing view and to sit surveying all that land that belongs to you? I know nobody's life is perfect but... I reckon Neeta Williams's life must come pretty close.

It's strange I never see the two of them together unless other people are around. Neeta seems to do her thing and Ted does his. Almost as if they have completely separate lives. It wouldn't surprise me if they have their own bedrooms, too. If I had the time to sit watching the whole evening, maybe I could discover some of this stuff, get some answers. But I think Neil might have something to say about that. So I'm stuck with trying to piece together the random glimpses I'm lucky enough to catch.

Neeta appears suddenly and sits on the edge of the bed with the small stack of garments on her knee. I adjust the binoculars to sharpen the focus as she unfolds one and holds it up. It's a small pink T-shirt, a child's, I think. Then she does the same with the second and third item, a little girl's frilly floral dress and a small pair of trousers. She covers her face with her hands for a few seconds as if she's upset and then she sets the clothing aside and stands up, disappearing from view.

It's odd because I know they haven't got any kids. Maybe that's why she's upset, who knows?

I wait a few more minutes but she doesn't come back. Reluctantly, I lower the binoculars and leave the room.

Neil and Albie get back home, nudging each other and laughing together as they tumble in through the kitchen door. I glance at the wall clock and see they're on time for once.

'Hey, love. You had a good day?' Neil kisses me on the cheek before sitting down heavily on a wooden chair.

'Mum, you'll never guess what... Ted says I can watch a movie soon in their cinema room!'

'That sounds amazing.' I smile to myself at my recent prediction to Keris. Reaching up, I take a couple of long glasses out of the cupboard and pour in cold water from the filter jug I've finally unearthed from the packing boxes. I push one across the counter to Albie. 'Did Ted actually show you the cinema room?'

'Not yet because they're decorating in there.' He takes a deep gulp of water. 'But he says it's just like being at the cinema and they've even got a popcorn machine!'

'Gosh, it sounds incredible.' I look at Neil, who is scrolling through his phone.

'Have Ted and Neeta got decorators in, then, Neil?'

He puts down his phone and frowns. 'No? Not as far as I'm aware. There have been no vans on the drive and Ted hasn't mentioned it.'

'Albie says the cinema room is being decorated.'

He looks blankly at me. 'Maybe, then. Dunno.'

'The house is massive, Mum,' Albie says, draining his water glass. 'I looked through the windows downstairs and it's like...' He looks around the kitchen. '... a thousand times bigger than this whole cottage.' Albie puts down his glass with a thump before heading for the hallway. 'Just gonna have a few minutes on my PlayStation. I'm nearly at the next level.' He scurries off before I get a chance to refuse him.

Neil is tapping at his phone screen again. 'You've been fiddling with your phone since you got in,' I say irritably. 'Why don't you go and have a shower and then we can all eat together.'

'Sorry, Neeta's just texted me.' He tucks his phone into his jeans back pocket.

'Oh?' I fold my arms and turn around, leaning against the worktop.

'Ted's gone out and she needs a delivery moving from outside the kitchen door to the back of the house.' He stands up without looking at me. 'I'll just pop up and do it for her. Shouldn't take long. What time are you aiming to eat?'

'You've just walked in! Can't it wait until Ted gets back?'

'Don't make a big deal of it, Lottie. I'll be back in twenty minutes, tops.' He leans down to kiss my cheek and I turn away, feeling tearful.

'That's hardly the point. If she thinks she can call on you outside of your working hours, you'll never get a minute's peace.'

'It's just a one-off, I'm sure. I want to add value at this early stage, show them I'm a useful person to have around.'

I hear Albie shout in frustration from the other room as I assume he fails to make the next level. This is supposed to be our happy time. Our worries behind us and nothing but a fresh start to look forward to. But at this exact moment, I feel lonely and frustrated.

I wipe a tear away roughly as Neil slips out of the door, repeating his promise not to be long. Maybe the key to feeling better is to focus on myself and what *I* want a bit more. I don't want to get paranoid as I've done in the past. That just ends up pushing everyone away.

And that's the last thing I want to do.

FOURTEEN

NEIL

He heads down the cottage path and out onto the hillside. Frankly, Neil is relieved to escape Lottie, who's been on the warpath since the moment he stepped through the door. She's over-tired, he realises that. For some reason she's started having nightmares about her childhood again and she hasn't had those since she began having therapy a few years ago.

When he's out of sight of the kitchen window, he stands for a few moments and takes in some deep breaths. The grass beneath his feet, the wide blue sky above him. The air is so fresh out here, it feels different to anywhere else he's lived. So cleansing and invigorating; he can't get enough of it. He feels like he never wants to be landlocked in suburbia again.

As he makes his way up to the estate, he reflects how much he loves Seaspray itself. Although the house itself is ultra-modern, Ted had explained that the gardens are hundreds of years old and they wanted to preserve the feel of that. Neil loves everything about the place, but the walled garden especially. It reminds him of the beautiful grounds of the stately homes his grandparents used to take him to on their weekly visits. Grandad Joe, a talented gardener, had sauntered around the gardens with Neil, pointing out the exquisite planting, explaining how certain plants flourished in different soils and complemented each other. After that, Neil had looked at plants in a different light. They were wondrous, living things that deserved to be respected and nurtured.

As he grew older, his love for the outdoors increased. Being amongst plants and walking in woodland had helped him through the most difficult years of his teens when his mother died. He'd gone to live with his widower grandad then, but only two years later, his beloved grandad had passed away too.

Neil had been an insular boy, not wanting to share or talk about his feelings and, in some ways over the years, nothing has changed.

Still, he credits Grandad Joe for igniting his love of gardening. It had given him a successful business for a good few years and now, another difficult period in his life is over and plants again have been instrumental in his fresh start.

On the way up to the house, Neil stops at a large flower bed at the side of a wooden bench and considers the layout. He takes out his notebook and pen and makes a quick sketch of the area. He's thinking honeysuckle planted at the vertical wall to hide the brickwork and maybe some Mexican fleabane or similar. Ted is laid-back and he's already reassured Neil he isn't the sort of boss to interfere.

'You're free to bring your own ideas to Seaspray,' he'd said as they'd stood surveying the grounds from the front of the house on Neil's first day. 'In fact, I positively encourage it. Tom was reliable and knew his stuff, but he was a bit stuck in his ways and struggled creatively, particularly as he started to overstep the mark and get involved in things that didn't concern him. Things that were nothing to do with the job. And that crazy wife of his... well, the less said about her the better.' Ted had fallen silent and taken stock for a moment before continuing. 'Sorry, I digress. What I meant to say is that I want you to think of the grounds as your garden, too. You should take pride in bringing fresh ideas and seeing them through to fruition.'

Neil had felt delighted at the prospect of being given a veritable free rein, but he was no fool. He hadn't missed the veiled warning that Ted had sent him about keeping his nose out of things that didn't concern him. He didn't know exactly what his boss was alluding to, but he didn't need to. If Lottie had heard the conversation, she'd be dissecting each word and phrase and reading much more into it. Sounded to Neil like Ted didn't appreciate his employees' wives getting involved in estate business and so he wouldn't be repeating what he'd said to Lottie.

Neil knew when he was on to a good thing and working for Ted was the best. So many of the jobs he'd seen advertised before Seaspray were limiting and prescriptive. People just looking for the legwork being done and not welcoming any creative input. Ted was offering all of it and that was enough for Neil.

He scribbles a couple more suitable plants down, feeling positive about the opportunity to make a difference here. Without doubt, this is his chance to impress Ted... Neeta, too. Ted has mentioned that she loves to spend time in the walled garden in the warmer months. 'She'll often sit and read for an hour on the memorial bench,' he'd said. 'That's her special place.'

Now, Neil runs his hand over the smooth wood of the bench. It's well made, but is well overdue for a good sand down and a fresh stain. He feels sure Neeta would appreciate this improvement and he will carry it out personally. He peers forward to read the small, oxidised brass plaque, its lettering already fading.

In Loving Memory of You.

No name or any other details. Some people are incredibly

private about stuff like that. Perhaps this was the kind of thing the previous gardener and his wife were too curious about. Neil won't be asking any more about it unless Ted or Neeta volunteer the information.

He glances over the other side of the garden and watches a young man in his twenties gather weeding tools together at the end of his shift. Ted is big on employing locals for his casual labour.

The requirements for labour fluctuate depending on the time of year but it's clear young, fit students like this guy are a mainstay at Seaspray. They carried out most of the menial, backbreaking work with ease and, best of all, there was a ready supply of them.

'I work on a win-win policy,' Ted told him. 'I pay a living wage when every other business around here, including the shops and cafés, all pay the students a minimum hourly rate.'

He's also flexible with them in fitting their hours around lectures and studying but he does expect them to work long shifts. Most of the labourers finish at 6 p.m. rather than Neil's own preferred finishing time of five. Still, it doesn't seem to put them off. There are at least a couple of students a day calling at the main gate to enquire about possible work openings during the week. Ted had told him that the local restaurants, on the other hand, with their unsociable hours and poor pay, often struggled to fill their flimsy seasonal vacancies.

Neil approves of Ted's fairness to his staff, particularly as it's great news for him. He won't have to admit a certain task might be too much for him physically because there will always be someone on hand to carry out the awkward jobs.

His thinking feels outdated, from a very unhappy time he's left behind. Still, there is no harm in remembering how far he's come from those dark, dark days when doctors warned him he may never walk again. It isn't something a man can easily forget.

The weeks after the accident had swiftly turned into

months. Neil's paralysis in the bottom half of his body remained but he'd steadfastly refused any kind of counselling help offered by the hospital. Lottie became his carer and, even through the pain and fog of misery, he'd felt a surge of love as she helped him wash his face and comb his hair. This would often be followed by a spike of resentment and hopelessness when he was forced to call out to her for something simple he needed, but could not get for himself.

Each day he felt sucked further into a black hole as he began to wonder how the situation could possibly resolve itself. If, indeed, it ever would.

Then one night, they went to bed and at about 3 a.m., Neil sat bolt upright.

'Lottie? I can feel something... I can feel something!' he hissed, shaking her awake. 'I've got pins and needles in my feet.'

After months of zero sensation below his waist, the pins and needles in his feet felt like a huge deal. Finally, it was the turning point they'd been waiting for in his long and arduous recovery. Slowly, over a period of a week, a little more feeling and then some movement returned to his lower legs. But although his physical state was improving, mentally, Neil was still in the iron grip of depression. He just couldn't seem to muster the hope for himself that his wife and the medics had. He refused physiotherapy. 'I'm not getting my hopes up, Lottie,' he'd said stubbornly. 'I can't handle any more disappointment. Let's just see how it goes.'

It was only later he realised he'd been afraid to put himself on the line, in case the new sensations were a false start and he'd find himself back at square one.

Then, on the last day of the summer term, Albie came home from school, impressed by a classmate's uncle who'd been in to talk to them during morning assembly. The guy had spoken about how he regularly competed in wheelchair tennis tournaments after doctors had told him he'd never walk again. He'd stressed to the kids how hope and belief can spur you to achieving what at first seems like the impossible.

'I told him about you, Dad,' Albie had said proudly, as soon as he'd ditched his rucksack and shoes at the door. 'I told him you're a fighter, too.'

Neil felt a warmth in his chest, a light behind his eyes. The next day, he agreed to attend a course of physiotherapy sessions at the hospital. Very slowly, step by step, he began to claw his way back from the dark place he'd started to believe he might be stuck in forever.

He looks around him now and feels a sense of peace, of gratitude. He's got a long way to go to put things right, to make it up to his wife and son, but he's doing everything in his power to reach that goal, every single day.

Neil resumes his walk up to the house. The impressive entrance, with its two white pillars and marbled portico bearing sculpted, potted topiaries, is clear of clutter. He glances up and down the perimeter but can't see any sign of a recent delivery.

The door opens and a barefooted Neeta steps over the threshold. It's still balmy out and she's wearing pink shorts and a subtle crop top that reveals just an inch of her flat stomach. He smiles and forces his eyes away from her long, smooth brown legs. There's no doubt about it: Neeta Williams is in great shape for a woman in her late forties.

'Thank you so much for popping back up, Neil. I hope I didn't disturb your plans?'

'Not at all,' he says cheerfully, pushing Lottie's fury out of his head. 'Always happy to help out. But—' he looks around '— did they put the stuff round the back in the end?'

'Sorry? Oh, you mean the delivery! Thankfully one of Ted's boys came up and sorted that all out.' Neil assumes she means the student he saw packing up in the garden as he walked up here. Neeta smiles and extends a slender arm, wiggling stiff fingers to test the air. 'So warm out here still, isn't it? I'm just about to take a tipple down to the bench. Care to join me?'

'Oh, I'd better not... Lottie's just started tea, so I ought to get back really. Nice thought, though!'

'Lottie won't mind you taking ten minutes out, surely? After all, a man deserves a drink when he's been working in the heat all day,' she says playfully.

Lottie won't like it one bit, but she's not expecting him back for about twenty minutes, anyway. And Neil doesn't like turning down any reasonable request from his boss. 'Sounds good, Mrs... Neeta.'

She smiles approvingly. 'Just wait here. You can help me carry the tray down.'

FIFTEEN

Neeta doesn't invite him inside the house but leaves him standing outside the door. He knows what Lottie would say about *that*. He watches through one of the big glass windows at the side of the door. He can see the entrance hall and Neeta padding elegantly through to the kitchen in her super-short shorts.

Neil presses his nose closer to the glass, looking up in wonder at the enormous glass staircase that rears up from the porcelain tiles through the centre of the marble interior. Each closed riser is mirrored with the chrome-railed sides flanked in glass with big chrome bolts securing it to the staircase. He gawps at the dramatic atrium that forms the roof, an intricate glass canopy that gives an incredible view of clear-blue sky, which, he imagines, transforms into a starlit canvas at night. He smiles, thinking Albie wasn't too far off the mark when he said it was a thousand times bigger than the cottage. Everything his eyes rest on is either white, silver, glass... there are no fabrics or textured accessories of any kind that might soften the look. It's clinical but also incredible. Lottie will be open-mouthed when she sees this place.

Beyond the hallway where Neeta headed is a glass wall that must lead to the kitchen. He can't see her but, through the slightly open door, hears the odd clink of glass and ice as she presumably sorts out the drinks.

A few moments later she appears, carrying a large tray.

'Let me take that for you.' Neil rushes forward, opening the door wide and relieving her of the large, heavy platter. It bears two cut-glass tumblers, half filled with ice, an open bottle of Whitley Neill rhubarb and ginger gin and four small tins of Fever-Tree aromatic tonic. There's a dish of olives and another filled with crisps. This doesn't look like a ten-minute drinking session and, as Neil picks his way carefully over the doorstep and outside, he's already running through the possible excuses he might give Lottie when he gets back down to the cottage.

Neeta scoots in front of him, leading him to the bench and Neil is treated to a view of her firm arse and neat waistline as they make their way down the garden. He places the tray carefully on the low table, fashioned in the same style as the bench. Neeta pours the drinks, heavy on the gin, he notices – handing him one and popping an olive into her mouth.

'Cheers!' They clink glasses and Neil takes a sip of the cool, sweet and sour drink. It tastes good.

'Well, now, isn't this nice!' Neeta smiles widely, showcasing her perfect teeth. He feels her watching him as he plucks an olive from the dish. Just before it reaches his mouth the olive slips from his fingers and lands in his lap. *Idiot*.

'Oops! Here, let me.' She grabs a small square drinks napkin and begins to gently pat his thigh. Neil feels his face inflame.

'Thanks,' he says hoarsely, taking the napkin gently from her. He glances nervously at the boundary wall and the gathering of trees over the other side. The cottage garden is beyond that. He's stood in that very spot and certain aspects of the main house can be seen but, thankfully, not the bench where they're sitting now. Lottie would screech like a banshee if she saw what

Neeta just did and his career at Seaspray would be over before it even starts.

Neeta's manicured hand strokes the wooden slats between them and he seizes the chance to get over the awkward moment.

'I'm going to sand the bench down and re-stain it for you. It's a lovely piece of garden furniture and deserves a bit of TLC.'

Her eyes alight briefly on the scratched bronze plaque and she pulls a tissue from the pocket of her shorts. Neil thinks he sees a shadow pass over her face as she gently wipes the small oblong of metal. He feels the warmth of the gin in his throat, the strength in the sun still beating down on the back of his neck. Before he can stop himself, before he recalls the subtle warning Ted issued earlier, he says, 'The plaque... is it a tribute to someone you lost?' Then no more than a beat later when he realises his mistake, he stammers, 'I – I'm so sorry, Neeta. I didn't mean to be intrusive.'

Neeta stands up, saying nothing for a moment or two. She traces the shadow of a small weed with a toe. 'This is my favourite part of the grounds. A place to come and reflect. Sadly, it's got a bit overgrown and neglected down here. I tripped on a cracked paving slab last year and sprained my ankle.'

She bends forward to point out the uneven area and her white crop-top rides up another inch. Then she drops the tissue and it floats down, landing a little way from her feet. 'Oh!'

'I've got it, don't worry.' He springs forward to pick up the tissue and plucks out the weed that's sprouting between two slabs, in one smooth movement.

'Thank you, Neil,' she says instead when he hands back the tissue. Their fingers touch and he feels a little spark pass between them. He notices her eyes linger admiringly on his biceps and he feels pleased. He's worked hard to build his body back up again. He might have had a mountain to climb to get mobile again, but there's nothing wrong with him now. Nothing that can't be sorted, at least...

'You know, I think it will be perfect if Lottie can get a part-time job locally,' Neeta says, as they return to the bench. Without asking him, she tops up their drinks.

'Yes, I think it would do her good,' Neil says, turning slightly from the brass plaque that sits between them. 'She's always enjoyed working and, of course, she gave up her job to look after me.'

'Yes, it was quite the sacrifice she made, caring for you in your time of need.' Neeta regards him thoughtfully. 'After your *accident*, I mean.'

Her emphasis on the word makes him look up sharply. 'What do you mean?'

Neeta smiles. 'I mean her being so selfless, that's all. Giving up her job without a second thought. But then what happened... it wasn't as if it was your fault.'

Unnerved, Neil reaches for the bowl of crisps. He feels scrutinised and he's not sure how to react. They sit in silence for a few moments. Birdsong is all around them, the heat still heavy on his damp skin. He's probably reading things into Neeta's comments. He's starting to realise it's just her way. She can be quite forthright in her manner and it takes some getting used to. But in fact, he has to agree that Neeta is spot on in that he also thinks it would be good for Lottie to work again. Even though they're almost out of debt now, a bit more money will always come in useful. They can think about getting a new car and perhaps booking a holiday abroad for the first time in years. Plus, in his opinion, Lottie needs something that might help keep her from getting jealous for next to no reason. He doesn't want to go back to *that* hellish existence again. To a wife who won't be pacified, refuses to be reasoned with.

Neeta takes a drink, the ice cubes in her glass chiming in unison with her gold and silver bangles. 'As we've said, it's no trouble for you to pick Albie up from school and bring him here. Ted and I would love to do stuff with him during the school holidays. He's so curious and intelligent, it seems a shame he's cooped up in that little cottage all the time.'

Neil shifts on the bench and can feel a small patch of damp at the bottom of his back soaking through his T-shirt. 'We do make sure he gets down to the beach and he's starting surfing lessons,' he says a little defensively. Lottie would rile instantly at Neeta's criticism and besides, she has always been guarded about Albie, not trusting anyone else to look after him before now.

'I'm sure that's the case and I didn't mean to sound critical.' She gives him a small smile. 'It's just having no children of our own, we'd love to see more of him. He's a breath of fresh air and we're not precious, don't mind a bit of mud on the carpet! I know Ted feels the same way, too. He's been like a big kid again, working on that tree-house.'

Neil chuckles. 'Well, thank you, Neeta. I'll speak to Lottie again. I'm sure she'll be very grateful. I know I am.'

'Fine. Well, then, I'll leave it to you.' She reaches over and lays a hand on his bicep. 'In the meantime, Ted's texted to say he's decided to go for drinks tonight with a few old colleagues of his. So I'm up for another drink, if you are?'

'Thanks, it's very tempting,' he says, feeling heat circling his neck, 'but I must get back. Lottie's making tea and she won't appreciate it if I'm late.'

'Of course. I understand completely.' She drains her glass and puts it back on the tray before standing up. 'I won't keep you any longer.' She smiles at him and then turns and walks away.

He feels torn inside like he's making a mistake and he should stay a little longer, but he also knows he belongs somewhere else. He must return to his wife, to his boy. He looks up at the house, the blue sky, the grounds so beautiful it almost takes his breath away. To have a life like this!

When Neeta turns her attention on him, his face feels hot like the sun. She's a laser that can see through to every secret part of him, to what makes him tick.

But he is a happily married man. So that's that.

Neil finishes his drink and enjoys the view, marvelling that her perfect pins look just as flawless from the back.

SIXTEEN

LOTTIE

Albie has just climbed into the bath when I hear the back door open. I glance at my phone screen. Six forty-five. He'd gone back up to Seaspray just after five-thirty so that's been a very long twenty minutes.

'I'm back!' Neil calls cheerfully.

'Upstairs,' I call as I leave the bathroom. I reach the top of the stairs and he's there, looking up and smiling at me from the bottom. He starts to climb. 'Albie's in the bath. He's had his tea and I've said he can have half an hour on the PlayStation before bed.'

'I'll go and see him then have a quick shower,' he says as he reaches me. I stand stiffly as he wraps his arms around me and gives me a kiss on the lips. 'Sorry I was a bit longer up there. Tell you about it downstairs.'

That's when I smell alcohol on his breath.

'I'll plate up then,' I say, shrugging free of him and going downstairs.

In the kitchen, I start to prepare tea. Albie's already had his, so it's just us eating. Who has Neil been drinking with? Neeta had said Ted was out in her text, so I already know the answer to *that* question.

I push my greasy hair from my forehead with the heel of my hand and think about Neeta's smooth perfumed skin, her designer clothes and dream lifestyle. She's already made a couple of flattering comments about Neil's appearance, which I take to mean she finds him attractive.

I slam the plates down a little hard and a tiny splinter chips off one of them. I don't know why I made hot food; a simple egg and cheese salad would have been so much better.

'Need any help?' Neil sidles into the kitchen, his hair damp from the shower. 'I'll set the table while you finish off.'

'Do you want a glass of wine?' I say, resentment coiling in my throat. 'Or have you had enough for one night?'

For a second, I'm reminded of my mum, who would so often address me with a sarcastic comment instead of saying what she was really feeling. Sometimes it's easier to lash out rather than open yourself to hurt. I always thought Mum's off-the-cuff remarks meant she didn't care, but for the first time, it occurs to me that maybe it was because she cared too much. She just didn't know how to articulate it.

Neil hesitates before replying. 'I did have a gin and tonic up there, yes. Just the one.'

'With Neeta?'

'What? No, no. I mean, Neeta was around but so was Ted. We sat in the garden; it's still lovely and warm out. We should get some garden furniture and then we can—'

'I thought Ted was out and that's why Neeta asked you to help with the delivery?'

'Apparently, he was on his way to a dinner but they cancelled, so he turned back. He'd just got home again when I got up there, so we had a drink together.'

'What had been delivered?'

'Huh?'

'The delivery you had to sort out. What was it?'

He takes a bottle of white wine from the fridge and reaches into the cupboard for two glasses.

'Luckily, one of the labourers had already sorted that.'

And yet Neeta had only just asked him to help out. So someone had sorted the problem before he arrived in about five minutes flat. I take the vegetables off the heat and see they're overcooked and mushy. I strain them at the sink, staring out of the window at the still-busy beach. Neil is relaxed and off-hand in his replies and yet something doesn't sit right. Too many beats of hesitation, the subconscious yawning when he talks about the delivery.

But what can I do? I've questioned him as much as I can on it and now I feel I have no option but to trust he's telling me the truth.

The cottage pie is disappointingly stodgy. Too much dry potato and not enough cheese topping.

He's chatty as we eat, telling me the plans he has for the small cottage garden.

'I thought I might lay a small patio area with a table and chairs and then we'll get you one of those comfy loungers with a nice thick cushion. What do you think?'

'Lovely,' I say, forcing down another mouthful of bland, dry food.

After tea, Neil tops up our wine and turns on the television in the lounge. There's a nature programme on about strange-looking creatures that live in the very depths of the ocean. He usually loves stuff like this but tonight he seems too wired to relax. I watch him from the chair, drumming his fingers on the sofa cushion, tapping his foot continuously.

Over the years, I've given so much thought to the last morning I saw my mum. The police asked me whether she'd been nervy or displayed any unusual behaviour, and I suppose they meant a bit like Neil is doing now.

However, unlike how Neil's acting, Mum had been the opposite. Chilled-out at breakfast time when she'd usually be rushing around, she'd sat and listened as I'd told her about the netball game I had after school.

'The team we're playing are really good at marking, but I think we can win,' I'd said, tucking into the hot, buttered toast she'd made me.

'I've got this feeling you're going to score tonight,' she'd said. 'I can't wait to hear all about it later.'

Had she said stuff like that because she'd wanted to lull me into a false sense of security? See me off to school before she disappeared to a new life where her problems with the police were behind her?

I'll probably never know.

Neil falls asleep watching television. His empty wine glass still clutched loosely in his hand, mouth slightly lolled open and softly snoring. I turn off the TV, prise the glass stem from his curled fingers then tidy up the kitchen. My clattering around doesn't wake him. I shake his arm softly when I'm ready to go upstirs.

We're not big drinkers. It was one of the things I liked about Neil. I suspect he had enjoyed more than one drink with Ted up at Seaspray and that's why he'd been evasive. His boss is well-preserved for his age, but the broken veins in his cheeks and red nose perhaps tells of a man who enjoys a few more whiskies on an evening than most.

Upstairs, we check in on Albie together. He's fallen asleep with the latest *Diary of a Wimpy Kid* in his hands. Neil tucks it under the bed and turns off the bedside lamp while I pull the quilt over his splayed limbs.

'I know you worry about him, but he's happy here, Lottie,' Neil whispers, sliding his arm around my shoulders as we look down on our boy. 'He seems to like his new school and he's going to love having a tree-house up at Seaspray. Given time, I think Ted and Neeta could play a big part in his life. They have a lot to offer him and Albie seems to really like them both, too.'

I look up at him, frowning. 'We only just got here. That's a big jump from him popping up there to earn a bit of pocket money now and then.'

He looks sheepish. 'I'm just saying. It's been the three of us for so long, coping with our problems alone. I think we've become a bit insular and that's not fair on Albie.'

'I'm not sure that's true. You might spend lots of time up at Seaspray, but I've met people like Keris. And Albie gets on brilliantly with Edie and is making other friends in his class. He needs to be with young people his own age, not a middle-aged couple with more money than they know what to do with.'

He follows me out onto the landing. 'I just think the Williamses have a lot to offer him, and if they express an interest in seeing more of him, maybe we should encourage that.'

'You mean like him going up there after school if I get a job?'

'Yes. I think it makes perfect sense.'

I flick on the bedroom light and draw down the blind. 'They've never had any kids, so they'll probably end up only wanting to have him in small doses once the novelty has worn off.'

He pulls off his T-shirt and pads across the room. I allow him to embrace me and I lay my cheek on his shoulder, the cold suspicion and annoyance running out of the soles of my feet and leaving only a warm softness. He smells fresh and lemony from his earlier shower when he lifts my chin and kisses me softly on the lips. I kiss him back and soon we're in a passionate clinch.

His lean, firm torso presses against my open pyjama top. His body feels hot and urgent against mine. It's been so long.

I take his hand and lead him to the bed, shrugging off my top as we lie down. I straddle him and press my face to his, my hair hanging loose, my heart racing. We kiss again and then, in one smooth movement, Neil flips me over so I'm lying underneath him. I feel his weight on me, his biceps flexed as his kisses travel down my neck.

I close my eyes and enjoy the tingle running up and down my spine. Until Neeta's face floats into my mind and I start wondering if he's thinking about her as he's loving me.

Her slim body, her perfect life...

His mouth travels further down to the top of my stomach before I push him gently away.

'Sorry,' I say softly. 'I'm really tired. Can we leave it tonight?'

He freezes for a moment and then rolls away from me, exhaling loudly. 'Sure, no problem.'

We lie there side by side in the dark, not moving, not speaking. The air feels thick and impenetrable between us.

I don't think I've ever felt so alone.

SEVENTEEN

The day starts well when I check my emails. An invitation from the sportswear company to an interview at 10 a.m. Monday morning if I'm available. I choose to see it as a sign I'm making the right decision about getting a job.

'That's a brilliant result,' Neil says with instant enthusiasm. As I recall, he was never that enamoured with me getting a job quickly until Neeta put forward her 'brilliant' solution.

'It's a great start,' I agree. 'I didn't expect them to get back to me this quickly.'

I send a reply accepting right away, noting the letter also says they're looking for someone to start with immediate effect, if possible.

Neil and Albie head up to Seaspray to work on the tree-house and I decide to have a wander down to the beach while it's still early. It's breezy but warm. I've dressed in a long-sleeved cotton top and some cropped canvas trousers with trainers. I'm OK going down the hill but I know I'll run out of breath coming back up. I need to lose the stone of extra weight that crept on and stuck fast while I stayed home to look after Neil.

I find myself idly wondering how Neeta stays slim. There's no sign of middle-aged spread on her hips and thighs at all. I'm a lot younger than her if she's in her late forties as I suspect and that just makes me feel even more of a failure.

When I'm about halfway down the hill, I stand and take in the vista as I drink from my water bottle. The sea looks azure-blue today and I can see little white foamy tips further out towards the horizon. There are a few dog walkers on the beach as well as runners, but there nearly always are, no matter what time of day. During school holidays, Keris warns me the place is always crowded out with tourists and day-trippers.

'Best to stay at home until they've gone,' she said. 'You won't find many locals down on the beach.'

I take out my phone and text Keris.

Got a job interview Monday morning at 10!

Her reply pings straight back.

Well done! See you later... you OK to bring Albie over about 4?

I send a thumbs up. Albie is having a sleepover at Edie's house tonight. I'd been a bit concerned because he'd grudgingly agreed when Edie had asked him but he'd said to me afterwards, 'Can I come home early Sunday morning, Mum? I want to help Ted with the tree-house.'

I'm hoping that once he's spending more time there in the week, he won't be as bothered about going up to Seaspray at weekends as well. As I've already said to Neil, he needs to be with people his own age.

When I walk to Seaspray, Albie is full of excitement.

'Mum, look! My tree-house is behind that little wood over

there.' He points to a small copse of conifers at the edge of the boundary. 'Ted says I can bring Edie to play in it but I don't want you to see it until it's finished.'

'OK, promise I won't look then.' I grin at Ted. 'It's really generous of you, thank you,' I say. 'I hope you don't live to regret it. You'll never get rid of him!'

Ted laughs, leaning on his spade. 'Albie's a lovely lad. Don't even know he's up here sometimes. It's the least I can do for him.'

'Well, it's really kind of you.' I look up at the house. 'Is Neeta home?'

He hesitates. 'I think she might be having a lie-down. She's felt a bit under the weather today.'

'Oh, I'm sorry to hear that. Shall I call in and ask her if she needs anything? I can pop to the general store no problem.'

'No, no,' he says quickly. 'Thanks, but we're fine. She has everything she needs and it's best she's not disturbed.'

'No worries. Tell her I hope she feels better soon. Albie,' I call out, walking up towards the house, where he's digging in a flower bed with a small trowel. 'Come on, time to go home.'

Albie looks up and scowls. 'I don't want to come home yet, Mum. Five more minutes... please!'

'Told you.' I grin at Ted as he starts to dig again. 'It's started already. He'll want to move in when that tree-house is finished.'

'Fine by me.' Ted grins. 'And Neeta would be delighted!'

I start to walk up to where Neil is unboxing some plants and I suddenly feel desperate for the loo. I should never have drunk so much water down at the beach. Just then, the door to the house opens and Neeta steps out to pick something up from a chair. She sees me, smiles and waves before going back inside. She looks spritely enough and doesn't seem in the least bit unwell.

This seems as good a time as any to call in. I walk up and knock on the door. There's no answer so I ring the bell.

'Yes?' I look up and see Neeta calling down from the balcony upstairs I've seen from the spare room.

'Oh, there you are, Neeta. I just popped up to say hi. It's a lovely day, isn't it?'

'Yes it is.' There are a few awkward seconds of silence before she adds, 'I'm just about to have a shower.'

She's still fully dressed and I'm dancing about here, so I pull a regretful face. 'Sorry to ask, but is there any way I can use your bathroom?'

'Not really, Lottie. Sorry... we've got problems with the flush. If you pop down to Neil's garden office, he's got one you can use in there.'

'Ahh, OK. Enjoy your shower!'

My face is burning. I feel embarrassed and annoyed she couldn't put herself out just to pop down and open the door. A house like that must have about half a dozen bathrooms, certainly a downstairs loo at the very least, so the flush excuse is a bit lame.

The thing that strikes me most, though, is the feeling of how odd our brief exchange was. There was some kind of undercurrent from her that I could feel well enough but not identify the source of.

I wonder if Neeta Williams is just one of those people who run hot and cold like the weather. I had a boss like that years ago. Each morning, I'd go into the office treading on eggshells because although she'd been upbeat and super-friendly the day before, I could never be sure exactly what mood she'd be in the next. And if I got it wrong, I risked being frozen out all week.

One thing I've learned from that unhappy time is this: the more nervously you act around people like that, the more power they draw from it.

· · ·

Back in the spare room at the cottage, I've worked out if I tilt the slats of the blinds to a certain angle, my view is almost as good as if they were fully open.

I keep popping up here to the spare room window at various times throughout the day. I'm ashamed but I can't seem to stop. It seems the lights all come on automatically early evening – in every room of the house – even though it's still light and often sunny. I assume it's because of the fantastic chandeliers they have in there. What's the point in having that stuff if you don't show it off to its full potential? Not traditional crystal confections but clusters of ultra-modern silver globes, a cascading crystal waterfall dripping down from the atrium. These sorts of elaborate furnishings need a lot of looking after and it suddenly occurs to me I've never seen any staff inside the house. Surely you'd have cleaners, or a housekeeper perhaps at the very least in a mansion that size wouldn't be unreasonable. Plenty of employees in the garden, of course, but inside, there only ever seems to be Neeta during the day. No visitors either. It is odd.

There's so much to see from here, even when there's nothing happening. Other people's routines are fascinating but there is something unusual that strikes me about Neeta and Ted's. He is often the last person working in the grounds when all the staff, including Neil, have left for the day. When he eventually goes inside the house, he always walks upstairs into the bedroom, I presume, to take a shower. When he emerges, sometimes in a white towelling robe and slippers, sometimes in shorts, T-shirt and sliders, he goes downstairs and the 'separate lives' phase, as I've labelled it, begins.

They don't eat together, they don't sit together, they don't appear to chat about their day. Upstairs there's a narrow landing that consists of floor-to-ceiling glass. They walk past each other along this landing and they both look at the floor.

I think about their fond touches, the dazzling smile Neeta

gives Ted when people are watching. 'Even after all these years, we still can't keep our hands off each other,' she'd told me.

But something is becoming increasingly clear the longer I observe the house: Neeta and Ted Williams are living a lie.

Bearing in mind that's not necessarily a healthy environment for my nine-year-old son to be around on a regular basis, this discovery concerns me as a loving parent.

So far as I can see, it leaves me with just one option: I have to find out why.

EIGHTEEN

Monday at 9.45 a.m., I park outside a large, grey steel warehouse with *JLG Sports* emblazoned across the front on the outskirts of Whitby.

I check in at reception and there's only me waiting. One or two staff walk by and I notice they're wearing JLG-branded clothing, including the receptionist. There are displays behind glass screens all around the walls including a section of kids' clothing. A full football range together with tracksuits and T-shirts. A glass cabinet houses accessories such as JLG-branded water bottles, towels and shin pads.

I pull my phone out of my handbag to turn it off and see that Neil has sent a text:

Good luck, you'll be brilliant!

My hands are sweating. I've realised I really want the job. I think I'd enjoy coming here, appreciate the chance to rediscover the part of me that's not a wife or a mother. This morning, I got dressed in black trousers, a smart green tweedy jacket and a white blouse. I applied a little make-up and twisted my hair up into a neat pleat. It felt good to give myself a bit of care and attention.

'Hi, is it Lottie?' A woman in her mid-fifties stands in front of me. She has on a pair of straight black trousers, flat pumps and a red polo shirt with *JLG Sports* embroidered in white on the pocket. I nod and stand up and we shake hands. 'I'm Mel Turner, the office manager. Come through!'

I follow her down a well-lit corridor and into a large conference room. I wasn't expecting a full interview panel, but there's nobody else in there.

'Take a seat, Lottie. We're going to keep this nice and informal,' Mel says, opening a folder in front of her. I spot my CV on top. 'I've had a good read through your application and I can see you're more than experienced enough for the role on offer.'

'Yes, I've worked most recently in a school admin role. But before that, I worked in retail accounts.'

'That's right and I see...' she turns a page '... you've acted as carer for your husband the last couple of years.'

I nod. 'Neil had a bad accident at work a couple of years ago. It was a scary time as we didn't know if he'd even walk again for a few months but since then he's made a full recovery.'

'That's great news. And you've recently moved to the area?'

'Yes. Neil got a job as an estate manager. Albie, our nine-year-old son, is at school and so the time is right for me to restart my own career.'

'And I'm very glad to hear it!' She beams. Then, 'You have seen the hours, I take it?'

She can't question me about childcare arrangements, but I know what she's getting at.

'Yes, and the hours suit me fine. I've got everything in place I need to fulfil the needs of the job.'

'That's great, thank you. We're a bit short-staffed in the

office due to recent expansions in our clothing lines. We're desperately trying not to get behind with the paperwork and also the purchase and sales ledgers. We deal with manufacturers in mainland China, so we need to ensure we have cover across the time difference.'

She asks me a few more things about accounting software I've used in my previous positions and then runs through salary details and staff benefits. 'If successful, you're entitled to twenty-five per cent off all JLG clothing from your starting date, which I'm sure will come in handy with a child at home!'

'It certainly will... and he's a football-mad one, too.'

She grins. 'You'll be entitled to four weeks of annual leave plus statutory days and bank holidays. I think I've covered everything; do you have any questions?'

'Just a couple. When's the starting date and when will I know if I've been successful?'

I wonder how many more people have applied and whether the fact there's just Mel interviewing me is because she's just going through the motions and has someone else in mind.

'I can answer both of those questions for you, Lottie. The starting date is as soon as you can... tomorrow would be ideal! And I can tell you right now that you've got the job. Congratulations!'

I'm walking on air when I get back to the cottage. I decide to park at the cottage before walking up to Seaspray to share the good news. Neeta and I will need to have a chat about how her looking after Albie will work.

Mel gave me my next two weeks of hours before I left. Although they're within the guide hours detailed in the job advert, there are more late finishes than I'd expected. Their Chinese manufacturers are a full eight hours ahead of the UK, so the best time to contact them is mid-afternoon. Over the next couple of weeks, on several days, I'll start at twelve noon and finish at six-thirty. Other days I'll work eight in the morning until two-thirty. Both shifts include a thirty-minute break.

I park up at the cottage. I'm wearing flat shoes, so I don't get changed. I text Neil to say I'm on my way up and he meets me at the side gate.

'How did it go?' he asks a little cautiously.

'I got the job!' I say with jazz hands.

'No way! That's amazing, come here, you.' He gives me a hug and a kiss. 'So proud, you knocked it out of the park.'

'Thanks, I'm chuffed! Oh yes, the other big news is... I start tomorrow!'

His mouth drops open and I explain briefly about the hours and how it's important I speak to Neeta today to get a plan together.

'She's up at the house,' he says. 'I saw her out on the upstairs balcony earlier.'

I head up the garden to the house and leave Neil loading plants into his wheelbarrow. There are several labourers around but I don't see Ted on my way up.

Before I reach the house, Neeta emerges from wide glass French doors at the side, carrying a magazine, a hat and a tall glass of water. She looks fabulous in a lemon midi-length dress with shoestring straps and a handkerchief hem.

She stops in the doorway when she sees me. 'Oh, it's you, Lottie!'

'Hi, Neeta, I came up to tell you in person that I just got the job!'

'Well, that's super news, congratulations!' She looks genuinely pleased for me.

'I'm really delighted. There's a snag, though... they want me to start tomorrow.' I wait for her reaction. Maybe I should have told Mel at JLG I'd have to let her know if I can start that quickly.

'My, they sound very keen to snap you up! I don't blame them, I would too.' She gives me a warm smile.

'It's incredibly short notice, I know, but I've got my hours for the next two weeks and I thought we could work out a plan about Albie,' I say, feeling a bit breathless with it all.

'Let's sit down and have a proper chat, shall we?' I wait for her to invite me inside, but she closes the glass door behind her. 'We can chat over there, under the parasol.'

I follow her down a winding little path to a small table set in a shady part of the garden. She has bare feet and her toenails are painted in a pretty pearlised pink. When we sit down, I shrug off my jacket and look longingly at the glass of cool water.

Neeta pops on her hat and studies my schedule of hours. 'So, on your early starts, Albie can come up to Seaspray with his dad first thing. When Neil starts work, Albie will come up to the house and then Neil can run him to school an hour or so later.'

I nod. 'And when I'm working lates, Neil will pick him up from school and he'll go back to Seaspray until his dad finishes? Are you sure that's OK?'

'Perfectly OK. It's all going to work fine, Lottie,' she says kindly. I suddenly feel a bit choked and can't answer her. This is the first time I haven't been there for my son. Before now, I've always taken jobs that fit in with his school hours.

'There's just one thing. What happens on the occasions you have to go out or—'

'Then Neil can take time off and make it up at a later date.' Neeta takes a sip of water and regards me from beneath the wide brim of her natural straw hat. 'You mustn't worry, Lottie. I give you my word I'll look after him like he's my own.'

'I can't thank you enough, Neeta. I really do appreciate it.' A single tear escapes but I manage to swiftly wipe that away and I don't think she notices. 'We also need to talk about paying you for providing childcare. Had you got a figure in—'

She holds up a hand. 'Zero. That's the figure. I consider it a privilege to be helping you out with Albie. He's a lovely boy.'

'Oh no, we can't let you do it for nothing,' I protest. 'It's a commitment. A big one at that.'

'Certainly. It's a commitment I shall take very seriously, but I'll be offended if you insist on trying to pay me, Lottie. Please don't fuss about it; it really is a pleasure for us to have him here.'

I thank her again, feeling overwhelmingly grateful and more than a tad guilty that I've been so mean about Albie spending time with her and Ted. I'm fizzing inside, grateful for the new job. 'Albie is going to love coming up here!' I look up at the glittering glass of the dazzlingly white house. 'Goodness, it looks so big when you're right next to it! How many bedrooms does it have, Neeta?'

'Five. All of them large doubles and three with en-suite bathrooms. People are often aghast there are just the two of us in such a big place, but we like the extra space in the living areas and the kitchen. The entrance hall is my favourite with its airy atrium. You don't get all that with a two-bed house.'

I nod, trying to think of something to ask whereby she'll finally stand up and say, *Why don't you come in and have a look?*

'Gosh, I don't think I've ever seen an atrium in a house! It's hard to tell from the outside, but is the house open plan? I imagine your kitchen has astounding views of the bay.'

She looks at me and I think I see her mouth tighten slightly. For a second or two she looks familiar again. Then the impression fades as quickly as it came and I think it must be just a mannerism that reminds me of someone else. 'Yes, the views are lovely. I suppose, similar to the ones from the cottage.' She checks her watch. 'Goodness, I completely forgot, I have a couple of important calls I need to make.' She stands up and looks regretful. 'I'm so sorry to cut our chat short, Lottie.'

'No, no, it's fine. Hopefully we'll get a chance to catch up better when I'm picking Albie up one day.' I stand up and hook my handbag over my shoulder. 'Thanks so much again, Neeta. We both really appreciate what you're doing for him.'

'No need to keep thanking me. It really is a pleasure.' She takes a few steps towards the house and then turns to give me a little wave. 'Enjoy the rest of your day. You have my number, so don't hesitate to text or call if you think of anything else I need to know.'

When she walks off, I turn and make my way back down to the lower gardens to find Neil before I leave.

The excitement about getting the job is still bubbling in my belly but there's one thing bugging me that I can't stop turning round and around in my head. I now accept Neeta doesn't want me anywhere near Seaspray House. What I don't know yet is why.

NINETEEN

The next two weeks are manic, but whizz by in a blur.

To give credit where it's due, the arrangements with Neeta run like clockwork just the way we planned it. I call her one evening to thank her for having Albie. As usual she courteously dismisses my thanks, then, just as I'm about to end the call, she remembers something.

'Oh, I meant to say, I've booked Luigi's for this Friday evening, eight o'clock. That's fine with you, I trust?'

I'm slightly taken aback because she hasn't said a thing about our meal out since mentioning it on her first visit to the cottage weeks ago and now, all of a sudden, it's booked. We'll be going in just a few days' time.

'I'll speak to Neil, but I think that should be fine,' I say. 'Thank you for booking it.'

'Neil says he's looking forward to it so I don't think you'll get any complaints from him,' she says. 'I've booked a table for five, including Albie. He says he really wants to come even though it's past his bedtime.'

I let it go. What else can I do?

'The tree-house is nearly done now, Mum.' Albie speaks

fast as he picks unenthusiastically at his cheese quiche and salad, his face bright and vibrant. 'Another few days and Ted says Edie can come up to see it!'

'That's brilliant, Albie. I can't wait to see it myself!'

'I've done loads of the painting, you know. And guess what? Neeta has helped with stuff in there and she says me, her and Ted are going to have a tree-house tea party when it's finished!'

Ted this and Neeta that... it's astonishing how much he seems to relish spending time with the Williamses. I'm lucky in that respect, I suppose. If he hated going up there, life would be so much more difficult.

'Don't you like the quiche, Albie?' He's pushed the same chunk around his plate for the past five minutes and he hasn't touched the salad yet.

'Not hungry,' he says, putting down his fork. 'Ted brought me some popcorn from the cinema room.'

When I'd got home from work on my first day, Neil fussed around a bit, made me a cup of tea while I got changed. 'We haven't eaten yet because Albie wasn't hungry,' he said.

'Have you eaten anything up at Seaspray?' I asked Albie.

'Neeta made me some sandwiches and I had cake!'

I looked at Neil disapprovingly. 'You're going to have to gently remind her it's a healthy snack only after school. He's not going to want anything at teatime if she stuffs him full.'

Neil had murmured something I couldn't quite hear, but I was distracted by a sudden thought.

'Did you go up to the house and eat there with Neeta?' I asked Albie.

He'd picked up the remote control and pointed it at the television. 'No, I sat in Dad's office.'

I looked at my husband. 'He's not allowed in the house?'

Neil had shrugged. 'It's hardly a case of *not being allowed*. He's been helping me in the grounds, so it makes sense he eats down there. My office is posher than some people's houses, I'll have you know. Nothing wrong with him sitting in there.'

'That's not the point,' I'd said. 'It seems to me that Neeta is just going out of her way to keep us *all* out of the house.'

Neil had given me one of his looks, as if to say, *here we go again.*

Since then, not much has changed. Albie still doesn't venture into the house and, judging by the popcorn he's just referred to, Ted made that inside and brought it outside to him.

But neither Albie nor Neil seem the slightest bit concerned about it all. Neil continues to reduce my concern down to me being curious and wanting to have a good look around Seaspray House. It might have started off like that but now, hand on heart, it isn't about that at all. It was unreasonable and even rude of her to deny my request to use the bathroom that day. It just doesn't make sense she'd be so defensive. But when it's my son who's being kept out of the house when I'm at work, it hurts all the more.

Midway through my second week in the new job, I come home with a large bag full of own-brand sportswear for Albie. He's been desperate for new stuff for ages and, finally, I'll be able to get rid of his worn-out gear.

'Surprise!' I say, setting the bag down in front of him.

He peers inside and then starts pulling everything out. 'Mum, this T-shirt is cool, it looks just like a proper Nike one!' He peels off his school shirt and puts it on. It fits perfectly.

JLG's designs are decent quality and, with my staff discount, the whole lot cost under a hundred pounds, which Mel says I can have deducted from my first month's pay.

When he gets to the football shirt with the number 7 on the back, his face lights up.

'This is so cool! I love my stuff, Mum, thanks!'

He leans over and gives me a big kiss on the cheek. A warm feeling floods through me, seeing my son happy and well after being the opposite of that only a month ago. I'm so glad I took this job. A full sports wardrobe that will last him at least six to eight months and I paid for it myself.

I work with a great team of people at JLG. Mel is a brilliant boss, laid-back, approachable and supportive. The other people in the office are really friendly and welcoming, too. I realise, one day when I get back to the cottage after a late shift, that I feel happy. For the first time in a long, long time, it actually feels like our new life is up and running.

A little later, I pop upstairs into the spare room. It's 5.50 p.m. and I can see two people moving around in the sun room. Infuriatingly, I haven't got a clear view because a couple of the blinds are slightly down.

Neeta and Ted stand in front of one of the clear windows, talking, which is an unusual occurrence when there's no one around.

At 5.55, the outline of another person passes in front of the window. I can see them moving like a dark shadow in the bottom half of the glass. There's definitely someone else in there but Neeta and Ted are not behaving like this person is a visitor.

'Neil!' I shout to him from the top of the stairs. 'Can you come up here? Come quick?'

I take a couple of snaps on my phone, zooming in but disappointingly the shots aren't very clear. A few seconds later Neil walks in. 'What's up?'

'There's someone in the house with Neeta and Ted. Look here, the sun room.'

He squeezes past me to the window and stares. Then he picks up the binoculars and fiddles with them for a few moments.

He frowns. 'I can't see anybody in there, but what are you doing spying on my employers again?'

'I'm not spying! I happened to bring something in here and just looked through the blind.' He twists one side of his mouth up, unconvinced. I peer out of the blind and I can see the sun room is now empty. 'They were in there,' I say, frowning. 'I saw them... and someone else was in there, too.'

'When I left the external gates were all locked up and they had no visitors. But even so, they are allowed to have other people in the house if they want to, you know. I don't know why you've got this obsession with them.'

Neil sighs and leaves the room without saying anything else. I feel like a fool, but I know what I saw. It's hard to be clear about why this feels strange, but something doesn't quite add up.

Something I can't quite put my finger on.

TWENTY

'It's no use denying it, I know something's wrong, Claire.' Yasmin Fuller reached for her daughter's hand as soon as they arrived home from the school run. 'You can tell me anything, I hope you know that.'

Claire kicked off her shoes in the hallway but didn't meet her mother's eyes. Yasmin had surprised her one day after school, stopping by to pick her up on her way back from shopping. She'd caught her walking up with Charlie, and Yasmin had lost her temper, embarrassing Claire in front of the other kids, yelling that she could no longer be friends with the girl from the Bellingham Estate.

After that, Claire had seemed to withdraw into herself, barely reacting to anything at all. Yasmin sighed, torn as to the best thing to do. She thought she'd probably worked out the reason her daughter had become increasingly withdrawn over the past few weeks. It had affected her far more than Yasmin expected.

Claire was a polite and kind girl and Yasmin's friends had

all invited her for sleepovers with their equally polite, kind children, and yet Claire only seemed interested in finding her way back to feral Charlie Price.

Claire walked upstairs with her head hanging while Yasmin headed for the kitchen to make a coffee. However long it took Claire to acclimatise to life without her best friend, Yasmin wouldn't go back on her decision. *Couldn't* go back on it because the Price girl had proven she was disturbed. For starters, she'd smashed the window the night Yasmin had sent her packing from the house that day: an original stained-glass panel broken beyond repair. They had no proof it was her; she'd somehow managed to stand just outside the scope of the front CCTV camera's lens, but Yasmin *knew* it was her... who else could it be? The damage had occurred only five minutes after she'd sent her on her way. A large flat stone from the driveway had hurtled in and only narrowly missed the family cat.

Over the last month, other inexplicable things had happened. The sorts of things that had never happened in their ten years of living here.

Graham found the dustbin had been upended after dark on a night with barely any breeze. It had taken him ages to clear up the stinking rubbish, strewn around the garden by nocturnal animals. A tracked parcel that the postman confirmed he'd delivered safely to the doorstep had mysteriously disappeared and, some time later, the contents – important land registry documents Graham needed for a forthcoming renovation contract – were found screwed up and trampled into the mud along one of the tracks that led towards the school. Then there had been the deep scratch down the side of Yasmin's car that...

She froze as she realised something. The spoon, loaded with instant coffee, hovered above the white porcelain mug as she held her breath and considered what had just popped into her mind.

When she released the spoon, coffee sprayed across the

white marble worktop. Yasmin walked out of the kitchen and upstairs. Claire was sitting on her bedroom floor watching TV, propped up against her bed with her legs stretched out. She didn't look up when her mother entered the room, but kept her eyes fixed on the television.

'Claire, darling. I need to ask you something.' Yasmin sat on the edge of the bed and muted the television. She patted the mattress for Claire to sit next to her. Reluctantly, her daughter stood up and perched on the bed, looking at her fingers twisting together. Yasmin reached to touch her hand gently. 'Claire, is Charlie Price bullying you at school?'

Colour flooded into Claire's pale cheeks and Yasmin immediately knew she'd found the reason for her daughter's insular and troubled mood.

'Claire?' Her child looked up, her sad eyes glistening. 'You have to trust me and tell me the truth.'

When Claire began to speak, Yasmin felt her mouth slacken. Her hand crept up to her face as she tried to cover her shock. Finally, she gathered her sobbing daughter in her arms and held her close.

She'd known something was wrong with Claire and had realised it was probably something to do with Charlie. Children fell out all the time and often they were best left to solve their differences themselves.

But what Claire had just told her was on a different level. It had chilled Yasmin to the bone and now one thing was absolutely certain: she'd have to do something radical to stop it happening again. And she'd have to be quick about it.

TWENTY-ONE

LOTTIE

FRIDAY

I've googled the restaurant, Luigi's, where we're eating tonight and discovered it's a family-run, traditional but pricey joint on the edge of the next town. I can tell immediately it's not trying to attract tourists by the location and the menu. Starters begin at twelve pounds with a steak setting diners back nearly forty quid each.

I intend to shelve the calorie counting at least for tonight. I'll take my lead from Neeta. She seems so effortlessly slim; it will be a good opportunity to see what sort of food she orders. Sadly, I'm not expecting it to be the creamy pasta dishes I adore.

'Neeta and Ted arranged this dinner so do you think that means they'll be paying for the meal?' I ask Neil as I apply my make-up sitting at my dressing table and he towel-dries himself after his shower.

'I don't know,' Neil says. 'I never thought about that. I suppose there might be some etiquette as to who's expected to pay but I haven't got a clue what it is.'

'I can't imagine they'll invite us and then expect us to go Dutch.'

He walks up behind me and whispers in my ear. 'Stop fretting. If we have to go halves, we'll go halves. We're a lot better off than we used to be. Not much left to pay off now.' He kisses me on the ear and walks back to the middle of the room.

He's right. We wouldn't ordinarily eat at a posh joint like Luigi's unless it was something like a birthday celebration. I could spend the next hour worrying what Albie's going to eat, too, because he's the pickiest eater on earth. That's one of the reasons I thought it best he doesn't join us. But Neeta was adamant he should from the off and, although it feels a bit like she's overruling me, part of me likes the fact she's regarding us as a family and doesn't want to leave Albie out. As Neil suggests, I'm better off not fretting about any of it. I'm determined to enjoy the evening.

I dither about what to wear for ages. Silly, really. Neil has already figured out what he's wearing in a minute flat: black trousers and an open-necked shirt with a smart-casual jacket, which he says he'll take off when he gets there. Albie said he wanted to wear his jeans and a smart shirt, which Neil said would be fine. And me? Well, I torture myself with thoughts of Neeta's designer wardrobe and Neil's throwaway comment about her being glamorous, which has stuck in my throat ever since like a thorn.

I suppose, with us not going out socially for the best part of two years and our relationship changing as a result of Neil's struggles to recover, I've stopped seeing myself as an attractive woman. I'd been a member of the gym at the local leisure centre before Neil's accident. I've never been a gym bunny with regards to weight-training or the high-tech machines, but I did used to enjoy the cardio classes and the odd stretch or yoga session. I got to know the regulars there and a small group of us graduated to meeting in the café afterwards for a coffee and chat. On top of the gym, and unless the weather was very bad, I used to make a point of always walking to work instead of taking the car. It was only twenty minutes there and back but I'd get a pace on and it helped me get in my ten thousand steps a day during the week.

When Neil was recovering, I did a lot of running about looking after him and Albie and the house, but the formal exercise got dropped and I finished my job too, as it all became too much.

Now, when it comes to trying on several of what used to be my favourite going-out outfits, I find that despite putting on weight, the shape of my body has also changed. Any spare weight seems to have pasted itself steadfastly around my waist, bum and thighs.

In the end, I decide to pair a forgiving black wrap dress with a nice red and black smart jacket I'd charged to our old maxed-out credit card from the LK Bennett sale a couple of years ago. A pair of black patent stilettos I've had for years complete the look. I go to town on my hair and make-up, though. The layers of my mid-brown hair are seriously overdue for a thorough trim but, once I'm home from work and have collected Albie from school, I unearth my ancient set of heated rollers and sit in them during the afternoon. When I take them out, my hair looks shiny and full of body. My make-up bag is in equal need of an overhaul but, after a quick search, I use a decent foundation and a near-depleted favourite lipstick I find a way of scraping out using the bottom of my eyeliner pencil. An oversized chunky crystal necklace and matching bracelet – a present from Neil from a few Christmases ago – adds a dramatic finishing touch.

Fifteen minutes before the cab is due to arrive, I walk downstairs and stand in the doorway of the living room. Neil looks up from tying his shoelaces. 'Wit woo! Look at you, gorgeous creature!'

'Thanks,' I say coyly. 'You scrub up quite well yourself. And who's this handsome chappie?'

Albie pulls at the collar of his shirt. 'This feels too small, Mum.' He frowns.

'It's snug but still fits you. Open a button or two if you like.'

'No, I want to look smart,' he says before turning away. He's growing up and I think he wants to be seen by Neeta and Ted as responsible after they've taken an interest in him and made flattering comments about what a big help he is.

In the hallway, I look in the mirror and feel gratified that I've done quite a good job under the circumstances. Nobody would guess my lack of resources... and low confidence. Maybe I should make the effort a bit more.

TWENTY-TWO

The cab drops us off ten minutes early for the meal. While Neil settles up with the driver, I take Albie's hand and lead him to the smoky glass doors of the restaurant.

Inside I can see subdued lighting and uniformed waiters gliding around.

'I'm starving, Mum,' Albie grumbles, pulling at my arm to go inside. 'I want pepperoni pizza and chips with loads of ketchup.'

It's Albie's favourite dish at the popular pizza chains and I noticed there was an upmarket version on the menu when I looked online. But I wonder if this place is too grand to cater to the chips and ketchup market.

Neil joins us and holds open the door while we step inside.

Immediately, a smart young woman in a black suit and white blouse appears in front of us. She has black hair slicked back into a ponytail, not a wisp out of place. Her feline kohl-outlined eyes sweep from my head to my toes in one practised movement and then linger a second too long on my husband. 'Good evening, do you have a reservation?'

'It's booked under the name of Williams,' Neil says. 'For eight o'clock.'

She moves to a large open book on a lectern and her face brightens. 'Ahh yes, you're guests of Mr and Mrs Williams. Would you like a drink in the bar area first or would you prefer to go straight to your table?'

I look at Neil and he says, 'I think we'll go straight to our table, thank you.'

'Of course.' She consults her iPad. 'Please, this way.'

As we troop through the restaurant in her wake, I'm mesmerised by the countless globes of soft light, all varying sizes and hanging at different lengths from the ceiling on flimsy copper wires. Subtle piped guitar music plays as a backdrop to a blur of chatter, clinking glasses and the chime of expensive-looking cutlery.

Luigi's menu might be on the expensive side, but the restaurant is not, as I expected, full of starched white tablecloths, confusing silver cutlery and stuffy dishes I can't pronounce. It turns out to be the opposite of that: under-stated and packed with casually dressed guests in that effortless way the wealthy often prefer. I realise with a jolt that I've got my look completely wrong. I'm far too dressed up and look incongruous amongst the other diners. I feel completely out of place, like wearing a sparkly cocktail dress to a picnic. I notice women in particular, their eyes sweeping quick as a flash over my ensemble as we weave our way through. The nervous excitement evaporates and I find myself wishing the ground would swallow me up.

The woman leads us towards the rear of the restaurant, a slightly quieter area where the tables aren't set so closely together. She points out one of four large booths set back down one side. She places the menus on the table. 'Here we are: Mr and Mrs Williams's favourite table,' she says with a smile. 'Sir, madam, young man, please take a seat. Someone will be along to take your drinks order shortly.'

'Can I have a bag of crisps if we've got to wait?' Albie whispers and I nudge him to shush.

At that moment, I catch sight of Neeta and Ted arriving in the smart foyer. Ted wears beige-coloured chinos with brown suede boat shoes and a short-sleeved powder-blue shirt. The gold Rolex Neil has been admiring catches the light as he raises a hand in greeting to someone out of my view. Behind him, Neeta looks stunning in a flowing floral maxi-dress in pretty muted colours that complements her dark hair. I catch a glimpse of sparkly flat sandals as she glides in, impossibly slim and elegant.

A rotund middle-aged man in a black suit approaches them. He air-kisses Neeta on either cheek and shakes Ted's hand. He takes a stack of leather-bound menus and leads them towards us. We stand to greet them.

'Oh my goodness, you look so handsome!' Neeta places both her hands on Albie's cheeks and kisses the top of his head. 'So grown up, like a teenager!' He blushes but I can tell he's flattered. Like most young people, he loves to think he looks older than he is. Funny how when you get into your thirties it's the opposite with everyone suddenly wanting to look younger.

Neeta directs everyone where to sit so we change positions slightly. She places me opposite Neil and nearest the wall. Neeta sits next to Neil and Albie and Ted takes his place opposite her and next to me.

'It's a family-run place, been in the same family for the past few generations,' Neeta remarks when she notices me looking around in awe at the endearing clutter and wall hangings. Every surface is covered but thoughtfully so, and all in an Italian theme. From Chianti fiasco bottles to colourful hand-painted plates and old framed photographs of the restaurant from decades before.

'It's gorgeous,' I say, running my hand along the scrubbed wooden table near the window we've been seated at. 'Feels more like Tuscany than the North Yorkshire coast!'

'Wait until you taste the food!' Ted grins, taking a menu from the wine waiter. 'We'll start with some fizz and then a couple of bottles of quality red with the meal. That OK with everyone?'

'Lovely. Thanks, Ted.' Neil beams.

'So, this will be your second drinking session together.' I give Ted a cheeky grin. 'And you sent him home smelling of booze last time!'

'I'm sorry?' Ted frowns, looking from me to Neil.

'The other week when you came back from your conference dinner.' I falter as Ted looks at me blankly. Clearly, he hasn't got a clue what I'm talking about. Then it all comes back to me... the feeling Neil was lying when he came home, his evasiveness. I glance at him now. His face has visibly paled and there's sweat beading his upper lip.

Neil sighs and runs his fingers through his hair. 'OK, so this is awkward. I think Lottie means—'

Neeta interrupts him. 'God, Ted, you've got a memory like a sieve! When Neil came back up to move that delivery and your dinner was cancelled... remember? You two sat drinking gin on the garden bench for ages!'

Ted claps a hand to his forehead. 'Sorry... sorry! Totally slipped my mind. Yes, Lottie! Our second drinking session, indeed!'

Neil's laugh comes out strange, too high-pitched. I watch as he quietly exhales.

I catch Neeta glance at Ted. The table falls into silence for a couple of moments. Albie looks up from his game. I'm confused... what just happened here? Were the three of them covering up for something?

Ted reaches for my hand and squeezes it. 'You have to

remember you're dealing with an old man here, Lottie. Some days I can forget my own name and that's really impressive!'

The three of them hoot with laughter. It's overkill and I look down at my hands.

'Mum, can I have a bag—'

'Albie!' I hiss. 'We'll be ordering soon. You'll have to wait.'

'What's up, buddy?' Ted asks him. 'Hungry?'

'I'm starving.' Albie frowns.

'He wants crisps,' I say stiffly, somehow collecting myself a little. 'Can you imagine, in a place like this?'

'If our little prince wants crisps then we must see what we can do,' Neeta chips in.

Our little prince, perhaps. But not hers. 'It's OK, Neeta, it won't hurt him to wait. He won't eat his meal if he fills up on crisps, either.'

But Albie's face is instantly transformed with a big smile when Neeta calls the waiter back and asks for a bowl of crisps to be brought over right away. I might as well be invisible. I glare at Neil, who hasn't said another word yet. He's getting a bit of colour back in his cheeks and smiles at me. I look away.

A few minutes later, Albie gets a small bowl of crisps, a glass of Sprite and, with his Nintendo Switch, he happily withdraws into his own world, zoning the adults out. I can't help thinking he'd have been better staying over at Keris's as I'd originally planned.

While Ted and Neil discuss the merits of Spanish versus Argentinian red wine, Neeta turns to me. 'You look stunning, Lottie,' she says. 'I love your dress and necklace.'

I feel my cheeks flush with embarrassment. 'I think I overdid it a bit,' I say, conscious of my blingy costume jewellery. A single tear-shaped diamond on an ultra-fine gold chain glints in the hollow at the base of her neck. I'm guessing it's at least two carats and it doesn't look like it's from Swarovski. 'I wish I'd put on a nice summery dress like you.'

'Nonsense, you look perfect,' she says kindly. 'I've dressed down a bit tonight, but I've dined here lots of times done up to the nines. Anything goes, so please don't worry.' She rolls her eyes. 'You must ignore Ted; he forgets what day it is sometimes and I'm not joking!'

'Hey, I heard that!' Ted grins. 'True enough, though. Very true.'

I force myself to shake off the strange feeling that they're all in on something. It's possible there's no cover-up and I'm just feeling over-sensitive because I'm so nervous and I feel like a bit of an outsider here.

Seeing that most of the diners have dressed down, I'm sure Neeta is just giving out compliments to reassure me, but strangely, I do feel marginally better after her pep talk. She just has this way of putting me at ease and making me feel good enough.

A drinks waiter appears, expertly holding a loaded tray aloft. He's dressed in a white shirt, sleeves rolled up to his elbows, black trousers and an apron tied around his waist bearing the embroidered 'Luigi's' insignia in an attractive flowing golden script.

He hands out perfectly chilled glasses of fizz.

'Cheers!' Ted raises and looks around for us all to do the same. 'To our new estate manager and his lovely family joining our Seaspray family. I hope you'll all be very happy here. Oh, and congratulations to you, Lottie, in your new job!'

I take a sip, determined to forget about my shortcomings and enjoy the evening.

'Cheers.' Everyone chimes in. Even Albie lifts his glass of Sprite, to Ted and Neeta's delight.

I'm already halfway down my drink and my throat feels pleasantly warm. I've kicked off my punishing stilettos under the table and surreptitiously slipped off the overkill bracelet, sliding it discreetly into my handbag.

Another waiter hands out the menus, reciting today's specials. I feel dizzy with delight keeping track of the number of staff attending to us. I see other diners glancing in our direction, perhaps wondering why we're getting extra-special treatment. I'd usually be one of those people so I'm happy to soak up the attention. Maybe one or two of those well-heeled women aren't feeling quite as snooty now, I think impishly.

While I help Albie to make his choice from the menu, the other three adults start talking about the Seaspray grounds and the work they're planning to do there. Neil really gets into his stride, making full use of the platform to push all his ideas and the value he's bringing to the job. It's great to see him like this but he's almost acting *too* keen to impress.

We order food and it's as good as I'd expected. Ted insists I have a glass of red wine with my garlic mushroom on ciabatta starter although I wanted to stick to fizz. He can't do enough for me, passing the salt and pepper to save me stretching, hailing the waiter as soon as I mention we need more water. While Neil and Neeta chat between themselves, Ted is very attentive to me and my son.

He wins Albie over in one sentence when he starts a conversation about football. 'Who's better then, Albie... Messi or Ronaldo? Got to be Ronaldo for me.'

Albie's face lights up. 'Me too, Ted! Ronaldo is the GOAT!'

'Ronaldo's a goat?' Ted frowns comically. 'No, he's not; he's a human.'

Albie bursts out laughing. 'GOAT means Greatest Of All Time! Ronaldo has scored more goals overall and he's the all-time greatest goal scorer in the Champions League.'

'Correct!' Ted finishes his red wine and reaches for the bottle. Without asking, he tops my still half-full glass up. 'And did you know Ronaldo also holds the record for most...'

I zone out at this point, smiling to myself at the unlikely

pairing of my now confident son and big, brash Ted, chattering on like they're sitting next to each other in class.

The wine has warmed me through and my sense of otherness has long since eased.

I slip my shoes back on, make my excuses and leave the table, heading for the bathroom, navigating a path through the packed restaurant. Every table is occupied and the waiting staff are expertly weaving in and out, steaming plates of food and trays of drinks held high as they avoid each other and obstacles like me: guests out of their seats who are skirted around with a polite nod and a smile.

The bathroom has ambient lighting and smoky mirrored walls. After I've used the facilities, I wash my hands and glance in the mirror. My hair and make-up have held up well, at least. Thanks to the wine and Neeta's comments, I feel a bit more confident about how I look now.

Back outside, I head for the rear of the restaurant and spot our booth tucked away from the other tables. My feet slow down as I take in what I'm seeing. Two heads bent closely together, whispering and laughing intimately together. Neil and Neeta. Ted is still chatting to Albie and doesn't look remotely concerned about his wife openly flirting with a younger man. Specifically, with my husband and his estate manager.

I brace myself and speed up again. I watch as Neeta's right hand, currently on the table top, disappears underneath as she reaches slightly towards Neil's thigh. He looks into her eyes and smiles and she says something to him. At that moment, he glances up and sees me. Sees my face, which must be pale and livid. I feel like up-ending the table.

He stands up quickly and the smile slides from Neeta's face. Ted and Albie look around, as do several diners around our table.

I feel dizzy and out of breath. Suddenly, Neil is at my side, his hand grasping my upper arm.

'Lottie, I can see you're not happy. Come on, come outside for a bit of fresh air, but remember this is my job on the line if you cause a scene.'

'I saw what you were up to! I saw you flirting with her... her hand, it... oh God.'

My conversation with Gloria at the school springs back into my mind.

Mrs Williams, Neeta – she's a stunningly attractive woman. Dripping with diamond jewellery and designer labels and yet she's got absolutely no ego.

'We were just talking. Ted was right there, for God's sake!'

'I saw you. Giggling, laughing... you were too close to her face!' I feel unsteady on my feet and sway a little. 'And that thing about the drinking... they were lying. You were all lying!'

'What? Listen to yourself, it's madness! We were laughing at a joke, that's all. Is that a crime?' Neil guides me expertly back out into the foyer and through the smoky glass doors, outside. 'You've had too much to drink, Lottie. You're blowing this up big time.'

'I... I feel sick.' I lurch towards a cluster of bushes and throw up. It's not the wine, but the churning in my stomach at what I just witnessed between my husband and Neeta Williams.

'Bloody great,' I hear Neil curse behind me. 'I can't believe this. You're blowing things up in your head; you're—'

'Is everything alright? Oh Lottie, you poor thing.' Neeta rushes out of the entrance and embraces me. I'm enveloped me in a cloud of sweet, floral scent that makes me want to throw up all over again.

'Where's Albie?' I say weakly.

'He's fine, don't worry. He's with Ted.' She hands me a tissue and I use it to mop my sticky mouth. 'Is it drink, or is it some kind of nasty stomach bug, Lottie?'

She looks at me, her face sympathetic and kind. I feel like crap. What did I see? Two people having a laugh on a great night out, or... the beginnings of a betrayal right in front of my nose? I can't start a full-scale row now. I haven't the energy and I'm doubting myself.

'She'll be OK,' Neil remarks. 'I'll probably just get her home now, if that's OK, Neeta.'

'Of course. Let me call you a cab. Ted won't want to leave yet without dessert or his complimentary shot of limoncello. It came on so suddenly, didn't it?'

'I... I—' The words won't come. I know what I saw and I want to tell her that, but... there'll be no going back from this if I confront Neeta and accuse her of groping my husband. 'Sorry the night's ruined,' I say stiffly. 'I wanted to have a good time more than anyone.'

'Of course you did; we all did. It's such a shame,' she says soothingly as if I'm a child. She slides her arm around my shoulder and squeezes gently, but I step forward so her hand slides away. Her voice brightens. 'Don't worry, we can do it again when you're feeling better!'

I press my lips together but don't reply. I'd rather stick sharpened matches down my fingernails than witness the two of them behaving like that again. I feel sick Neil sees her every day up at Seaspray and there's no way Albie will continue going up there after school.

I'll get childcare for him. I'll give up the job.

Anything but allow Neeta Williams to poison every area of my life.

TWENTY-THREE

SATURDAY

Neil sleeps in the spare room and, the morning after the disastrous meal at Luigi's, he brings me a cup of tea. It took me hours to get to sleep, replaying the awful evening second by second in my head. Then when I did finally drop off, I woke up sweating in the middle of a nightmare.

'Oh, thank you so much,' I say coldly. 'But I could've made my own tea.'

'Please, Lottie,' he says wretchedly. 'I beg you, can we just put last night behind us? Ted has already texted to say everything is cool and they're looking forward to me taking Albie up there this morning.' He pulls on a T-shirt and a pair of jeans. 'You just focus on drinking plenty of water and feeling better.'

He's trying to say I was drunk last night but I wasn't. 'You can try and put a spin on it, tell yourself I was out of it, but I know what I saw. And I know you lot were covering something up about that drinking session in the garden, too.'

'How many times do I need to say it? Nobody was lying, nobody was covering anything up! Look, I know how it must have looked, but I keep telling you, I swear to God it wasn't like that! We were drinking, laughing... maybe we shouldn't have been sitting as close but—'

'I saw her hand, Neil. She touched you under the table. Exactly where, I don't want to imagine.'

'She patted my thigh, that's it. She told me a funny story about a guy she once knew who went weight training and got flattened by a bar-bell weight he couldn't handle. She said, "I can see by your thigh muscles it wouldn't be a problem for you," and she patted my thigh.'

'God. How pathetic.'

'I know, it's cringeworthy. But my point is, that's all it was. It wasn't as sinister as it looked. She didn't have her hands down my trousers!'

'Oh, silly me, nothing to worry about then.' I can feel my eyes flashing dangerously at him. 'We won't mention how *embarrassing* it was, how *disrespectful*. And, the worst thing of all, how you were both oblivious to a nine-year-old sitting directly opposite you.'

'Albie was embroiled in his football chat with Ted,' Neil says, deflated. 'He didn't pick up on anything untoward, I can guarantee that.' He sits on the edge of the bed and grasps my hand before I can snatch it away. 'I'm sorry, Lottie, OK? I got carried away with the occasion, the drink, the warmth... I'm an idiot. I won't let it happen again. I swear.'

'I heard something a while ago down in the village. There's a rumour Ted and Neeta aren't the perfect married couple they pretend to be at all. That in private, they live separate lives.'

The fact I haven't heard anything of the sort and it's a conclusion I've come to myself is beside the point. It feels good to voice it.

He scowls. 'What? Where did you hear that?'

'I overheard a conversation.'

'That's clearly rubbish. It's just gossip.'

'Is it?'

'Ted and Neeta seem very happy to me and I see them more than anyone.'

'People in happy relationships don't usually behave like Neeta did last night.'

'Lottie, I told you, it wasn't what it looked like. I swear that's the truth. Don't you believe me?'

I look at him and he folds his arms around me, nuzzling my neck. The answer is no. I don't believe him at all. I think he's trying to exercise damage limitation, knowing how much trouble I could cause if I lose my temper.

I pull away and pick up my tea.

'You'd better go,' I say frostily. 'You don't want to be late.'

TWENTY-FOUR

NEIL

He can't wait to get out of the cottage; he needs some space to think. Lottie had handled last night badly. He acknowledged he'd played a big part in that but what was he meant to do when Neeta became over-friendly at the table?

Neil thought he was going to throw up himself when Lottie had innocently asked Ted about the drinking session in the garden. Neeta had stepped in and saved his bacon, but Neil had been completely unnerved when Ted instantly played along. I mean, how many men, realising the gardener had been drinking with his wife while he was out, would leap to that man's defence?

Lottie is no idiot and she'd been able to sense the awkwardness. It had been a close call and Neil didn't know what he'd say to Ted about it when he saw him this morning.

Despite all that, the point Neil had tried to get through to his wife was that the Williamses hold all the power in their relationship. They are Neil's employers but have made it clear from the outset they consider Neil and Lottie to be friends. By offering unpaid childcare for Albie, Neeta has enabled Lottie to get a part-time job. In addition, Albie is very fond of both Neeta and Ted. They've both witnessed their son's confidence increasing almost daily as Ted has got him involved in renovating the tree-house, and offering him responsibilities on the estate for a bit of pocket money.

By anyone's standards, they've landed on their feet in Whitsend Bay and he's found himself a job that will enable them to pay off the remaining debt by this time next year and build a good, solid lifestyle.

So even though Neeta pushed things a bit far last night, he finds it astonishing that Lottie would willingly put everything they've gained on the line and end the evening early, instead of keeping quiet and having it out with him when they got back. She'd shrugged off Neeta's attempts to make amends outside the restaurant and hadn't even said goodbye to Ted before getting in the cab.

'Why is Mum upset?' Albie had asked him on the way home as Lottie had stared blearily out of the window as the cab had sped past streetlights and glowing shop windows. 'Is she mad at me, too?'

Neil had done his best to reassure Albie, but his son wasn't stupid. He knew that something was wrong and that the night had been ruined. Thank God Ted hadn't taken Neil to task for having a laugh with Neeta in the same way Lottie had.

'Nothing wrong with having a giggle over a drink,' Ted had said, slapping Neil's back when he'd felt moved to explain there had been nothing in his chat with Neeta. 'We're all friends together now.' He hadn't mentioned the drinks in the garden issue.

Although Neil would never admit it to Ted or Lottie, he had, in fact, been shocked how full-on Neeta had behaved after a few drinks. At one point, when Lottie was still in the restaurant bathroom, he'd become worried Ted might suddenly break off his footie conversation with Albie and ask him what the hell he thought he was playing at. But although Ted had glanced over a couple of times, he'd simply smiled knowingly, even winked at Neil once and gone back to chatting to Albie as if he found it all completely normal that his wife was flirting with the hired help.

Frankly, he'd found that a bit weird. Neil had even wondered, in that split second, whether Ted was the kind of guy that got off on seeing his wife flirting with other men. That theory would also be backed up by Ted's readiness to lie about his supposed drinking session with Neil.

When Lottie went to the bathroom, Neeta had begun talking about her favourite areas of the grounds and had quickly got quite saucy. She'd leaned in closer and confessed that she had, on occasion in high summer, sunbathed naked close to the trees on the main lawn. She'd also hinted that Neil should call in for drinks on the occasions Ted went to the wholesaler's or to one of his boozy business networking meetings where he met old colleagues in the building industry, which could last all afternoon.

'Even when he gets home, he's usually fast asleep for the night within ten minutes,' she'd stressed, her hand slipping from the table at that moment and brushing his thigh before she'd placed it on her own leg.

That's when Neil had looked up and seen Lottie advancing rapidly, her face like thunder. If he hadn't stopped her in her tracks like he did, she'd have probably screamed the place down. Thank God he'd been able to think on his feet this morning and come up with the story about the guy in the gym who Neeta knew, which had seemed to pacify her somewhat.

That's what people didn't realise about Lottie: she had a hidden temper and once her fury was unleashed, she could quickly become a different person altogether.

TWENTY-FIVE

LOTTIE

Neil insists on taking Albie up to Seaspray to finish off the tree-house.

'We can't just cut everything off, Lottie. We have to fully discuss this so we don't blow everything we have out of the water. Please, just let's take a couple of days, OK?'

I know in a way he's right. I feel like packing up and leaving everything behind but we can't do that. Things must be thought through more carefully, even though I'm still disgusted with Neeta's behaviour last night.

I pop down to the general store for a few basics like bread and milk. It's only my second time in here, but it must boast one of the best views of any small shop on the coastline, tucked away as it is on the side of the sea with expansive views towards the horizon.

There's usually a cluster of customers outside the door when I pass. A snaking queue of young mums with pushchairs, kids in damp swimwear with bare feet and accompanied by parents and grandparents. Most are customers who, judging by their sandy feet, come here straight from the beach probably for drinks and snacks. Today, because I'm early I presume, there is no queue.

'Be with you in a sec,' someone calls out as I enter.

Inside, the shop is clean but cluttered. Still, I get the feeling the large, rather brusque lady behind the counter knows where every single item is.

The walls are packed with shelves and tinned goods and packaged food items like long-life cakes and biscuits. There's a small section housing fresh bread, croissants and cakes from a local bakery. A long refrigerator runs the length of the serving counter, stocked with cold and cured meats and also deli items such as readymade sandwiches, Scotch eggs, pork pies and cheeses. Everything the tourists might want for an impromptu beach picnic.

The woman looks up from refilling a section of the deli fridge with cellophane-wrapped, filled rolls. 'What can I get you, love?'

I put a rye boule and a litre of milk on the counter. 'I'll take half a pound of bacon and a big piece of Cheddar cheese, please.'

She gives a curt nod and reaches for a pair of plastic gloves before touching the food. She stares for a moment before looking back at her hands.

'Is your husband the new gardener up at Seaspray?'

'That's right. We've moved into the cottage on the grounds.'

She nods. 'And how are you finding it, up at Seaspray? Have you met Ted and Neeta yet?'

I take a breath and smile. 'Oh yes, I've met them both. They seem like lovely people.'

'And have you been invited up to the house yet?' She picks up a pair of silver tongs but waits for an answer.

'Not yet, but—'

'Tom and Mary Gooding, they never went up to the house, you know. Imagine that... working for them all those years and never getting invited up there.' She grabs a piece of waxed paper and picks up a good-sized chunk of cheese, holding it up with the tongs. 'This one alright for you?'

'Perfect, thanks.'

'Very glamorous people, the Williamses. See them out and about now and again at some posh event or other. Other than that, they tend to keep themselves to themselves. Who can blame them, I suppose. Fancy cars, designer clothes, bags of money.' She chuckles, sliding the cheese into a bag. 'They're hardly going to want to mix with the likes of us, are they, now? Smoked or unsmoked bacon, love?'

'Unsmoked, please. I've heard they do a lot in the community. Saving the library from closure, helping to fund repairs to the church roof.'

'Oh yes, they do all that and more. Can't fault their generosity and yet...' She plonks a small stack of bacon on the digital weighing scale. 'There I go again, I've said too much again. I confess, it's a fault of mine.'

'Please, go on. I'm interested.'

She inclines her head and gives me a crafty smile. 'Us locals, we have a saying in here: "What's said in the general store, stays in the general store." Do you get my drift?'

'Absolutely.' I mime zipping my mouth. 'Received and understood.'

'I've lived here for thirty years now. Nine years ago, Neeta and Ted Williams appeared from nowhere, knocked down a perfectly lovely Victorian house and built a glass and metal Fort Knox up there.'

I think about the framed photograph of the original house I found upstairs. 'Was the old house not a listed building?'

'No, but it still put a lot of folks' noses out of joint around here, that I can tell you. That glass box they built sticks out like a sore thumb up there where everyone can see it. It's not in keeping with all the other dwellings around here at all. Remains a mystery how they got it through the planning process but there you go. Money talks, doesn't it?'

'Where did they move from?'

'That's just it... nobody knows! I mean, most of the people around here are dazzled by the Williamses' wealth and the generosity they show. Might sound cynical, but any improvement they fund is always well-attended by press and plastered all over social media.'

'Is that what people think, that they do it for the attention?'

'No, no. They're generally held in very high esteem. There are just a few of us grizzly old stalwarts who aren't as impressed as the other ninety per cent of Whitsend Bay.' She wraps the bacon before popping it into a paper bag. 'Don't get me wrong, the Williamses have done nothing to me or anyone I know. It's just a feeling. That's all. A feeling that something doesn't sit quite right with the two of them.'

I nod slowly. 'Do you think they might just be really happy in their own company and want to keep themselves to themselves? Some people have a very strong, close marriage and don't let anyone else in.'

'You'd think so, but something doesn't add up.' Her voice drops quieter again. 'See, for all they're the perfect couple when they're out and about, they apparently don't get on behind closed doors. Mary Gooding told me that here in this very shop.' I wonder what happened to the 'what's said in here, stays in here' maxim she'd just recited. 'Ted is always out on the estate and he often goes away for the whole weekend. Neeta hardly leaves the house and when she does, it's usually on her own and she's back within the day. Mary found it all very odd. Used to prey on her mind, it did.'

'Where do they live now, the Goodings?'

'Nobody's heard a thing from them to date. Just upped and left after a disagreement with their employers. But I've said enough, anyhow.'

I pay for my shopping and thank her before leaving the shop feeling vindicated. Mary Gooding obviously came to the same conclusion as I did about the Williamses' relationship. What else might she have witnessed? What I'd give for a conversation with her... and yet nobody seems to know where they've gone.

Still, it's reassuring I'm not on my own. Not everyone is enamoured with our glamorous neighbours.

When Neil and Albie get back mid-afternoon, Albie is full of it. Neil goes straight back out again, supposedly to pick up some DIY bits he needs for various jobs in the cottage but I get the feeling he's staying out of my way a bit. Very sensible. I'm still seething inside.

Still, it's hard to stay irritated when Albie is so buoyant and full of enthusiasm. Instead of chilling out with his PlayStation or watching TV, he sits with me in the kitchen as I tackle a pile of ironing.

'Guess what, Mum? I've started doing my own regular jobs now for Ted up at Seaspray, not just helping him and dad with their jobs. Ted's giving me extra pocket money!'

'What kind of jobs?'

'Weeding, sweeping up and—' he covers his face with his hands and supresses a yelp '—he's going to look at making me a proper games room in one of the spare rooms after Christmas!'

It's all a bit over the top for a nine-year-old. They'll be moving him in there next.

The shopkeeper's words come back to me. *Tom and Mary Gooding, they never went up to the house.* So far that applies to all of us.

'That's incredible, Albie. You're a very lucky boy.' I fold the school shirt I've just ironed and pick up one of Neil's T-shirts. 'Did you see Neeta today, too?'

He nods, pouring a drink into a glass. 'She brought some

homemade cookies and lemonade outside to us. Oh yes, and I nearly forgot!' He dashes back to the door and returns with a carrier bag. 'Neeta sent you some, too.'

I open the bag and take out a pretty Fortnum & Mason tin, beautifully decorated with a picture of the iconic shop. I open the lid and there's a small, lilac, handwritten sticky note affixed to a piece of greaseproof paper.

To dearest Lottie,

Hope you're feeling better.

Sending love and home-baked cookies, Neeta

I remove a piece of greaseproof paper to find half a dozen chocolate chip cookies. They look perfect enough to sell in an artisan bakery.

'They look nice,' I say, replacing the paper and lid and placing them on the side.

'Neeta says I can help her bake some biscuits one time. She says they have this massive oven with a real fire in it.'

'Sounds like an Aga,' I say, thinking how every time Ted or Neeta promise Albie something that involves him going inside the house, it's always set at some indeterminate time in the future.

'Yeah, *the Aga*. That's what she called it. I wish we lived in that house, Mum, it's so cool.'

A twist of envy pokes at my chest. I'm delighted Albie's had such a good day – of course I am. It's just that... I look around. I was feeling proud of how cosy our little space looked, and now I realise this is just the biggest poky room in the Seaspray gardener's cottage. It's not even our own place.

I sound petulant and ungrateful and I'm not. Really I'm not. It's just that last night's diabolical display aside, Neeta and

Ted's life seems so perfect, so happy and picture-postcard, it makes everything around it seem lacking.

'Mum?' Albie is studying my expression. 'I really like it here at Whitsend Bay and living next to Ted and Neeta. Can we stay here forever?'

'Oh Albie!' I put out my arms and, for once, he allows me to give him a cuddle. 'This is our home now. Our life is here, and I'm so pleased you love it.'

My heart sinks as I hear myself make what sounds very much like a promise and yet, last night, I would have packed up and gone back to Nottingham in a heartbeat given half a chance.

I eye the boxes waiting to go up to the box room. 'Why don't you drink your juice and watch a bit of TV while I finish tidying round?'

Albie nods happily and reaches for the remote and I pick up the first box and take it upstairs. I set it down on the floor of the tiny spare room. It's dim in here and lovely and bright outside. I kneel on the bed and pull the blind strings to open the slats to an angle that allows the daylight to flood in. At that moment Albie calls upstairs.

'Can I have another cookie, Mum?'

'Just one more; you don't want to spoil your tea. It's macaroni cheese tonight, your favourite,' I call back, stepping back out onto the landing.

I pop down for the other box and place it next to the first one. The room is transformed with the light. If Neil could perhaps board the loft for storage then I could paint this a pretty colour and put a little sofa in here and a desk. It could be a quiet space for us to use rather than a dumping ground as it is at the moment. The cottage is so small; we should cherish and utilise every inch of space we have.

I move over to the bed again, pick up the binoculars and peer out of the window. Ted is sitting outside on the balcony, and Neeta stands in the doorway of the room. I realise, as they are both in their dressing gowns, it's probably part of their master bedroom. They both hold short, fat glasses, possibly containing gin, I think.

Neeta is talking, her free hand waving around in the air. At first I think she's just animated while she's speaking, but when she juts her chin forward and becomes agitated, I realise that she's shouting at Ted.

Through the slats of the blind, I twist the handle and slowly push open the window enough so I can feel the fresh sea air and... as I'd hoped, hear the angry strains of Neeta's voice.

The direction of the breeze is in my favour and carries some of her accusatory words.

'Don't you dare... blame... without you!'

Slowly I twist the blind and lift one of the slats up so I can see the balcony.

Ted glances at her a couple of times during her rant but appears to be largely ignoring her in favour of the view of the ocean. It occurs to me, if I were that angry, his reaction would only serve to infuriate me more. I'm clearly right because, suddenly, Neeta steps fully out of the balcony and shouts directly into his face.

'It's your problem too!'

I hear every single word she shrieks, each one punctuated by a beat of silence before she utters the next.

His hands fly up in a 'what do you want me to do about it?' manner and they both stare each other down for a few moments before Neeta turns to go back inside.

Then I let out an involuntary gasp and my hand flies to my mouth as her arm lifts and she launches her glass straight at her husband.

TWENTY-SIX

The second Neeta launches her glass at Ted, he jumps up out of his seat. His back is facing me but it's not hard to imagine, seeing his jerky, quick movements, that his face is a mask of fury. Neeta's actions back this up when she freezes momentarily and then turns and flees inside the house. Ted follows swiftly, knocking his chair over in the process.

I stand there, peering through the blind. Neeta shouldn't have done that but... my heart is thumping and Ted is acting aggressively and I feel like I definitely need to do something... but what, exactly? Ted is much bigger and stronger than Neeta, but I can hardly ring the police on the strength of him looking annoyed.

I run downstairs and see Albie is still happily watching television.

'You OK?' I ask from the doorway of the lounge.

'Yeah,' he says vaguely without taking his eyes from the screen.

I push my feet into Neil's old Crocs and slip out of the kitchen door quietly, heading down to the bottom of our small garden. It's been a pleasant day and the air is still warm. I take a deep breath in, tasting the tang of the salty sea air on my tongue.

When I peer through the trees, I have a partial view of the empty balcony. I can see the sliding doors to the bedroom are still open, so I stay still and listen. Nothing. There's no shouting or even raised voices.

I feel somewhat relieved. If it had been obvious the Williamses were fighting, I'd have felt obliged to do something. Apart from ringing the police, I would have had no choice but to try and contact Neil, or to go round there and check Neeta was OK.

Everyone knows that domestic violence victims often suffer in silence. Violence within relationships transgresses all sorts of boundaries and just because the Williamses are a well-respected, wealthy and much-liked couple in the community, it doesn't mean that Neeta isn't being terrorised behind the luxurious glass and steel walls of Seaspray House.

After another couple of minutes of standing there, my head cocked, listening for sounds of distress, I go back inside.

It's another hour before Neil gets home. I'm playing Albie's favourite board game, Frustration, when the kitchen door opens.

'Hello, you two,' Neil says, upbeat. 'Having fun?'

I decided not to ring him in the end as there was no evidence of any distress from the property. Now, seeing him upbeat and happy at the end of his working day, I debate whether to tell him at all.

While he takes a turn on the board game with Albie, I finish off the meal I prepared earlier in the afternoon: a slow-cooked pork ragout and buttery mashed potatoes, washed down with a bottle of good quality red wine. One of Neil's favourite meals.

Albie's already had his tea and didn't finish it due to scoffing too many of Neeta's home-baked cookies, I suspect. When they've finished their game, he sidles up to me as I'm giving the ragout a final stir.

'Can I watch some TV in my room, Mum?' He assumes a pleading tone. 'Just for thirty minutes?'

His face lights up when I readily agree. The last thing I want is him soaking up the negative energy that still exists between me and his dad.

When Neil comes down from his shower, I'm already eating.

'Oh, I thought we were going to eat together.' He looks crestfallen.

'Yours is in the oven keeping warm,' I say curtly.

He takes two large wine glasses from the cupboard and uncorks the half-bottle of Merlot on the side.

'Cheers.' He hands me a glass and holds his up. I take the wine but don't clink his glass. I inhale the wine's bouquet and swill some around my mouth.

'Oh, right. Still like that, is it?' His expression turns surly. He puts his glass on the table and walks over to the oven to get his plated meal out. When he gets back, he sits down and looks down at his food. 'Can we just call a truce, be normal with each other just for the next thirty minutes, Lottie? I know you're angry and for good reason, but... please let's just try and be civil while we eat.'

He picks up his cutlery as though it's a done deal. But I'm not ready to talk about the weather yet or what's on television tonight.

I say, 'I'm curious. What are they like together, the Williamses?'

He puts his cutlery down with a clatter, swallowing his food and reaching for his wine. 'I guess that's a no then, right?'

'Indulge me.'

Neil frowns and takes a gulp of wine. 'I think I've said before that they seem happy enough. They've been married a long time so they've got that easy way with each other.' He loads his fork with mashed potato before adding, 'Saying that, I haven't seen that much of them together. Neeta mostly stays up at the house.'

'Doing what?'

He shrugs, chewing his food. 'Just stuff, I guess. She sits out reading on the patio quite a bit.'

'You've never heard them arguing or anything like that?'

'No.' He looks at me and inclines his head slightly. 'Why all the relationship questions?'

'I'm interested, is all,' I say quickly.

'Ha! I know that look. Something's piqued your interest.'

I have two or three seconds at most to decide whether to tell him what I saw, or say nothing. My head buzzes pleasantly with the effect of the wine and I take another sip. Sod it.

'I saw them arguing earlier. They were out on their bedroom balcony at the side of the house.'

Neil is immediately riled. 'What? Have you been spying on them again?'

'Don't be ridiculous!' I feel heat flush into my face.

'I'm sorry. But... if they find out, they'll probably fire me.' He frowns.

I've kept quiet about visiting the spare room vantage point because I know he'll moan, exactly as he is doing now. 'I heard them,' I say. 'I took some rubbish out to the bin and I heard them shouting. So I walked to the bottom of the garden and looked through the trees. Like anyone would.'

'What were they arguing about?'

'I don't know. They were just angry with each other. Shouting and then...'

'Then what?'

'Then Neeta threw her glass at him.'

Neil's mouth drops open. 'She *what*?'

'It looked nasty. He jumped up and to be honest... I thought he might hit her. I'd have had no option but to call the police if he had.'

Neil's face darkens. 'No, that's absolutely never an option, Lottie. There would be no going back for us from there.' He picks up his wine glass and stares down into the dark liquid. 'Besides, they're entitled to have a spat in private if they feel like it.'

'Excuse me? If it had been the other way around and Ted had been the aggressor, I'm sure you'd have been shocked.' I put down my glass a little harder than I mean to and the wine wobbles violently within it. 'If I see any man hitting a woman, I'm going to be straight on to the police no matter what you or anyone else says. Anyone with a decent bone in their body would do the same.'

'From what you've just said, Neeta was the aggressor, so Ted isn't at fault.'

'You don't know, you weren't there.'

'Fair comment, but...' His voice tails off as he hesitates.

'But what?'

'I have seen Neeta giving Ted the odd filthy look. One in particular when I first started the job.'

'Really? You never said.'

'I suppose I thought I might have imagined it. Plus, a lot of the time, they seem to be the opposite of argumentative together.'

'When people are watching them, you mean?'

He sighs and puts down his drink. 'Lottie, let's stop talking about this now. What's the sense in us being at loggerheads over *their* relationship? Maybe you just caught them at a bad moment out on the balcony, I don't know.' He pushes his food away. 'I really like this job. Whatever their relationship is like in private, Ted and Neeta are great bosses. I think I'm going to do well here and the last thing I need is for you to... for you to—'

'Mess it up? Is that what you mean?'

'I didn't mean that. I just don't want you to get the idea something's wrong and then set about gathering evidence to support your claims.'

'I know what I saw,' I say simply. 'I'm not the enemy here.'

'Fine. But please, if you're worried about anything in the future, then promise you'll ring me first? Not the police.' He sighs and reaches across the table, squeezing my hand lightly. 'Dinner was fabulous, thank you. Can we just forget about the Williamses and focus on us, please?'

I stand up. 'I'll clear the table and make some coffee. Will you just check if Albie's OK upstairs?'

He nods, seemingly relieved. 'Course and I'll take a quick shower while I'm up there. You know, he'd be heartbroken if we left the bay, Lottie. Let's keep that in mind and try to make things work. It's our relationship that's important, not Ted and Neeta's.'

TWENTY-SEVEN

SUNDAY

I wake in the early hours from a nightmare and lie awake for a long time, listening to Neil's soft snores and the first light creeping in around the edges of the curtains. I use the time to do some hard thinking and I conclude – rightly or wrongly – that I should draw a line under the whole sorry saga of what happened between Neeta and Neil at the restaurant.

So, mid-morning when Neil takes Albie down to the beach to see what they can find in the rockpools, I determine it's the perfect chance to speak to Neeta to clear the air after Friday night.

There aren't many excuses I can find to go up to the house, unlike Neil, who works up there, and Albie, who is spending increasing amounts of time up at Seaspray. I'm certainly not willing to put up with the behaviour I witnessed at the restaurant, but now I've calmed down a bit, neither do I want to wreck our nice new life after a slip-up that Neil swears will never happen again. It will also give me a chance to see Neeta after the balcony incident and satisfy myself she's OK.

I wave the boys off and transfer the two remaining cookies out of the Fortnum & Mason tin into a small Tupperware container, wiping out the tin in readiness for its return.

I change into a knee-length blue shift dress and flat white leather sandals, then leave the house, locking the door behind me. It's not yet 10 a.m. but the sky is clear and blue and dotted with fluffy white clouds shaped as if a child had drawn them. My stomach churns as I walk across the level ground and start the short climb to Seaspray. I want to speak to Neeta about what I saw last night but I'm not sure how to do it. I certainly can't tell her the truth: that I was watching them from the spare bedroom window.

As I walk, I look up and realise I can't see the bedroom balcony or window from this angle. The area the altercation took place in is completely screened by trees. Unless you stand in one particular corner of our spare bedroom, that is. It occurs to me that, if the trees are left to grow unchecked, this time next year, the view from the spare room window will also be obstructed.

But for now, I have a small, temporary window of opportunity to glimpse inside the Williamses' very private world. It feels like I was always meant to witness their altercation, to see the real people behind the masks they wear.

Instead of walking to the high, wrought-iron front gates with the buzzer, I keep going until I reach the side entrance that I know Neil and the labourers use. It's also the entrance for any deliveries. Because of this, Neil has said that the gate often looks closed but is left open even on weekends, so if I ever need him and can't get him on the phone – signal can be notoriously bad at the top of the hill – I should try that entrance first.

As I approach, I'm convinced the gate looks locked but I push it firmly and it clicks open. I close it behind me and begin to walk through the grounds and up to the house. I admire the smooth emerald sheet of grass and the colourful borders that frame it as it sweeps up towards Seaspray House.

I spot a couple of labourers weeding at the far side. Neil told me that Ted often gets the students to work a good chunk of their hours over the weekend when they haven't got lectures.

Close up, the house is bright, white and enormous. There's so much glass and very little wall in some places. I'm walking close to the side of the building, so I can't see the impressive pillared porch that looks down the drive to the enormous gates.

The sun is already hot today; I can feel it reflecting back at me two-fold off the white stucco walls. I wonder if Albie is having a good time wading through the rockpools. I glance inside the house as I pass the first big window. It affords a side view into an enormous airy inner hall. I slow down so I can take more in. There are glass stairs at the centre of the room and the floor space is vast like a hotel. I continue walking and then see something that stops me in my tracks. I stand behind a short run of wall from where I've got a good view of Neeta. She's sitting on the floor, her back to me, rocking back and forth gently as if she's upset and trying to comfort herself.

What should I do? I can hardly bang on the window and appear from nowhere.

I start walking again and head around to the front door. There is a long narrow piece of glass either side of the extra-wide front door. I can see that Neeta is holding toys of some description. A couple of soft toys in her hands and more scattered in front of her. Before I can overthink it, I ring the doorbell.

I stand in front of the door so when she looks up, I'm not staring at her through the glass. After a few moments, the door slowly opens a few inches and she peers out.

The groomed, elegant Neeta I'm accustomed to seeing has been replaced by a woman who looks like someone else altogether. Her hair is unkempt, sticking up in uneven tufts;

mascara is smudged under her eyes. She's wearing baggy cropped linen trousers and a creased T-shirt.

'Lottie?' Her voice emerges high and strained. She was not expecting me at all and I wonder why she even opened the door. 'What is it?'

'I'm sorry, Neeta, I didn't mean to disturb you. I just wanted to return your tin.' I hold it up. 'It was so kind of you to send the cookies and—'

'How did you get in?' Her eyes are staring, glazed almost. She hasn't blinked for a while.

'I... the side gate was open. I thought I'd walk up through the gardens and... sorry. I didn't mean to give you a scare.'

For a few awkward seconds we stand looking at each other in silence.

She glances behind her and pushes the door closed another inch. 'I can't let you inside,' she whispers.

'That's fine, Neeta. Don't worry, I just... please, take your tin.' I push it towards her. She's acting very odd and I don't want to add to her obvious distress. She doesn't say anything, doesn't move. I have no choice but to broach the subject. 'Neeta, are you OK? Can I just come inside for a few minutes? I'll just stand here in the hall.' There's no response. 'I can see you're upset and if I can do anything to help, I—'

'You can't come inside!' she says shortly and I take a step back.

'Why can't I come inside?' There it is. The question that's been bugging me for weeks. 'Are you OK? Is there a problem in the house that—'

'Nobody can help me. I don't need any help. I...'

Her voice trails off to nothing and a haunted look settles on her face. She's scaring me now. She looks suddenly older, her face folding into creases I've never noticed before. This is a woman who is very obviously suffering... but how? 'Neeta, please. Just let me in and we can have a chat—'

She stumbles back a little and inadvertently releases the door. The weight of it forces the hinge to open wider. I glance behind her, at the pile of toys on the floor. There's a little pink trike in there and photographs scattered from an open album, but I'm too far away to see any detailed images.

Neeta's hand reaches out, grasping the tin. Then the door closes to again. She's gathering herself a little. The agony has gone from her eyes and the creases have softened.

'I'm sorry, Lottie,' she says quietly and calmly. 'But I can't let you in. Not today. I'm feeling unwell, you see.'

'Of course. That's fine.' My arms drop to my sides. 'Is there anything I can get for you? I could go to the chemist if you need—'

'Thank you, I'm fine. I just need some space, some time to rest.' She looks down at the tin. 'If that's all...'

My eyes slip past her to the toys on the floor again. She told me they couldn't have kids but those toys look well worn. Used.

'Just call me if you need me,' I say. 'Sometimes all it takes to feel better is to offload to someone.'

'Thank you,' she says and, as I turn to leave, she raises her hand. I see a line of dark little bruises on the underside of her forearm.

My breath catches in my throat. 'Neeta, your arm... what did you—'

'Please, Lottie, go home. I'm fine and I trapped my arm in the door. I know you mean well but you need to leave.'

'Look, if you decide you want to chat, you can call or text me any time and I'll—'

But before I can finish the sentence, she closes the door in my face with a soft *thunk*.

TWENTY-EIGHT

When they return from the beach about an hour or so later, I make Neil a cup of tea while I listen to an amusing and well-crafted tale from Albie about the monster crabs and foot-long eels he's apparently spotted in the rockpools. I make him a slice of toast and when he's happily settled watching TV, I return to Neil in the kitchen.

As succinctly as I can, I relay what has occurred up at the house.

'It wasn't just that she seemed unstable. It was the bruises on her arm... they looked like finger marks. Like someone has had a hold of her. It fits with the altercation on their balcony.'

Neil shakes his head. 'If you're trying to say Ted's responsible for that then you really are way off the mark. Did you ask Neeta about her arm?'

I nod. 'She said she'd trapped her arm in the door, which is rubbish. I know finger-mark bruises when I see them.'

Neil looks away and takes a sip of his tea. 'All I know is that Ted is one of the most decent men I've ever met.'

I shake my head in disbelief. 'Just because you get on well with him doesn't mean he's not a monster behind closed doors.'

'A *monster*? Listen to yourself! I see Neeta and Ted every single day so please, give me some credit. I'd soon pick up if they had an abusive relationship.'

Neil's questionable grasp on domestic abuse, and what it might look like, is worrying. But I'm not going to try changing his mind about that right now.

'Neeta looked terrible and those soft toys were just weird. Why would you have a load of used soft toys if you've got no kids?'

'I don't know... a hundred reasons!' Neil runs a hand through his hair in frustration before letting his arm drop. 'Maybe she's collected them for a local charity sale. Maybe she just likes them! Who knows? It's her own business.'

He's getting more agitated and I force myself to keep calm in the face of it. 'You can get as annoyed as you like, Neil. But you didn't see her... she looked, I don't know, like she was on the edge of something, you know?'

'No, I don't know! You and your crazy assumptions.'

'That's not fair!' I'm instantly riled. I feel my face start to burn and I jab a finger at him. 'There's something not right up at Seaspray and I've decided that Albie isn't going up there any more.'

'Is that right?' He clenches his jaw, his eyes suddenly wild. 'Well, you need to remember he's my son too!'

'I don't care what you say. Something's off-kilter in that house and as caring parents, we can't send our son up there pretending everything is fine.'

'Don't be ridiculous, Lottie. You can't stop Albie going up there just because Neeta didn't want to open the door to you,' Neil rages, slamming down his mug of tea so hard it spills onto the table.

'It's more than that. The bruises on her arm looked like finger-marks and—'

'You need to stop this! What about all the times in the past you've been anxious and hidden away when you can't face the world? If you'd opened the door to a neighbour, you'd probably have looked pretty rough too, and we both know you sure as hell wouldn't have let them in! Neeta must have had her reasons and in any case, it's not a crime.'

I'm incredulous.

'Why are you defending her like this? You hardly know either of them!'

'Well, I see a lot more of them than you do and I like to think I'm a fairly good judge of character. I reckon I'd be able to tell if they were hiding something.'

I stare at him, biting down on my tongue. I've hidden one detail of my childhood from him for years but he's never guessed *that*.

I turn my back on him and stare out at the blue sky. There's a bit of wind about this morning and far below us, the sea looks choppy and restless.

When I turn back to Neil, I say, 'If that's your opinion then fine. But I'm stopping Neeta's school runs and childcare. Albie's not going up there every day any more.'

'Ahh OK... and what about your job? How are you going to carry on if you've nobody to help out?'

'I'll make other arrangements if I can; people do, you know. But I'll quit the job, if necessary. I'll get something else.' I know my answer will infuriate him but I don't care. 'My priority is my son. Nothing else matters.'

Neil looks at me coldly. 'What you've said is pure speculation, every bit of it. And speculation can be a dangerous thing.' He shakes his head and the expression on his face turns to something else... sadness, confusion maybe. 'You know, I think you should get some help again, Lottie. Find yourself a counsellor.'

'Oh really? Just me? If anyone needs a shrink, it's probably Neeta Williams.'

He ignores my comment. 'All I know is if you continue with this... this crazy obsession... you're going to destroy everything good that's happening in our lives. And I can't allow that to happen.'

I give him a cool look. 'I see. And what are you planning to do about it?'

Neil turns away from me without answering. He grabs his phone and then he walks out the door without looking back.

TWENTY-NINE

Some issues in life were so difficult to face, Yasmin told herself. There was no handbook, no easy or right way to tackle them. On occasion – and certainly in a situation like this – you just had to take a breath, be brave and get on with it.

She had finally succeeded in getting Claire to open up and tell her the shocking truth about what was wrong and so, now, the moment had arrived when she had no option but to speak to Kay Price. The way some people lived their lives... it was as though they had no idea at all how to avoid certain disaster. It was everyone's decision how to conduct themselves, of course, but now Kay's life had bled into her own and Yasmin could not, *would* not, allow things to continue the way they were. She'd known Kay for years. When the girls were small, they'd bump into each other at the primary school. She'd lived her life in a decent manner in those days; Yasmin had even thought she'd make a good friend. Kay's life had changed beyond recognition now, but despite her fall from grace there was still a glimmer of hope because it was in Yasmin's power to save Kay from herself. And that's exactly what she intended to do.

Yasmin drove through the rabbit warren of streets on the infamous Bellingham Estate, comfortable in her new Mercedes, insulating her from the dreary but unseasonably humid weather with its cream leather interior and heated seats. She turned her head this way and that, her fingers tapping to the radio playing discreetly in the background. Most of the ex-council houses on the fringes of the estate had been privately purchased and were kept neat and presentable, but as Yasmin drove deeper into the bowels of the deprived residential area, the feel of the place changed. Some gardens resembled skips with unwanted furniture dumped underneath boarded-up windows. She turned in to Kay's road and parked at the bottom end.

Number forty-two was a pebble-dashed semi that shared an overgrown patch of front lawn with the adjoining property. One of the upstairs windows was broken and the front door was wooden and cracked. Yasmin got out of the car and shuddered as a booming heavy bass beat emanated from the house next door. What must it be like, trying to raise your child in a place like this?

It was fair to say Charlie was generally an unlikeable girl, but Yasmin felt a twinge of guilt when she recalled how the girl had once begged to come inside to play with Claire when she'd walked up to the house from school. Despite her pleading that day, Yasmin hadn't realised the extent of the poverty and lack involved in her life. Now, after her disturbing chat with Claire, Yasmin realised the child's resentment and rebellious behaviour was understandable.

Now she was here, all Yasmin really wanted was to get back inside the comfortable interior of her car and drive away, but that had never been her way. When people needed help, something in her changed gear. She'd been that way at boarding school, stepping in to defend more vulnerable kids from the meanest girls. She always instinctively knew how to make other people's lives better, even when they hadn't yet realised they needed rescuing themselves. And Kay Price was a prime example.

Yasmin brushed down her jacket, hoisted her Radley handbag over her shoulder and marched up the short front path. There was no bell, so she hammered on the door loudly in an attempt to compete with the pounding bass from next door's open windows.

After a few moments of holding her breath to avoid inhaling the strong smell of cannabis threading its way under her nostrils, she heard a click from inside the house. The door opened and Kay peered out from the gloomy hallway, her eyes wide and cautious.

'Oh... Mrs Fuller, it's you!' She opened the door a little wider and seemed to be about to invite her inside but then appeared to think better of it. She glanced past Yasmin to the road. 'Is... everything alright?'

'I wondered if I might come inside for a chat, Kay? I need to speak to you about some concerns I have that are better discussed privately.'

The other woman hesitated and for an awful moment, Yasmin thought she was going to refuse her access. Then she sighed and opened the door.

'I'll apologise now for the state of the house; I wasn't expecting any visitors today.' She wrinkled her nose. 'Come in quick, Mrs Fuller, you'll get high as a kite standing out there.'

Yasmin stepped into the small, dank hallway away from the stench of weed, but immediately started coughing. She held a hand up to her face and looked around for the source of the irritation.

'Sorry, it'll be the damp.' Kay indicated a sinister-looking trellis of black mould rising up from the skirting boards. 'We've got it in all the rooms. Nothing you can do about it when it gets a hold.'

Aghast at her casual acceptance, Yasmin said, 'I think you should speak to your landlord, Kay. Breathing this in is extremely hazardous to your health.'

'Yeah, I know. I tell Charlie to sleep with her bedroom window open but it's hard in the colder months when the house is already freezing. There's no heating upstairs, see. Our landlord's not the most compassionate person and any complaints I make, he has one stock answer for me: *Feel free to find somewhere else if you're not happy.* Easier said than done when you're on housing benefit and you struggle to meet the rent as it is,' she says, her voice redolent with a hopeless inevitability.

Yasmin immediately recognised this was a woman who believed there was nothing she could do to change her bad fortune.

Kay led her into a small living room off the hallway that smelled equally as bad. There was no carpet in here but mismatched rugs had been scattered over the floorboards. A two-bar electric fire sat incongruously against a flat wall, facing a two-seater sofa that sagged badly in the middle. Cheap ornaments and multicoloured blankets had been used in an attempt to inject some cosiness and character into the dreary, damp space.

Yasmin noticed Kay's quick snatching movement as she reached for an empty bottle of vodka from beside the shabby armchair before sliding it behind a cushion. 'Please, sit down, Mrs Fuller. Can I get you a tea or a coffee? I'm sure I must still have a drop of milk in the fridge.'

Yasmin declined the drink and Kay looked relieved. 'There's an awkward conversation I need to have with you, Kay, and I'm afraid there's no easy way to say what I've come here to talk about.'

'Don't worry on my account.' Kay waved Yasmin's concern away. 'Takes a lot to shock me these days.'

Yasmin nodded before speaking bluntly. 'I'm afraid Charlie has been bullying Claire.'

'She's what?' Kay looked alarmed. 'Are you sure about this? My Charlie thinks the world of Claire.'

'That's as may be, but there's no doubt about it. Charlie has been taking the money I give Claire to spend at the tuckshop at breaktime. She's also pulled her hair several times, pushed her over and thrown her school reading book in a rubbish skip outside the school gates.' Yasmin pressed her lips together.

'And Claire's told you this herself?'

'Yes. I'd noticed she'd been a bit withdrawn over the last couple of weeks. I sat her down last night and we had a good chat. She got very upset and told me what's been happening.'

Kay's cheeks flamed. 'I can't apologise enough, Mrs Fuller. When Charlie gets home, I assure you I'll punish her for this. I'll send her to her room and then I'll—'

'There's something else, too,' Yasmin continued, her expression grave. 'Can I ask, Kay, do you have a boyfriend called Duncan?'

'Duncan?' She laughed nervously. 'I wouldn't say he's my boyfriend exactly. He's a friend. Just a good friend, that's all.'

'And he comes to the house when you're not home?'

Kay frowned. 'Sometimes, yes. He'll sit and watch TV until I get home. I have a little cleaning job, you see. Three nights a week. It helps me out because Duncan will watch Charlie while I'm working.' A frown appeared. 'Why do you ask?'

'Claire told me she'd threatened to tell the teacher if Charlie didn't stop bullying her. Claire told her she didn't want to be friends with her any more and that's when Charlie broke down crying.'

'My Charlie broke down?' Kay said, bemused. 'That girl's as hard as nails, so I find it difficult to believe.'

'She confessed something very troubling to Claire. To quote her exact words, "Mum's boyfriend, Duncan, gets drunk when she's at work. Sometimes he tries to kiss me and when I push him away, he hurts me."'

'Oh no, no. Duncan wouldn't do that,' Kay said faintly.

'Charlie showed Claire some of her bruises,' Yasmin continued. 'On the top of her arms where he's grabbed her and also around her neck. It's probably fairly easy for you to check.'

Kay's face drained of colour. 'She's insisted on wearing a polo-neck jumper every day even in this muggy weather we're having. I thought it was strange, but I never...' Her eyes glistened. 'He... he's been violent with me once or twice when he's had a drink, but I never thought he'd hurt Charlie. I mean, I'd never have left her alone with him if I'd thought that, Mrs Fuller. You've got to believe me.'

'I do believe you, Kay. But this situation can't be allowed to continue, you must realise that.'

'I know. I've tried to finish things with him a few times but... he just comes around anyway, banging on the door all hours of the night until I let him in.' Kay's moist eyes shone as she looked around the room. 'When I was Charlie's age, I wanted to be a teacher, can you believe that? I imagined myself living in a neat little house, married to a caring chap and having a couple of kids and a dog. And I always wanted a caravan so we could go to the seaside.' She laughed bitterly. 'Instead, I'm barely existing in this dump, raising my daughter in a place where the police won't come out for robberies, never mind to a drunken man hammering on the door.'

Yasmin felt a deep stirring within her. Some people might shun Kay in view of the hash she'd made of life for herself and Charlie. Now, even poor Claire had been affected by Kay's disastrous life choices. But Yasmin took a different view. It was in her power to help this wretched woman and her daughter, just as she had forfeited further education at the age of sixteen to become a full-time carer for her own terminally ill mother.

Yasmin opened her handbag and took out a clean, folded tissue. She handed it to Kay, who tearfully thanked her and took it with a shaking hand.

Yasmin cleared her throat. 'I know it must seem like all is lost, Kay, but really, it's far from that. I wish you'd have confided in me earlier, well before it got to this stage.'

'I'm sorry, Mrs Fuller, I never thought of speaking to you... I mean, I know you have such a busy life and I wouldn't dream of intruding but—'

Yasmin reached out to pat Kay's cold hand. 'You mustn't worry about that now. We are where we are, and this is what we're going to do about it.'

THIRTY

LOTTIE

SUNDAY

There's an undeniable gulf opening up between my husband and I. Important decisions like Albie's wellbeing that we just cannot agree on are forcing us apart.

I had to agree to Albie going up to Seaspray with Neil because they're finally going to finish the tree-house today. I feel terrible when I realise, after all the hard work he's put in, Albie isn't going to be able to use it.

I'm going to be the worst parent in the world for weeks on end when I tell him, but that's OK. One day when he's older, he'll understand why I did what I did to protect him.

I hear Albie laughing and see they're back from Seaspray. But they don't come inside. Instead, Neil grabs Albie's football and they start kicking it about in the garden.

I walk upstairs and go into the spare room.

I take a sip of water before picking up my phone and opening the camera app before putting it back down on the small table next to me.

It's 5.18 p.m.

Pushing my arms behind my back, I link my fingers and stretch.

5.19 p.m.

I pick up the phone, unlock the screen again and point the camera at the house, pinching open the screen to maximise the zoom.

Neeta walks into the sun room on the ground floor. She is followed by Ted. They leave the door open and both turn to look behind them.

I wait, glancing at the clock on the wall.

At 5.25 p.m. exactly, a small shadowy figure appears – from where, I'm unable to discern. It's so hard to see, to make out any details, just a series of shapes and shadows that are hard to pin down.

Ted sits on the sofa facing the big window and Neeta joins him. They both look over the shadowy side of the room I can't see properly, and they begin speaking to someone.

For me, it's the final proof that I've been right all along. The Williamses are living a lie and I know now exactly what that might be.

I think this couple, who have told everyone they live alone, are hiding something. *Someone.*

I think about what I've seen so far. The Williamses arguing on their balcony, the shattered glass that made Ted jump up out of his seat and pursue Neeta into the house like he might throttle her amid a haze of red mist. Then seeing the worrying bruising on Neeta's forearm and, finally, the third person I'm now convinced is in their house. The pieces to this jigsaw are beginning to slide into place, but there are still some key parts to pin down.

I need to escape from the cottage for a while. I decide to take an easy walk down to the beach, using the time to fill my lungs with the salty sea air in an effort to clear my mind.

I walk along the shoreline and back again. I listen to the rush of the water, taste the salt from the sea air on my tongue.

As I look up towards the top of the hill, I see a figure saunter into view. The person stands there, looking down. Watching me approach. I don't yet need to wear glasses, but I have noticed distance is a bit more blurred than it used to be. I can't quite make out the detail or whether it's a man or a woman. But there's nobody else around they could be watching, so I guess it's me they're waiting for.

The sun is weaker and broken up by cloud now but walking up the steep hill doesn't seem to be getting any easier. I unzip my fleece, relishing the cooler air around my neck. I keep my eyes on the uneven terrain in front of me, avoiding clumps of reedy grasses and the knots of old roots.

Who lives inside Seaspray House that never comes outside? Why is Neeta paranoid about anyone going inside?

I wish I could talk this over with Neil, but I'm 99.9 per cent sure he'd be furious at me for even mentioning it. And after our argument this morning, I'm best to not get him any more agitated. There's one thing I can't allow to continue that's going to cause uproar anyway. Albie can't continue to go up to Seaspray until I'm reassured there is no danger to him there.

I look up the hillside again and see the figure is still standing there. I keep my eyes pinned on them and when I get close to the top, I can see much better. I laugh and wave. 'Keris, hi!'

'I heard they used to use donkeys to move up and down this hill in the old days,' she teases cheekily. 'Reckon you could do with one today.'

I force a laugh. 'I'm just taking it easy. The tortoise wins the race, remember?' When I reach the top, I tug at the neck of my T-shirt, panting for effect. 'Isn't Edie with you?'

'She's with Albie. We walked up to the cottage and Albie

insisted on taking her to Seaspray to see his finished tree-house. Neil said it was OK and took them up.'

My throat tightens. I need to stop the kids going up there, whatever it takes. The problem is, how do I tell Keris to keep Edie away without telling her I've been spying on the Williamses from my spare room? I like Keris, but I haven't known her very long. If somebody I'd met a few weeks ago told me the same thing, I'd probably think they were a bit odd.

We walk down the short path and I unlock the cottage door. 'Can you stay for a coffee?'

'Thought you'd never ask.' She grins and sits down on the chair closest to the door.

I fill the kettle, flick the switch, stand and stare thoughtfully out of the window for a short time before I realise she's watching me.

'You're distracted,' she says. 'Like you've got something on your mind?'

I'm about to deny there's anything wrong and start babbling on about what I'm planning to bake for the school's summer fayre when I change my mind. 'You're right. Something is bothering me. But... the question is, can I trust you to keep it to yourself?'

She pincers her fingertips together and performs a zipping action across her mouth. 'Scout's honour, I won't say a word. Who would I tell, anyway? I haven't got much in common with most people in the bay.'

'Even so, they'd all be very interested in what I'm about to say.'

She sits forward on her chair. 'Go on then. You've got my full attention now.'

We take the coffees through to the living room. I set the tray down and Keris takes a mug and I tell her I witnessed Ted and Neeta arguing on their balcony. Lines of disappointment etch the corners of her mouth and she interrupts me before I've finished speaking.

'I suppose most married couples bicker from time to time.'

'It was a bit more than a bicker. Neeta threw a glass right at him.'

Her mouth drops open. 'She what?'

'She threw it right at him and he jumped up and chased her into the house.'

'Good God! Hardly the behaviour you'd expect from the golden couple.' She frowns as something occurs to her. 'When you say he chased her, he didn't hit her or anything, did he?'

'Not that I saw but he looked angry, as you'd expect, I suppose. But... there's more. It sounds crazy, but I think there's someone else in the house.'

'Huh?' She frowns, in a lack of understanding.

'I've seen someone in there. I can't see well enough to get a good look at them, but it's another person and they're definitely not a visitor. Neeta won't let any of us near the house; we've never even been inside! Now I think I know why.'

'My God.' I'm surprised at the strength of Keris's physical reaction. Her face pales and she looks at me with wild eyes. 'Don't take this the wrong way, but how did you see all this? It's a private estate, right? They're not overlooked.'

'Unless you're looking out of the window of our spare room,' I say quietly.

'No way! Can I see?'

I look towards the door nervously. 'I don't want Neil to find us snooping,' I say. 'He'll go mad. He never believes me when I express concerns about Ted and Neeta.'

'I'm sure they'll be a while yet, exploring the tree-house. Come on... we'll be quick!'

Upstairs in the spare room, I open the blind slats and hand Keris the binoculars. She fiddles with the focus wheel and then gasps. 'Who knew you had such a brilliant vantage point up here! I can totally see how you watched their argument on the balcony now.' She peers through the binoculars, looking this way and that before turning to me. 'I wonder if Mary and Tom Gooding used to peek out from this window, too?'

'I guess they couldn't fail to know about it,' I say, thinking about the part-written letter I'd found when we first moved in. Mary Gooding had definitely got her suspicions like me that all was not as it seemed up at Seaspray, but we still didn't know much about the manner in which they left the cottage. Still, I decide against going into too much detail with Keris.

I think I've said enough for now.

THIRTY-ONE

Yet again, I haven't slept well. I've been thinking about the argument I witnessed on the Seaspray balcony.

It's fully possible – highly likely, in fact – that they may have fallen out over Neeta and Neil cosying up at the restaurant. I hope so because nobody wants to see a replay of *that*. When you distil what actually happened between the two of them, it's embarrassing: wealthy older woman fawning over the hired help.

I choose to believe Neil when he said there was nothing in their playful exchange but I'm not sure that was the case for Neeta Williams. If she is unhappy in her marriage, then maybe she's hoping more might come of it.

Still, last night when Neil and the kids returned from Seaspray and Keris and Edie left, Neil and I agreed we'll leave the childcare arrangements as they are for another week before we review them. Despite me feeling so resolved earlier in the day, he's just got this way of making me feel like I'm being overly dramatic and unreasonable.

Yesterday, I arranged with Keris we'd take the kids down to the beach after school. After Albie waxing lyrical about his surfing lesson at 4 p.m., Keris has ended up booking Edie a couple, too. I know finances are a struggle for her right now, but like most parents, she'll willingly go without herself rather than expect Edie to.

It's 3.50 p.m. when we get down to the beach. The sky is cloudless and the sun feels strong on our skin. I'd insisted on slathering Albie in high-protection sun cream before we left the cottage.

'Mum, we'll have our wetsuits on soon. We don't need cream on,' he'd complained as I slopped cream on his arms and face.

'We've still got to walk down to the beach and, like the instructor said, there's a lot of stuff to go through before you even go near the water, so you'll be standing for a while in the sun.'

After we've signed them in, they're allocated surf boards. Most of the other parents leave them to it but we watch as they begin learning how to balance on them standing on the sand before they even get to put a toe into the water.

'Let's grab a coffee,' I suggest to Keris after we've stood watching them for a while. 'We know they're safe here.'

We tell one of the instructors where we'll be if they need us and then walk down to the coffee shack by the beck.

The sun is beating down from a pure blue sky, but there's a light breeze that feels refreshing on my face as we walk. It's a perfect day and yet my heart feels heavy.

'Are you sure you're OK, Lottie?' A perceptive Keris shoots me a sideways glance after a couple of minutes of us walking in silence. 'I've been thinking about what you told me yesterday and I know you're really worried.'

'I'm fine,' I say quickly. 'It's just wondering what the best thing is to do, I guess. I mean, as Neil is always telling me, it's not a crime to have someone living in your house that nobody else knows about. It's just creepy as hell.' I sigh. 'Sorry, this is supposed to be a fun afternoon, I know.'

'Hey, no need to apologise. I totally get how you feel, especially with Albie going up there regularly.'

When we reach the beck, I tell Keris to grab a table and I join the queue to get our lattes. The coffee shack is right on the beach. There are lots of tables and chairs outside on the decking that surrounds it, but no seating inside. The glass doors on two sides retract all the way back so the place is completely open to the elements. Keris told me that she's often called down here on a drizzly day to find a note pinned on the door to say it's closed for the day. 'That's how they roll around here.' She laughs. 'Their opening times are shaped by the weather.'

On the plus side, when it is open, it's well worth a visit because the views of the beach and sea are incredible. As I queue, I can hear the ebb and flow of the water even above the buzz of people chattering around me. Down on the sand, kids clutch buckets and spades and squeal with delight as they dodge the water.

On one level, Whitsend Bay is everything I hoped it would be and more. But after the events of the last few days, it feels like I'm carrying a storm cloud around with me, hovering constantly above my head. One I have no shelter or protection from.

I can feel the yawning gap growing daily between my husband and me. He doesn't seem to realise that the Williamses are sucking him and our son into their web. Doesn't seem to believe anything I try and tell him about them.

'Hi, can I help you?'

I jump to attention as the man behind the counter addresses me and order two regular lattes and two flapjacks.

I carry the tray over to Keris, whose fingertips are currently blurring across her phone screen. 'Sorry,' she says, finishing off and putting it face down onto the table. 'I couldn't resist using the five minutes to catch up on my emails.'

'You're allowed a break, you know.' I put the tray on the table.

'You don't know my boss. She doesn't know what a finishing time is.' She looks at the tray. 'Ooh flapjack, nice!' She nibbles off a corner and we sit looking back up the beach.

From here, I can see the kids in their yellow and black wetsuits, still standing on the sand exactly where we left them. Their neon-green boards shine on the sand beneath their feet.

Directly in front of us, the sea glistens in sapphire-blue patches, darker by the cliffs and a lighter, bluey grey as it rolls back and forth on the sands. I take a sip of coffee and stare at the water.

Keris puts down her polystyrene cup. 'So, what are you going to do about what you know?'

'The first thing I'm going to do is finish working,' I say. 'Put an end to Albie going up to Seaspray most days. It's not going to go down well, particularly as Albie loves it up there.'

Keris nods. 'Edie says his tree-house is so cool. But I can see your reasoning. Have you told Neil yet?'

'I've told him and it didn't go down well. For now, we're meeting in the middle and we've agreed to reassess in a week. But that's just to buy me some time.'

Her phone buzzes and she turns it over to look at a notification before placing it down again. 'I just want you to know I'm here to get stuff off your chest, if you need to. For what it's worth, I think my reaction would be exactly the same as yours.'

'Thanks, Keris, I appreciate it.'

It's not easy to talk about anything remotely personal for me because I have a problem trusting people since my mother left. During my time in therapy, the counsellor had established this fact on my first session.

'Building effective communication with other people is like

travelling through a series of layers. Each one gets closer to the complexities of who you really are,' the counsellor had explained to me. 'The deeper you go, the more vulnerable you are. But there's the catch. You have to trust and go deep to get the most from your relationships.'

It had made perfect sense to me at the time. I'd longed for a good friend to talk to for so long, but the thought of exposing my soft belly also made my blood run cold. Mum had left so suddenly and she'd never contacted me even once, to check if I was OK. I moved into the care system where I remained for three years, leaving my school and hometown behind. I developed a metaphoric coat of armour. I kept everyone at that first shallow layer and it worked. Nobody ever disappointed or hurt me because I didn't let them close enough. It kept me safe; at least that's how it felt at the time.

After that, I believed I'd never find that trust in a person again. Particularly not in female friends. It was like that until I met Neil at the age of nineteen.

'I know it's hard to open up sometimes,' Keris says now matter-of-factly and tracing the foamy lip of her cup with a finger. 'I'm exactly the same. When you're a single parent living in a new place, you quickly learn to keep it all inside. Keep all your problems to yourself.'

I look at this woman, her open expression, her wispy, purple-tipped hair and I feel a rush of affection. I might not have known her very long, but she's supportive and a good listener.

'I know you've been through a lot,' she says. 'But you can offload your worries on me any time you like and I'm not going anywhere. I'm happy to wait until you trust me.'

THIRTY-TWO

'I do trust you,' I say. 'But the last thing I want is to burden you with all this stuff.'

'Not a problem. I've got as long as you like,' Keris says and then checks her watch. 'Well, until the surf lesson finishes, anyway.'

I grin. 'This is going to sound crazy – in fact Neil has decided I'm crazy – but I feel like my husband and son are slipping away from me. Or being taken away.'

She frowns. 'How so?'

'Neeta and Ted. They're...' I press my fingertips to my forehead. 'They've been kind, can't do enough for us on one level, but... gosh, I don't know how to say it. Everyone around here thinks so well of them.'

'Just say it, Lottie. I'm not going to judge you.'

I know that's true. Keris takes people as she finds them. She's open and accepting.

'They seem to be one thing, but I'm not sure if that's an act.' I think for a moment how best to explain what I mean. 'They appear to be this perfect couple: everything rosy in their life and they want to share their good fortune. But underneath, I don't think they're like that at all. I think they have a hidden agenda.'

I still don't think I've articulated it very well, but Keris is nodding.

'I think a lot of people are a bit like that,' she says. 'But what do you think their hidden agenda is?'

'I don't know. That's probably not even the right term to use. I just know they seem to want something from us – from Neil and Albie anyway – something more than Neil just being their employee. And as you know, they agreed for Albie to go back there after school.'

Keris nods. 'You saw that as a godsend when Neeta offered, right?'

'Yes, I did. But not any more.'

'What's changed your mind?'

'Albie never wants to come back to the cottage when I get home. I mean, what kid would? He's got a tree-house, they're fitting out a games room and he's treated like a little prince. I get this feeling Neeta loves it, too and it's probably because... well, this is where I betray confidences. But she told me that her and Ted, they couldn't have children. She said it was for the best and they'd accepted it, but I didn't get that impression, not really. She looked sad when she talked about it.'

'You think she's pushing it with Albie because she'd have a kid?'

'Sort of, I suppose. But there's other stuff... oh, I don't know. It sounds crazy when I say it out loud but I found the beginnings of a letter that I think Mary Gooding wrote. It was clear from the few lines she'd written that she thought there were sinister goings-on in the house. There's that shadowy figure I told you about and Neeta acting odd, looking at kids' clothes and stuff.' I glance at my watch. The surfing lesson finishes in twenty minutes.

'Don't worry, we've plenty of time,' Keris says.

'There's other worrying stuff that's happened.' I tell her about the meal at Luigi's and her mouth drops open.

'No! She was feeling him up in front of you... and Albie was there, too?'

'Well, that's just it. Neil said she wasn't doing anything of the sort and it's all in my head, but... he did admit she was flirty with him. And Ted never batted an eyelid!'

'Jeez, they're not swingers, are they?'

I let out a little laugh but the more I think about that idea, the less funny it seems. 'I wouldn't think so, but... well, you never know, do you?'

'What else?'

'Well, there's the fact that both my husband and son spend hours up there but, to date, have never been in the house. Neeta has also gone to great lengths to keep me out.'

Keris's eyes widen. 'Yes! I can't believe you've not been in there, yet!'

'Yesterday, I took her a biscuit tin back. Neil had told me about the side entrance being open mostly and I walked up through the grounds, so I didn't need to ring the gate bell and I surprised her. I saw her through the window; she was clearly upset and surrounded by all these soft toys.'

'What? My God, how creepy!'

'I thought it was, seeing as she hasn't got any kids or grandkids, but Neil said she could've just collected them for a charity sale or something. Anyway, she came to the door and she looked awful. Not ill, but... stressed out and wretched, if you know what I mean. I asked her if I could come in and she said no, outright. She said she couldn't let me inside. Neil's telling me I'm being unreasonable, but you seem to react in the same way as me. I just don't know what to think.'

We sit in silence for a few moments and then Keris leans forward, glancing around to make sure nobody is close enough to hear what she's about to say. 'Want my opinion?'

'Course,' I say. 'That's why I've told you, to see what you make of it all. As an impartial bystander.'

'If I were you,' she says slowly, her eyes burning into mine, 'I'd get your family away from that couple as soon as you possibly can.'

THIRTY-THREE

NEIL

When he'd returned from a perfectly nice time at the beach with Albie yesterday, he'd walked into Armageddon. Lottie has ramped up a notch in her paranoid surveillance of Neeta and Ted.

The first thing he did was to try and talk Lottie into keeping on with the childcare arrangements at least for the foreseeable.

'Let's face it. Whatever is happening between Neeta and Ted, it could just be a drink-fuelled one-off,' he'd said reasonably when she'd calmed down. 'Albie is so happy up at Seaspray and you said you enjoyed your new job. It just seems impulsive to disrupt absolutely everything on the strength of one altercation.'

'I don't want him seeing any of that stuff, Neil,' she'd said. 'It's not healthy.'

'That's just it... nobody has ever seen them behave that way.' He'd sighed. 'I mean, you wouldn't have seen it if you hadn't been...' He'd searched for a phrase that sounded better than *spying on them*. 'If you hadn't been watching them.'

'That doesn't make what happened right,' she'd snapped.

'None of our business, though,' Neil had said firmly. 'You

checked on Neeta, offered her help and she was fine and Ted was his normal self. Tempers obviously got frayed and a glass got broken in the process.'

'I can't believe the spin you're putting on this,' Lottie had replied. 'This narrative of "it was just a disagreement".'

'Likewise, I can't believe you're making such a far-fetched drama out of what you saw for a few seconds!'

'So how do you explain Neeta's bruises?'

He'd raised both hands and pressed them to his temples. 'I don't explain them because it's none of my business, Lottie. She insisted she'd trapped her arm, so who are we to delve deeper than that? We're not her keepers.'

Round and round in circles they'd gone, neither of them really knowing if they were right. 'Look, how about we agree to disagree, just for this week. We'll keep an eye out, see how it goes. At the end of the week, we'll chat again and see how we feel?'

Clearly as tired of the arguing as he was, she had miraculously agreed.

But it's getting harder and harder to keep discounting the stuff Lottie is telling him. Yes, she's always had a hyperactive imagination and because of her mum leaving when she was a kid, she has a tendency to quickly get jealous and insecure.

The thing is, Neil knows the Williamses are a strange couple. He'd never stoke the fire by confiding in Lottie, but they've got a strange relationship, too. They'd put on an act for him when he first arrived, but they now barely speak to each other and will happily walk past each other without so much as an acknowledgement.

They never have any visitors and, to Neil as an outsider looking in, the house seems like a sterile palace, not like someone's home. It concerns him that despite the promises they're making to Albie about him seeing a movie with Ted in the cinema room and baking cookies with Neeta, he's never allowed inside. Ted and Neeta certainly don't seem to have any content-ment there. Ted often goes out at the end of the day or stays in the garden until late and what Neeta does all day and evening is anybody's guess.

Neil can't discuss his concerns with Lottie because she'll raise the roof and blow everything out of the water and, as a result, a sinking feeling is growing inside him. This isn't go to end well, he can feel it. But what can he do? At the end of the day, he's just as bad as the Williamses.

He loves Lottie and his son and he continues to betray them both in the worst way possible.

When he gets up to the estate, he walks directly to his garden office, raising his hand by way of a greeting to a couple of the part-time gardeners who are dotted around, working on the flower beds.

He's just sat down at his desk when Ted appears at the door.

'Morning, Neil! Before you start, Neeta wants to see you up at the house.'

'Oh!' He stands up, trying to cover his surprise. 'Fine, OK. I'll pop up now, then.'

'Good man. Door will be open, so just knock and go straight in.'

Neil stops moving and stares at him.

'What's wrong?' Ted says.

'Are you sure to go straight in, Ted? It's just that... well, I've never been inside the house before.'

'Well then, it's your lucky day, isn't it?' He grins and winks before disappearing off down the path, whistling.

Cautiously, Neil starts walking up to the house. He feels nervous because if he does as Ted says and just walks in, Neeta may well take offence. No. He decides it's better to knock and wait. That's the safest way.

He needn't worry; when he gets up to the house, Neeta is already waiting at the door.

'Neil! Thanks for coming!' She's dressed down in a pair of wide-legged linen trousers and a matching vest top. She has tan leather sliders on her feet and less make-up than he's seen her wearing. No red lipstick today, just natural nude lips. She opens the door wider. 'Come inside. Welcome to Seaspray.'

He walks into the cavernous hallway and just stands there looking around.

'It's even bigger than I'd imagined,' he murmurs, transfixed by the staircase. He wonders if she's going to show him around but she beckons him through.

'Let's sit in the sun room for our chat.'

Chat? Chat about what?

It feels like a fist is slowly tightening in his stomach. Has Neeta seen Lottie watching them from the spare bedroom? If so, what can he say?

'Sit where you like.' She sweeps an arm around the sun room and he chooses a cream leather armchair. He looks at the bookcases, sparsely furnished, and then he sits and stares at the view. 'Can I get you a tea, coffee or perhaps something a little stronger?'

'No, no thanks,' Neil says. It's just after eight in the morning and she's plying him with drink!

Neeta moves closer. 'Are you sure?' she chides. 'You might just need one when I'm finished speaking.'

He looks at her. His lips feel tight and dry, as if they might split. 'Really? Why's that?'

She sits in the chair next to him, fans out her hands and inspects her bright pink manicure. When she looks back up, she smiles at him.

'Ted and I, we're going to need your help with something.

Something very important that has to stay just between us, for now.'

'OK,' he says, drawing out the word. His heart is racing now. What is it she wants him to do? 'What is it?'

'Ha, not so fast,' she says, giving him a wide smile. 'Let's play a little game to prove we can trust each other. First I want you to tell me something, Neil. I want you to tell me the truth about what you've been hiding from your wife.'

At the end of the working day, he opens the cottage door and steps into the kitchen. He feels shellshocked. His knees are shaking and he doesn't know how he got through his shift.

Lottie spins around from the kitchen sink and her mouth falls open. She leans forward and squints at him. 'Are you OK? You look... are you ill?'

'I'm OK,' he says faintly. 'I think I might be coming down with something, so I'm going to have a lie-down.'

'Before you do, I want to speak to you about something,' Lottie says. 'Something really important.'

He can hardly stand up, but he nods and says, 'Go on.'

THIRTY-FOUR

LOTTIE

'I don't know quite how to say this, so I'm just going to come out with it: I'm certain there's someone else in that house... someone who is concealed most of the time. And... I know you won't like this... but if we can prove the person is there against their will, I think we should consider confronting Neeta and Ted.'

Neil grips my upper arms a little too tightly and presses his face close to mine. His eyes look wild and red-rimmed.

'Lottie, listen to me. You have to stop this. You're going to get us all in trouble if you continue with these crazy accusations against them.'

'They're not accusations,' I say, shrugging free of his grip and stepping back. 'They're facts. There's something strange happening inside Seaspray and we need to find out what it is. Our son spends loads of time up there; he could be at risk.'

Neil throws back his head and laughs. It disturbs me slightly... he seems a bit manic. 'That's the most ludicrous thing I've ever heard! Why? Ask yourself, why on earth would Ted and Neeta be concealing someone in their house? I would've seen someone coming and going. You're risking everything with your ridiculous theories.'

'That's just it... I don't mean a visitor. I mean someone who is living there who never comes outside. Like a prisoner or something.'

His face... I've never seen darkness descend on him like this. His eyes look almost black, his mouth pinched and hard. He moves forward, towering over me. 'Don't you dare,' he says from behind bared teeth. 'Don't you dare do anything crazy or I'll...'

'You'll what?' I square up to him but inside I'm quaking. 'Don't *you* dare threaten me.'

'I'm not going to let you ruin our lives, Lottie. Things are hard enough right now.'

'Hard enough? You're always saying what a fantastic life we have here! I'm not going to let you whitewash the truth. If the Williamses are up to something, people need to know the truth about this so-called perfect couple and we need to keep Albie away from them.'

'What you're saying, it's slander! You've got no proof whatsoever for your groundless accusations.'

'Well, I don't need your permission and I won't be intimidated.'

His voice drops lower and he stares at me with those dark eyes. 'You don't know what you're getting into here. Back off. Do you hear me?'

I still feel shaky, but I don't let it show. 'What do you mean by that? What *am* I getting myself into? I'll do what I think is right for me, for our son.'

'You can't just take him away out of the blue. Ted has spent a fortune renovating the tree-house for him.' He releases his hands, shakes them out. 'Look, let's be reasonable. Let's just calm down. We can cut down on Albie being up there, OK? Let's do it gradually and not get too silly about this.'

. . .

It's 2.32 a.m. I'd felt so exhausted when I got into bed last night, I honestly thought I might sleep through.

But I've been dreaming again. Mashed-up images of the past, my mum's face drifting into focus and then quickly fading out again. I'm a mess.

I feel really thirsty and I have a fuzzy head that's being further aggravated by worrying about keeping Albie safe if there's an unknown person living at Seaspray House. Worries grow ten times bigger between midnight and 5 a.m. and this one is no exception. I know I won't go back to sleep if I just lie here letting it terrorise me.

Neil is sleeping heavily and snoring lightly. I'd usually elbow him gently so he'd turn over and fall quiet, but there's no point doing that as I know from experience I won't sleep now anyway. I need to get up and do something else until my head empties of the troubling memories and present worry.

I slip out of bed and, after visiting the bathroom, I grab my robe and head downstairs. I fill the kettle and stand at the kitchen window, dazzled by the scene before me. The sky is clear and the moon shines like someone hung a polished silver coin in the sky. Down the darkness of the hillside, I can see the shimmering silver tips of the waves as the ocean moves back and forth under the lunar pull.

Mum always loved day trips to the seaside. I try my best to keep happy memories at the forefront of my mind but it's hard to erase that look she gave me the last time I saw her. The day she left for good and never said a word.

The kettle boils and disrupts my unfocused stare out of the window. I make a cup of tea and, as I turn to put the dirty teaspoon in the sink, I catch a movement at what I think is the bottom of our garden. I turn off the light and stand back a little, waiting.

There it is again. The moonlight highlighting a shape darting amongst the conifers that act as a boundary between the cottage and Seaspray House. Then clouds drift across the moon and it's suddenly too dark to see anything.

I put my mug down on the kitchen counter and tiptoe lightly back upstairs, heading for the box room. I slip inside and close the door softly behind me. I climb onto the single bed and inch right up close to the window, lifting a single slat of the blind to see out. The moon is out again, and I have a pretty good view of our garden and the land underneath the Williamses' bedroom balcony from here.

I sit there, perfectly still. Waiting. But there's no further movement that I can see and I begin to wonder if I'd imagined it... or if I'd seen a nocturnal animal.

But it was too tall for a fox. Far too large and quick for a badger.

Deep down inside I know what it was I've seen. It's a person.

Someone has been watching me.

THIRTY-FIVE

After confessing the living hell her supposed boyfriend, Duncan, was putting her through, Kay Price sat quietly and obediently listened to Yasmin Fuller's plan to sort her life out.

Kay felt calmed by the surety and confidence of Yasmin's calm manner. A better life sounded so easy, a simple case of following three easy steps that Yasmin outlined.

'First, you pack up a few essentials now and come with me. Secondly, we pick Charlie up from school later with Claire. Thirdly, I put you both in a small bed and breakfast establishment out of town for a few days. We have a small flat near us for rent you can have once it's ready. The tenants vacated last week and Graham is redecorating.'

Kay's eyes widened. 'It sounds a wonderful plan, Mrs Fuller, and I wish with all my heart it could come true. But Duncan will never allow it, you see. He'll track me down, find me and start his pestering all over again.'

'I can assure you that if you agree to my solution, Duncan will never be a problem for you again.'

'But how? I mean...'

'It's very important we keep things simple, Kay,' Yasmin said firmly. I only need one of two answers from you. Do you want to escape this life and make a fresh start? Yes, or no?'

'Yes! Yes, of course I do. But I can't live too far from here because of my cleaning job and—'

'I'd like to employ you as a childminder for Claire. She doesn't need a full-time nanny at her age and I don't need the expense that option incurs, but I do need someone I can trust to look after her after school regularly for a couple of hours. There'll be some household duties like cleaning and I'd also need you to provide childcare for her in the school holidays, make sure she's getting enough fresh air.'

'Oh yes, I could do that no problem, Mrs Fuller!' Her face brightened. 'I think I could do that job very well.'

'There is one thing, Kay: I would need you to take care of Claire in our home and give her quality attention.'

Kay nodded. 'Course.'

'What I mean is... how can I put this... Claire is a sensitive girl and she needs time to get over the trauma of Charlie's treatment of her.'

'I understand and I can't apologise enough for what happened, Mrs Fuller.'

'So you're happy for the time being at least to care for Claire without having Charlie around? I think that's what she needs to refocus and get her confidence back, you see.'

'No problem,' Kay said easily. 'Charlie's thirteen next month. She's old enough to look after herself.'

'That's settled then.' Yasmin stood up and dusted down her jacket before glancing at her watch. 'Let's get your things together and get you out of this godforsaken place. If necessary, my husband can come back with you and pick up the rest of your things.'

. . .

Everything went to plan and just two weeks later, Kay and Charlie moved into a neat little flat just a ten-minute walk from the Fullers' house. The walls were clean and white, not a spot of mould to be seen. It had central heating, a sparkling white kitchen and, best of all, a view of the park with its trees and green lawns.

'Anything you need, any problems, just drop me a text,' Yasmin had said several times. As usual, she waved away Kay's effusive thanks. But this kind, caring couple had transformed Kay and Charlie's lives.

Kay wondered if she'd ever felt as happy in her entire life and Charlie adored her bedroom so much, she barely came out of it! Then one day, about 2 a.m., the entrance door buzzer started blasting through the silent flat. There was no intercom camera but once she'd roused herself from a deep sleep, Kay rushed to the door to answer it, fearing something was wrong. She snatched up the handset.

'Hello?'

'Let me in, you sly cow! Did you really think you could get away from me this easily?'

Kay slammed down the phone, terrified. How had Duncan found her so soon? His slurring and yelling reminded her of the vicious personality change that took place when he was drunk. The amiable man who'd do anything he could to help disappeared without trace as he neared the bottom of the whisky bottle. Kay had downplayed his violent nature to Yasmin the day she came to the house, but Yasmin's revelation had shocked her. She had never suspected for a moment he'd also been terrorising Charlie.

'Mum? What's happening?' Kay turned to see Charlie barefooted and standing in her nightie, rubbing her eyes. She'd had to sleep in her clothes at the old house because of the cold. They both had. Kay refused to go back to that and she steeled herself. She would not allow Duncan to drag her back to the swamp again.

Loud, incessant hammering started on the entrance door downstairs. She peered through the security peephole to see several neighbours down the corridor with their doors open and craning their necks nervously in their dressing gowns. If anyone was foolish enough to open the exterior door for him, Duncan sounded in an angry enough state that he'd probably try to break down the flat door.

Behind them, a sharp crack on the living-room window sent Charlie running in there. Kay heard her scream. She rushed through to see Charlie jumping back from the curtains.

'It's Duncan, Mum. He's lobbing stones up at the glass!'

Kay knew then there was only one thing to do. She picked up the phone and called the number she'd been given. Yasmin picked up on the third ring and Kay told her what was happening in one long babble.

Thirty minutes later, Graham arrived with the police and Duncan was carted off to the station. A day later he was charged with affray and criminal damage to private property.

A month later he was sentenced to a year in prison and while he was serving his sentence, someone beat him up so badly, doctors told him he'd walk with a permanent limp.

All this, Kay learned from Yasmin. 'You mustn't worry. He won't be bothering you again.'

Kay never asked how Yasmin had found out so much information but she got the impression the Fullers had ways and means of always getting everything they wanted some way, somehow.

They were certainly not the sort of people you'd ever want to cross.

THIRTY-SIX

LOTTIE

TUESDAY

Today is an eight o'clock start at work for me, so Albie goes up to Seaspray with Neil. It's a real wrench to let him go.

I feel sick with worry when I think about what I saw last night. I couldn't sleep a wink when I went back to bed and when Neil woke up, I was ready and waiting.

'I went downstairs for a drink in the early hours and I saw someone skulking around outside,' I say, my chest tight as a drum. 'I know you'll say I imagined it but I didn't, Neil. I know what I saw and it was real.'

To my surprise, he doesn't automatically discount my claim. 'That's odd. I'll speak to Ted this morning, see what he makes of it.'

That pacifies me for now but I'm still so troubled about whether I should resign from work. Sure, we can do with the extra money, but I worry about the influence of the Williamses on Albie. Neil seems to be their number one fan and, although he's listened to my fears this morning, generally he thinks I'm blowing all this stuff up in my head. I just don't know what to do for the best.

The day flies by and just before I finish, Mel stops by my desk to say how delighted she is with the progress I've made since starting the job. 'You've cleared all the ordering and invoicing backlog and, for the first time in months, I feel like I can breathe again.'

I feel a twinge of regret I'll probably be leaving the job soon. It feels so good to be recognised as being competent at something other than caring for my husband or being a mum. I love being a parent and I wouldn't have changed my time at home caring for Neil, but it's so refreshing to use some of my office skills and experience and air another side of who I am. But I can't see the situation resolving itself.

I'm still concerned about events at the weekend and especially seeing what I believe was a figure at the window. I'll feel so much better when Albie stops going up to Seaspray. It's so exhausting to constantly watch for problems in others and then, if I spot any, spend time trying to convince Neil I'm not imagining it.

Later, I've got the radio on, the sun is out and I'm in the kitchen making a family favourite for tea, when the back door opens and Albie breezes in, his face fresh and smiling.

'Hi, Mum,' he calls out. 'What's for tea?'

'Macaroni cheese. How did school go today? How was footie practice?'

'Good. Everyone thinks I'm really good at tackling.'

I look over at him, my heart sinking when I see him beaming. He's got a light tan and looks so healthy compared to the pale-faced boy who arrived after a chest infection. I hate that I have to disappoint him, but it's for his own good. His safety. Then I notice something else.

I stop stirring the cheese sauce. 'Whose top is that?' I squint against the light to get a better look. The smart zip jacket has a navy body and lighter blue arms. That's when I see he's wearing matching trackie bottoms, too.

'Cool, isn't it, Mum?' he says excitedly, running a flat hand down his sleeve. 'It's a CR7 tracksuit... Ronaldo's very own brand! Neeta bought it for me and gave them to me this morning. And look at this...' He walks around the table and lifts his leg up, wiggling his foot. 'New Air Jordan trainers to match!'

I'm speechless. When he comes closer, I reach out and touch the fabric of his top. The material feels soft and flexible. Expensive. The gold-embroidered logo is large and designed to be seen.

'Where are your other clothes I gave you to change into after school?' I say faintly, taking the pan off the heat. 'The gear I bought you from JLG Sports?'

'It's in that bag by the door,' he says dismissively, slipping one of the trainers off and studying it. 'Nobody else in my class has got these trainers. I've never had any this good in my whole life.'

He takes the other one off and places them both reverently on the floor. 'Ted said I look just like Ronaldo!'

While Albie is still cooing over his new footwear, I pick up my phone and google the clothing range. Seventy-five pounds for a kid's CR7 tracksuit... and I can hardly process the next cost... nearly *two hundred quid* for the trainers.

'Albie, I'm sorry but you can't keep these things. Neeta should never have bought them for you without asking me and your dad first.'

'What? They're mine now, so I can keep them and besides...' He snatches up the trainers and holds them close to his chest. 'Dad thinks they're great. He says he wouldn't mind some.'

'We need to talk about this, Albie. We'll need to—'

'You always ruin everything!' He stands up, his face puce and eyes shining. 'I didn't even want to come back for tea because it's boring down here!' He storms out of the room. I hear him stomping upstairs and then he slams his bedroom door so hard I swear the cottage shudders on its old foundations. I freeze in shock for a moment. This isn't Albie. He doesn't behave like this.

What kind of message is it, buying a kid of nine expensive things like that for no particular reason? Maybe if they were a Christmas present or even a birthday gift I could begin to justify it, but out of the blue? It just feels wrong.

The money will mean nothing to Neeta and Ted, of course, but I don't want Albie getting an appetite for designer sports gear. There's no way we can stretch to that kind of expense on a regular basis and, at the rate he's growing, he'll only be in it for a matter of months.

I'm sure Neeta will have bought him the stuff out of kindness. She's got no kids of her own to spoil and money is no object. To her, no doubt, the outfit wouldn't even have seemed that expensive and she wasn't to know I've just forked out for a new sportswear wardrobe for him. But what on earth was Neil thinking of, approving of it? He knows only too well we can't sustain this kind of expense for Albie.

Neil gets back thirty minutes later. 'Good day, Lottie?'

I empty the cooked macaroni out of the pan and into an oval dish.

'It was a good day until I heard what Neeta's done. With your full approval, apparently.'

'Christ, what's wrong now?' he snaps, wheeling around to glare at me. 'Just lately, you're griping on about something new every time I walk in the door.'

'Sorry? I'm not!'

'Well, it seems that way when you're on the receiving end.' He sits down to take off his boots. 'Go on then, fire away. What's up now?'

I grate some cheese onto a plate. 'Neeta's bought Albie some ridiculously expensive sportswear. But you already know that.'

'The Ronaldo stuff? Yes, I've seen it. I thought it was lovely of her.'

'I've just bought him a load of stuff from JLG or had you forgotten about that?'

'No, I haven't forgotten,' he says slowly and in a very patronising manner. 'His new stuff hasn't changed that. He's still got the stuff you bought him and he can wear both.'

'But he's not going to want to wear both, is he? Not when he's got this new fancy stuff!' I unroll some foil and rip it off noisily. 'Do you know how much that gear costs? The trainers alone were nearly two hundred quid.'

'Yes, that's because they're Air Jordans.' He walks over to wash his hands at the sink.

'Neil, we can't afford for Albie to get an appetite for designer clothes.'

'Here we go again. The lad's quite rightly excited to be treated and, true to form, you're taking it to the nth degree to find a disagreeable ending.'

Neil sounds really fed up and a wash of dread travels down my spine. He spends the day with people with money who make him feel good about himself and then comes home to grumpy old me. Is he getting tired of our life together?

It's always the same. The old fear of being abandoned, of being left alone.

THIRTY-SEVEN

SATURDAY

When Neil announces he's taking Albie into Whitby so they can climb the famous 199 steps to the abbey, I decide, on the spur of the moment, to do something different, something daring and, for me, challenging. I'm going to drive to Pocklington, the market town where I grew up. Where I lived until Mum left.

I dress practically in jeans, trainers and a white cotton T-shirt before filling the car up and setting off for the ninety-minute drive inland. Pocklington sits at the foot of the Yorkshire Wolds. When Mum left and I was forced into the care system, I left my hometown and never returned.

I never felt a pull to come back – quite the opposite, in fact. I ran from returning. But the dreams... so many dreams of being in the house again, being young and confused, the fear and abandonment translating to cockroaches and woodlice climbing up my legs in nightmares and waking up panting, drenched in sweat.

'Have you ever considered returning to the area?' my therapist had asked once when I'd described what felt like a haunting of the past I could never escape from. 'As an adult now, you're empowered to face your fears. You're no longer a young girl at the mercy of other people's decisions. This could be a gift you give yourself, instead of keeping on running.'

But I'd never seriously considered it. Not really. There is nothing there for me any more. It had just been me and Mum back then, no other family. The only real friend I had was long gone, too. And yet, since we've lived at Whitsend Bay, it feels like the past is calling to me. I'm dreaming about the place most nights. The house. My bedroom. Waking up with that cold, damp fear again and not knowing why.

It's not a bad journey. A couple of snaggles in various places, no long delays. Plenty of time to change my mind, though, and I nearly do. But something pushes me forward, urging me on.

I'm not interested in the centre of town: the marketplace where we'd sit and eat chips, or the handful of arcades that line one side of the square.

It's the house I want to see.

I don't know why. I've spent my time trying to push the memories of it away. And yet now, something is pulling, tugging at me to take notice. Like a frayed rope lying on a riverbank that you suddenly realise is attached to an invisible weight that lies underneath the deep, dark water.

I drive into the immediate area and right away, I can see how much the place has changed. The corner shop Mum would send me to for a pint of milk or loaf of white bread has been extended and refurbished into a Tesco Local. New-build houses line the stretch of waste ground I used to roam around after school, sometimes watching the boys play footie for something to do until they all went home for their tea. Then I'd try and find a corner out of the wind or sit in the bus shelter, if it was raining, until Mum finally got home from work.

My hands tighten on the steering wheel as I turn right and then follow the road through a steep left bend before entering the street of my childhood. I wait for the rush of nostalgia when I see the small, scruffy house where Mum and I lived.

But the rush doesn't come. Somehow, I must have managed to turn up the wrong street.

I drive up to the top and then back down the next road. I recognise some of the houses here, people we used to know, although they've all got new windows and new front doors. At the bottom, I pull over and check the street sign. Just as I thought, this is Montague Street, so that means the one next to it is Pullman Street, where I used to live. I *did* take the right turn after all.

I set off again, my insides feeling tight and uncomfortable. There's no car behind me, so I turn in to Pullman Street and crawl past the row of new-build town houses where our house used to stand. A hard nut of disappointment pushes down in the pit of my stomach. I wanted... needed... to feel something today. Anger gnaws at my throat. I feel cheated of the chance of putting something to rest.

I pull over and get out of the car. I walk towards the top of the street. From here, I can see a brand-spanking-new medical centre standing where our primary school used to be. I never had many friends there, although there was one girl who was always nice to me. I've forgotten about her just like everything else. Now, as I stand here, grey clouds scudding above and threatening rain, I feel a sense of loss as the thought occurs to me: I'll never know the kind of person she might've grown into. That thought makes me incredibly sad.

A single tear rolls down my cheek and I wipe it away with the back of my hand. It's only now I'm here I realise what it was I'd hoped to find here today. Something like an anchor, or a sense of belonging. Even though this is an unhappy place that's linked to an unhappy time, it's all I've got from the early days.

It's where I started out and I left in the hope of building a better life, a completely new me.

The astonishing thing is that up until this moment, I honestly thought I'd succeeded.

I turn left and walk to a new, small area of grass where there are a couple of wooden benches. This used to be part of the scrubland and, as far as I can tell, is one of the last areas that hasn't been covered in smooth, new concrete.

I sit down and stare at the grass, thinking about all the hours I've spent here. I always seemed to be cold and alone but I just accepted it as the way my life was, in that way children do. Trying to get through each never-ending day. When Mum was still around, I never thought about the future, or what life might be like if I could get away.

A scuffling noise at the side of the bench snaps me back into the moment. An older woman clutching shopping bags hovers hesitantly.

'Is it... are you...' She peers closer, her eyes disappearing into slits.

I stare at her a moment, trying to place her familiar face and then it clicks. She's our old neighbour from the street behind ours.

'Mrs Cornell! How are you?' My heart is pounding. It was unrealistic perhaps, but I never banked on seeing anyone while I was here.

Her face lights up. 'I'm fine, lovey, how are you? I come to sit here every day if it's fine, you know, to think about the past and I saw you and... well, you're all grown up! I'd recognise that lovely curly hair anywhere, though, and that pretty face of yours.'

I laugh and look down at my hands. 'I came to see the old house but they've built new homes there,' I say.

'New houses everywhere you look.' Mrs Cornell frowns. 'All new people here now, mostly. Hardly anyone I used to know.' She looks at me, her pale eyes soft. 'Your mum, did she ever…'

'No,' I say quickly. 'She never got in touch again.'

'I'm so, so sorry. Terribly hard on a young girl.' She glances around before leaning forward and speaking quietly. 'For the record, I never believed what they were all saying about her.'

'I try not to think about all that now,' I say. The last thing I want to do is get into a full-blown reminisce of what had happened back then. I'd hoped to lay ghosts to rest, not rake up more bad memories.

'Course. But it's funny, you turning up out of the blue after all these years because there was someone here last week asking questions about that very time.'

I stare at her, my heart rate picking up to a sickening thud. 'Asking questions?'

'A woman. She was knocking on doors on our street, asking if anyone knew your mum. She had her old address and everything.'

My chest tightens. 'Really? Did this woman leave a name?'

'Not with me. She claimed she was working on the history of the area, but she didn't seem interested in anything else but your mum.'

The vulnerability begins to stir.

Then Mrs Cornell brightens and fishes in her jacket pocket. 'I just remembered, I took a picture of her when she came to the door!'

I sit up straighter. 'Oh that's brilliant, well done! What made you do that?'

'We've had some con people coming round here pretending they're from British Gas. One old fella a few doors down asked them in and had his pension stolen and he'd only just picked it up from the post office. Pays to be careful these days, doesn't it? Bear with me a minute, I'm not great with this phone. I know how to use the camera but finding the actual photographs is another matter altogether.' I wait patiently as she scrolls through the icons, tapping the phone screen. Then she's flicking through dozens of thumbnail shots before triumphantly holding up the phone. 'Here she is!'

She angles the screen towards me to show me the photograph. Taken covertly, it's a little grainy as you might expect, but she has captured a front view of the person's face and so I recognise who it is immediately.

I stare at the image, a wave of confusion washing over me. I blink, try and make sense of the implication of what I'm looking at.

'Do you recognise her?' Mrs Cornell watches my face, hungry for a reaction. But I still can't speak because I'm grappling with the knowledge that the person who's been asking questions is my new friend, a person I thought I could trust.

The person in the photograph is Keris Travers.

THIRTY-EIGHT

I can't tear my eyes away from the picture on Mrs Cornell's phone until she clears her throat and tries to lower it. Then I realise she thinks I'm acting weirdly.

'Is everything alright, lovey? Do you recognise this person? She didn't mention you.'

'No, no, it's just that she was asking questions about what happened back then; it makes me feel strange. Can you tell me exactly what happened that day, and exactly what she said?'

'Well. I was just sitting there in my living room, looking out of the window. I spend hours there, see, in the armchair. It used to be my Joe's favourite place to sit and I find a little comfort in that when I'm feeling a bit low. I like to just watch people passing by, especially at school times with the children. It's very quiet on our street now. All my friends like your mum have moved on... in one way or another.'

I nod and feel a twinge of guilt. I never thought about other people suffering because Mum took off. It wasn't just me she left.

'Anyway, I saw a young woman – the one in the photo. She was still over the road at that point, knocking on doors. When someone answered, she'd speak briefly to them and in each case, I watched them shake their head and close the door. And then she'd move to the next house. She seemed very determined.'

'Did you call her over, ask her what she was doing?'

'No. She didn't look dodgy and, truthfully, I thought she might be selling something. She had no products or anything, but you don't need actual goods these days, do you? Everything's ordered on one of those iPad things,' she says, looking baffled. 'Anyway, when she got to the last house, she crossed the street. From my upstairs bedroom window, I can see all the other houses on my side of the road and I spotted her coming up towards my place. That's when I remembered the British Gas crooks. When she knocked, I opened the door right away and she said, "Hello, I'm looking for someone I used to know who lived on the next street."'

'So she knew all the details?' I murmur.

'That's right, she gave me your mum's name and her address. So anyways, I said, "Oh yes, I knew her well. She was my friend and it was an awful shock when all the trouble happened." She perked up at that, having tried all those other doors with no luck. She started asking me all sorts there on the doorstep. I'm no pushover and I said, "I'm not saying another thing until you tell me why you're asking all these questions."' Mrs Cornell folds her arms smugly. 'People think you're daft, you know, once you get past sixty-five. I was only saying to the postman the other day that—'

'Sorry to interrupt, Mrs Cornell,' I say quickly. 'It's just... what other things did she ask you?'

'Oh, what *didn't* she ask! She wanted to know everything, you know, about what happened with your mum.' I take a breath and wait. 'I said, "I'm not going to discuss serious matters like that on the doorstep," and that's when she asked if she could come inside for a chat.'

'You let her in?'

'I did. Perhaps I shouldn't have, but...' Mrs Cornell looks sheepish. 'Well, she looked like a nice young woman despite her having purple hair. I like to think I'm a good judge of character and she seemed honest enough, if you see what I mean.'

Honest! Keris Travers had targeted me since Albie's first morning at school when we met her and Edie on the hillside. Supposedly by chance, but now I know that can't be the case.

'I made her a cup of tea and I'd made some little coconut buns because it was a Friday and I often bake on a Friday morning and she had a couple of those too... said they were delicious! I remember thinking it was unusual for a young woman these days; they're usually trying to starve themselves to fit into the latest fashion, aren't they?'

I smother a sigh. It is hard work keeping Mrs Cornell on task. 'Did she tell you why she wanted to know all this stuff?'

'She did. I said, "Are you a police officer?" Although I didn't really think she could be because I don't think police officers are allowed knock on doors asking questions without their uniform on. But there again, a few weeks ago I watched a programme about undercover detectives and some of those look like the drug dealers they're trying to catch, with their long hair and shifty appearance. So I suppose you never know.'

'She denied being a police officer?'

'Yes. She said, "I'm not police, I'm a..." – now let me get this right.' She thinks for a moment, before continuing. 'That's it. She said, "I'm a private investigator."'

Despite trying to keep a neutral reaction until Mrs Cornell has spilled everything she knows, I fail to stop my mouth from falling open. Rather than dissuade her, it seems to give her new energy.

'Yes, that's exactly what she said: "I'm a... private investigator,"' Mrs Cornell clarifies, looking pleased with herself. 'And I said, "Well, I hope you're not out to rake up old gossip and cause trouble because we had enough of that at the time it happened," and she said, "Oh no, not at all. Someone has hired me to try and find out what really happened, and what better place than to start here."'

'Did she say who had hired her?' I say faintly. This sounds like a smokescreen to me. Is Keris really a private investigator, meaning her job as a freelance PA is a lie? Could she actually be a journalist, interested in my mum for her own gains to rake up the story again?

'She didn't, I'm so sorry. But she did say there were still so many unanswered questions and she called it a cold case. So she's starting at the beginning and looking into it all herself.' Mrs Cornell regards me curiously. 'I mean, I suppose it's good news, isn't it? That she might find out what happened and people will know all that stuff that was said at the time was nonsense.'

I stare ahead of me at the green space in the small park. A couple of pigeons are fighting over a scrap of something that's too small for me to identify.

The more time that passes, the more I realise how hard I've tried to run away from what happened here. But the horror was too big; I was never going to escape it forever.

Mrs Cornell can't figure out why I'm so unhappy. She doesn't know that Keris Travers has been pretending to be my friend, obviously all the time trying to get insider information.

'Tell you what, why don't you come back to mine and I'll make us a nice cup of tea and a slice of malt loaf. How does that sound?'

I watch the light in her eyes dim when I tell her I must get back. 'I'm so sorry, Mrs Cornell. I promise I'll visit you again soon and we can chat about the old days. I can dig out a few old photos and bring them with me. How's that?'

'That would be lovely,' she says half-heartedly. She probably thinks I'm just saying it to get away.

'Tell you what, give me your phone number.' I key it into

my phone and then send her a text. 'There, you have my number now, too,' I say, when it beeps. 'We'll get together soon, I promise.'

I say goodbye to Mrs Cornell and walk back to the car. When I start the engine, the fury is burning strong in my chest. I put my home postcode into the satnav, but I'm not going back to the cottage. Not yet.

First, I'm calling to see my so-called friend Keris Travers.

Find out what the hell she's doing and, more importantly, who she's working for.

THIRTY-NINE

After leaving Mrs Cornell's house, I start to feel shaky so I pull over in a layby next to some fields on the outskirts of Pockling-ton. A headache is building at the base of my skull, so I wind down the window a little and stare out across the crops just to take a minute before the long journey ahead.

I can remember cycling along this lane once with the only friend I had at school. It had been a cold day in late autumn, just before everything changed forever. The wind had whipped through our hair and I only had a thin coat on, so I'd been freezing cold. But we were laughing and screeching as torrential rain and then sleet had blasted our faces. We'd stopped at an old hollowed-out oak tree, which had afforded us some cover until the worst of the weather had passed.

When I'd got back home, Mum hadn't got annoyed about my wet clothes as I'd thought she might. Instead, she'd warmed up a tin of Heinz tomato soup and we'd shared it in front of the two-bar electric fire.

So many unhappy times and yet here's a good moment that's managed to survive that time. What if Albie only remem-bers the bad stuff? Me trying to confiscate his new sportswear, me stopping him visiting Seaspray House and me forcing him to give up his new tree-house. It occurs to me that maybe, just maybe, I've been unfair to Mum. How hard must it have been for her, struggling to raise me and work two jobs just to try and make ends meet? Nobody's childhood is all pastel pink, is it? Parenting spans the full spectrum of colours despite our best efforts.

I watch the wheat swaying gently. It shines like pure gold in the sun, catching the light as it sways in the warm breeze. In August it will be harvested – torn and chopped from the ground – until the whole cycle begins again.

Why would Keris go all the way to Pocklington, knocking on doors and asking questions about my mum? It doesn't make any sense. Right now, I don't buy her claim that someone is paying her to do so. I mean, *who*?

The muscles and tendons at the top of my shoulders feel taut and sore. I grimace and dip my chin, massaging the base of my neck but it doesn't help. When I start the car, the satnav informs me it's a seventy-five-minute drive. That's plenty of time to think about what I'm going to say, what I'm going to do with the information I've just discovered.

What I really want to do is go home, close the curtains and lie down. Shut the world out.

But I'm not going home. I'm going to get the answers I need.

Keris lives in a rented flat in a bay-fronted, brick-built detached house that's been converted into two accommodations. Flat 11B is upstairs and I've only dropped Albie off here a couple of times. Once I had a coffee but mainly she comes to the cottage. The bay is much livelier our side of town, so she usually brings Edie over to us. There are very few amenities here on the edge of town on this modest housing estate, but maybe that's part of the 'strapped single mum' cover she uses.

I park the car and walk towards the tiny paved front garden. There are posts complete with hinges at the opening to the property, but no gate.

I know Edie usually goes to a Young Scientist club on Saturday afternoons between two and four, so I'm praying Keris is alone and we can talk freely.

I press the doorbell for her flat in the front porch. There's no intercom so I have to just wait. After about thirty seconds, I ring again. Finally, I hear footsteps approaching on a tiled surface. The front door opens and Keris's face lights up.

'Lottie! This is a nice surprise!' Then she takes in my expression. 'Is... everything OK?'

'Can I come in? I need to talk to you.'

'Course! Come through.' While she closes the door behind me, I have a proper look around the small, dim hallway. There are patterned terracotta tiles on the floor and a console table with a couple of items of unopened mail on it. There's just one other door and that's for the flat marked '11A'.

I follow her upstairs.

'Edie's at her science club until four, so we can have a coffee and a proper natter. It's gorgeous out today, isn't it? I hate being stuck in, it feels like such a waste of sunshine, but I had lots of work to catch up on. It's been a busy week.'

I bet it has.

She doesn't seem to notice I'm not responding to her inane chatter.

She unlocks her flat. Inside, the small entrance is painted white with tasteful pastel-coloured framed prints on the wall. There's a large photograph of Keris and Edie in a silver frame on a small table also bearing a wooden dish that she tosses her keys into.

I slip off my shoes and follow her into a bright, sunny lounge. It's one long room with a glossy white kitchenette one end, overlooking the back garden. There's a tiny bistro set with two chairs. The table top is scattered with pens and a colouring book still open. Edie must have been sitting there before going to her club. The other half of the room is given over to a cosier living space with Aztec-style rugs and raffia floor lamps.

The house itself looks bland from the outside, but Keris's flat is clean, neat and modern with its thoughtful decoration and light wood flooring. More framed photos of Edie are scattered across furniture and walls.

She indicates I should sit on the beige modular sofa and I perch in front of a flat-screen television that's fixed to the wall above a glass-fronted realistic-flame electric fire.

'I'll put the kettle on. Coffee OK?' Keris says brightly, ignoring my dark mood.

'Coffee's fine.'

She potters around, chattering about nothing, spooning coffee into two mugs and tidying away Edie's colouring book and pens. When the kettle has boiled, she makes the coffee, adds milk and brings the drinks over, placing them on coasters on a low coffee table before sitting at the other end of the sofa and looking at me.

'Are you feeling alright, Lottie? You seem awfully... quiet. Has something else happened between you and the Williamses?'

I feel sick, rather than quiet. I say, 'It's not the Williamses who are giving me a problem, it's someone else.'

'OK...' She draws out the word before picking up her drink and taking a sip. 'So, are you going to tell me what's wrong then?'

I look at her. 'Have you ever thought you were getting to know someone well, someone you considered a friend and even trusted with looking after your child? Then you find out they've been lying to you all along about what they do for a living and it feels like a sledgehammer slamming into your skull. Has that ever happened to you, Keris?'

She puts down her coffee and looks at the floor.

'How did you find out?' she says, her voice soft and low.

'I went for a drive today. Back to Pocklington... an area I spent time in as a child but then you probably know all about that. I bumped into a kind lady there I've known a long time and she told me about the woman who'd been knocking on doors and asking questions about someone who lived on the next street. What I want to know, Keris, or whatever your name might be, is why are you asking questions in my old neighbourhood? Why are you so interested in me?'

'It's not *you* I'm interested in, Lottie, and my name is Keris. I didn't know you had links to Pocklington and whatever you might think, I do consider us to be good friends and Edie adores Albie, as you know.' She ignores the derogatory noise I make in my throat. 'I'm interested in trying to trace a woman called Kay Price. Do you know her?'

I don't respond.

'Price was accused of abducting ten-year-old Claire Fuller eighteen years ago. She disappeared before police could arrest her and the case has never been solved. My clients have reason to believe the parents of Claire knew far more than they claimed at the time and in trying to locate Kay, I was hoping to piece together exactly what happened at the time from the people who were actually there.'

'Kay Price was never formally charged by police. The local community decided she was guilty by means of a kangaroo court and that's why she ran.'

'Possibly, but Claire has never been found so it's a bit of a coincidence.' Keris sighs. 'Look, Lottie, I want to come clean with you. I confess I did lie to you about my job as a PI, but most people run a mile if you identify yourself as such. Were you there throughout it all? Where did you live?'

'Who are your clients?' I say, my voice steely.

We stare at each other for a few long seconds and then she

says, 'Tom and Mary Gooding, the people who used to live in your cottage. I swear I had every intention of telling you the truth as soon as I'd figured out all the missing pieces.'

I'm confused. She's just been talking about the abduction of Claire Fuller and my mum and now she's switched to talking about Tom and Mary Gooding?

'So you have two jobs to investigate right now and I'm connected to both of them?'

'I was just about to tell you—'

'Why did the Goodings ask you for help? Did they live in Pocklington, too?'

'No... no, that's not it.' She presses her fingers to her forehead for a moment before looking at me. 'Look, this is going to come as a shock to you, Lottie. I didn't realise you had any connection to the area Claire Fuller was taken from or that you might know Kay Price. I—'

'Then what *is* the truth? What are these missing pieces you've talked about?'

'There's no easy way of getting this information out, so I'm just going to say it.' Keris falls quiet for a couple of long seconds. 'Neeta and Ted Williams aren't the people you think they are and they haven't always lived at Seaspray House. They used to be called Yasmin and Graham Fuller, they lived close to Pocklington and they're the parents of Claire who went missing.'

The room starts to spin, but Keris keeps speaking.

'The Goodings are convinced Ted and Neeta Williams staged the disappearance of their daughter and that Claire has been held captive for all these years.' Keris stares at me.

I can hardly breathe. The person I saw... surely that can't be...

'Over the years Tom and Mary saw things, tried to ignore them because they wanted to keep their jobs. Then something happened, an incident, just before they left the area. Mary Gooding had been suffering from increasing stress and anxiety.

One day she snapped and confronted Neeta. Asked her if there was someone living in the house. Mary went to the police, who dismissed her claims as groundless. Ted and Neeta invited them to take a look around and they found nothing. Apologised. It all blew up in Mary's face. Things got out of hand and that's when Ted dismissed them.'

'The child... Claire... where do the Goodings think she's been held captive all this time?' I whisper.

'You're not the only person that has reason to believe the impossible,' she says, pinning her eyes on mine. 'Mary Gooding is convinced she's in Seaspray House.'

FORTY

I stare at Keris. I can't speak.

Neeta's strange routines, the shadowy figure I've seen inside the house, the creepy sighting of someone skulking outside in the early hours of the morning. The aggressive argument on the balcony. Neil's dismissive reactions that made me feel I must be imagining it all. Seeing things. Being a drama queen.

Keris takes my silence as cold fury.

'Lottie, I'm so sorry. I should have told you before now and you have to believe me... I honestly had every intention of doing so. But when you said Neeta was adamant they had no kids and then you felt sure you'd seen someone in the house... I felt like I was getting closer to the answers I need. I've been playing for a little more time and didn't want to tell you and then you freak out and blow my cover.'

'You were in Pocklington asking about Kay Price,' I say hoarsely.

'Yes, but I had no idea you used to live there! I had no idea you'd know all about the case of Claire Fuller. It quickly dropped out of the papers, her parents left the area and now, people barely remember it at all.' Keris covers her face with her hands briefly before letting them drop. 'Did you know Kay Price? She was Claire Fuller's childminder. I've been following any lead I can and so I went to Pocklington to try and find her, but her house no longer exists. That's why I went knocking on doors, but there's hardly anyone left there who remembers that time. I suppose you know the Fullers accused Price of knowing about their daughter's disappearance, of having something to do with it. But police found no evidence to support their accusation. Then Price disappeared overnight and the Fullers, and many locals, believed Price had taken Claire abroad. Despite the involvement of Interpol, no trace was ever found of them. Despite all their efforts, the police finally agreed it looked like Price had managed to get Claire out of the country and somehow evade detection.'

I feel my breathing getting shallow. 'I know that Kay Price had a daughter herself,' I say carefully. 'Why would she leave her own child behind and disappear abroad?'

'Exactly. There are lots of details that don't make sense, I know. There are still internet sleuths out there who maintain that Price had a contact abroad who paid her a lot of money for Claire.' She hesitates before adding, 'For whatever reason someone might want to buy a child... I don't want to even think about.'

A rush of indignation travels through me. 'That theory is disgusting. It beggars belief.' Then I add sadly, 'Kay would never have done that.'

Keris looks at me with interest. 'I'm guessing you would have been a similar age to Claire Fuller at the time she went missing. Did you know Claire? Would you be prepared to speak to me about what you remember?'

I can feel something building inside me. All those years ago and yet... the pain is as sharp yesterday and ready to explode.

Keris frowns, her investigator's nose sniffing out an inconsistency. 'Lottie, did you or your family know Kay Price well?'

My throat tightens so severely I bring up a hand to rub it. Somehow I have to get this out, release the secret that I've tried so hard to bury since the day Mum left and I was taken into care. The secret I've not even found the strength to tell my husband.

'Claire Fuller was my best friend at school. I was known as Charlie in those days.' My voice cracks but I know I have to say the words. It's now or never. 'And Claire's childminder, Kay Price?' I take a breath. 'She's my mum.'

FORTY-ONE

Keris is either a world-class actress, or she is genuinely shocked at my revelation that I'm the daughter of Kay Price. My instant impression is it's the latter. She opens her mouth to respond several times but no words emerge.

'I was just thirteen when it happened and I find it difficult to recall the details,' I say. 'I guess that's because I've tried to block it out my whole life. Claire had gone missing and I recall people outside the flat shouting. Someone threw eggs at the door and then police came round to question us. Then a couple of days later, Mum had gone. She just disappeared.'

'Did your mum leave you a note?' Keris says, regaining her composure. 'Anything that gave a clue as to why she took off so suddenly?'

'She'd been really panicked by the growing animosity towards her, not sleeping at night and hiding away in her bedroom during the day. But the day she left, she was there in the morning and seemed a bit calmer. When I came home from school she'd gone. Two days later they took me into care.'

'Had she taken anything with her?'

I think for a moment. 'Not much. The police asked me the

same thing. She'd taken a few clothes and the boots she liked to wear. I noticed her handbag had gone, her phone and stuff. It was hard as a kid to know what to check on and I was so confused.'

'Natural that you would be,' Keris says gently. 'Before she left that day, did Kay tell you her version of what had happened, or what she thought might have happened to Claire?'

I sigh. 'I've thought about this a lot, but no. She just seemed... confused and upset all the time. She was scared of the police coming to the house again, but I think that was just because she felt like everyone seemed to believe she, the child-minder, was guilty of something. And I felt that, too.'

'And when you got older, did you ever try to find your mum?'

'No, but... I thought about it plenty of times.' I look at my hands. 'As time went on and I got older, I got angrier that Mum had just left me behind like that. I couldn't get it out of my head, that she'd dumped me like a piece of trash and taken off with Claire. I decided if she didn't want me then I didn't want her either. I didn't want anything to do with that horrible time. My full name is Charlotte, but I left Charlie behind and I started calling myself Lottie. I started to actively forget everything I could about Mum. I... I've never told Neil the full story about my past. I mean, he knows Mum left and that screwed me up a bit. I told him I burned all the photos I had of Mum, which I did. But I never told him what they said she'd done, or about Claire's disappearance.'

'What do you believe happened, Lottie?'

'Honestly? I don't know.'

A memory floods back of when I was about fifteen years old. Mum had been gone a couple of years by then and I was living in a care home miles away, waiting hopefully for a foster placement that never came. I know now I was too old, too troubled for couples to want to take me on. I heard two people talking on the bus one day. 'How does that work, though? You decide you don't care about your own kid any more and abduct someone else's child instead? And no ransom demand for the Fullers? Doesn't wash.'

'Maybe the kid had a nasty accident and the parents tried to cover it up 'cos they were to blame,' one guy suggested.

'Yeah, they're wealthy. They have a lot to lose if they get sent to prison for negligence,' the other added.

All the news channels were covering it and people were phoning into radio stations to give their opinion. Two sides were formed. Supporters of the parents who believed the child-minder had abducted Claire Fuller for reasons known only to her and fled the country, and their accusers who believed the parents were involved in some terrible way that they'd figured out how to cover up.

'Is it a possibility in your mind that Kay did take Claire abroad for some reason?'

'I guess so... at first. There were even a couple of spots of Mum and Claire in the first year. One couple claimed they saw them together at a market in France; another swore they'd spotted them on a Spanish beach. But ultimately, neither came to anything although I took it as evidence she'd left to start a new life with a better daughter.'

'Over the years, you must have considered what else might have happened,' Keris remarks.

'I did, but I couldn't remember that much about the circumstances. I'd blocked so much out. I just kept coming back to thinking Mum must have taken Claire. Nothing else fitted. Claire had gone, Mum had gone... it seemed obvious to everyone. But I wonder... in the end, did Mum do it for money? Did someone pay her to take Claire? It still doesn't make sense because she was always so grateful to Yasmin for getting us out of our really shitty life, I can't believe she'd ever do the dirty on them.'

Keris watches me steadily. 'I'm sorry to mess your head up even more about this, but consider this: what if Claire never went missing in the first place? What if her parents faked her abduction and used your mum as their scapegoat?'

'Why, though? What would they gain from that?' It just doesn't make sense. Try as I might, I can't reconcile Keris's claims with Ted and Neeta Williams. They are totally different people to what I remember of Claire's parents.

'Let's just say, for argument's sake, there had been an incident beforehand that nobody else knew about. Just say Claire was maimed by an accident caused by her parents' neglect. Maybe they left out some drugs or medicine with dire consequences... she could have overdosed. I'm plucking ideas out of the air just as an example, but if something like that *did* happen, Claire's parents would be liable for prosecution. They might even go to prison.'

When I think about this dispassionately, together with the conversation I overheard on the bus all those years ago, it doesn't sound as stupid as it first seems. It still makes my head hurt.

Keris has more to say. 'The theory gets complicated because Neeta – as I suggest we continue to call her – has changed so many key features about herself.'

If this woman, Neeta, was once Yasmin Fuller then her eyes are not as cold as I remember. Her lips are not as thin and mean. Filler, Botox... she looks younger than I'd expect. Maybe even a facelift? Her voice is more cultured and easier on the ear. Her nose looks sculpted, her jawline tighter. She's probably forty-odd pounds lighter. All this is well within the realms of possibility with surgery. If someone was determined to look different, that is.

And yet... I feel a sense of dread wash over me that I failed to miss that she's someone I used to know. I should have picked up *something*.

I think about the creepy feeling I got when Neeta first visited the cottage. The sense that I'd seen her before. The dreams about the past that started as soon as we moved to the bay that I'd put down to being in closer proximity to the childhood home I'd lived in with Mum.

'If it's true, I feel so stupid, so clueless, that something didn't click straight away.' I rub my forehead. 'I mean, I should have spotted definite signs.'

'Neeta has had extensive cosmetic surgery,' Keris says. 'She and Ted changed their names and although he's not gone to such extreme lengths, he's changed his appearance, too. You were just a kid, Lottie. Don't be too hard on yourself.'

She's being kind, but I'm still so irritated with myself, and embarrassed, too. I barely saw Ted – or *Graham* as he was in those days. He always seemed to be working away on his building business and I never stopped overnight. I saw his picture in the local newspaper when Claire disappeared, but I didn't know how his voice sounded, how he carried himself. These are the things that are difficult to change about yourself.

'You said Mary Gooding was convinced they had Claire in Seaspray House,' I say. 'Where are the Goodings now? I'd like to speak to them.'

Keris nodded. 'I'll get in touch, explain who you are and your own suspicions about Ted and Neeta. Then we can go over there together. I know Mary has been unwell, so leave it with me and I'll see what I can do.'

'Let's just say the Fullers faked Claire's disappearance for whatever reason. Why would Mum still leave like that?'

'They'd already orchestrated a smear campaign against your mum, so she might have fled abroad to escape prison if she felt the police were going to arrest her.'

I consider this. If this was true then it meant Mum had put her own needs first and left me behind, a kid, ill-equipped to deal with the fallout. Every time I think about her these are the mixed feelings that come up. That's why I realised a long time ago it's best not to overthink that time.

'There's one thing we haven't touched on that makes the most sense of all,' Keris says. 'Money.'

'Money?'

'You know, the one thing that never fails to amaze me in all the cases I've worked on or read about are the fixes people will get themselves into for money,' Keris says. 'Did you know Claire's parents allegedly received donations totalling over a million pounds after their daughter's supposed abduction?'

I take a sharp breath in. 'I didn't know that.'

'Yep. And just to be clear, that's purely money for their personal use. It wasn't given to a charity and donations are completely tax-free. You've heard of high-profile cases in the past where parents have done something similar, staged a crime or said their child has gone missing to get public sympathy, right?'

'Yes, but... who in their right mind would keep their child a prisoner just so they were a bit better off?'

'A hell of a lot better off,' Keris corrects me. 'I've already done some background investigation, and when Claire went missing, Ted – Graham Fuller back then – appeared to be a successful businessman. But, actually, you don't have to dig that deep on the Companies House website to see that his business was headed on a downward slope at that point in time.'

'The police must have seen that, too.'

Keris shrugs. 'Maybe. But I'm guessing they weren't thinking along the lines of why he might have abducted his own daughter. They clearly didn't link the two facts.'

'Are you saying it might have been Ted's idea to stage Claire's disappearance?'

'Who knows. But what I am certain of is that those donations transformed their lives. They didn't spend the money travelling around Europe to look for Claire or to bring publicity to their cause. They didn't employ any private investigators to look into the case and try to find crucial details the police may have missed. They stayed put for about ten years and then, from what I can see, they just spent it on buying an old neglected house on a hill for a very competitive price and Ted built Seaspray from scratch himself at cost. The accounts of his building company show that he did very well in the first years after Claire disappeared. People were sympathetic and gave him more business than ever.'

I hold my head in my hands. Taking such possibilities on board hurts like a physical pain. All these years I've blamed Mum and yet... is it possible she felt she had no other way out than to run away? Now I'm older I can understand how blind panic might have made her act so impulsively.

'I know this is a lot to take in, Lottie, but there's one other thing that really bothers me.'

'What's that?' I'm dreading what's coming next.

'Look, call me a cynic, but I'm not a believer in big coincidences,' she says, never taking her eyes off mine. 'And now I know your huge connection to the Claire Fuller case, I can't ignore the obvious. Neil getting the Seaspray job meant it would put you in direct contact again with the Fullers: the very people that accused your mother of a terrible crime. That kind of coincidence leaves a nasty taste in my mouth. So, taking all that into consideration, how exactly did Neil hear about the job?'

'He posted his CV online and an agency contacted him with a view to applying.' As I say the words, the back of my neck prickles. Is it possible that, somehow, the Williamses saw his details and recruited him on purpose? 'I know what you're getting at, but why would the Williamses ever want to set eyes on me again? Surely if they'd got away with a crime for so long and completely reinvented themselves, they'd hardly want to draw attention by risking me recognising them?'

As I say the words I'm thinking again: *How? How could I not realise who the Williamses are?* I did feel some vague sense of déjà vu when I met Neeta, but I discounted it. I had zero trust in my feelings, my instincts. I've been the same since Mum left. But if Mum did take Claire away, what if Keris is right and the Williamses brought me back solely to exact revenge? All the worrying I've done about Neil and Albie... perhaps I'm right to be concerned because now Neeta wants to take *my* family away to settle an old score.

'I wish I had the answer to why they brought you back... if that's what happened. All I know is that something feels off about how you and your family got here. The Goodings told me they were pushed out, that Ted and Neeta came up with a spiteful story designed to drive them out of the close community.' Keris reaches out and grabs my hand. 'Lottie, I'm sorry I kept my true identity away from you, but I didn't realise your previous involvement with the Williamses. I thought you were just the new couple who'd come to live in the cottage.'

'You set out to get to know me, though. That first morning I saw you and Edie on the hillside, you made an effort to come over and start chatting.'

'It's true, but I never expected to really like you. I couldn't have known Edie and Albie would become best friends and that we'd get on so well. Lottie, this might be your chance to find out exactly what happened back then and if your mum was involved in any way.'

'I saw someone creeping around outside in the early hours... was that you?'

'What?'

'Doing your... investigations, or whatever you want to call it.'

Keris shakes her head. 'Of course it wasn't me. I'd never leave Edie alone in the flat so I can skulk around in the dead of night! What did you see?'

'Someone... just the shape, the movement. Between the cottage and Seaspray.'

She frowns, thinking. Then she says, 'Look, there's so much to make sense of at Seaspray. If you can find it in your heart to trust me again, we could do it together. What do you say?'

The truth is, I don't know what to say. It's true she's lied to me. Yet, in a way, I can see why she wanted to chat to me that day. I never expected our kids would get on so well either, and I do believe she didn't have a clue about my link to the case, as Kay Price's daughter. As she says, that's one too many coincidences that need to be looked at.

'What have you got in mind?' I say slowly.

'If you can observe the house whenever you can, try to get more detail of whether they have someone in there and where they're being held. I'll do more work in the background. I'll speak to the Goodings, so you can meet them. But in the meantime, there's one thing you *can't* do.'

'What's that?'

'You mustn't tell Neil what we're doing. He's the link between Neeta Williams and you. If she somehow gets an inkling that her cover has been blown, we may never find out what happened to Claire and your mum. Surely you must see that?'

I think about Neil's reaction to anything I've said about Ted and Neeta and how he's always tried to discount my doubts or ridicule what I've seen. The way it seems Ted and Neeta are commandeering both my son and my husband.

'I won't tell him everything, but there's no way I'm going to let Albie continue to go up to Seaspray. If you're right and the Williamses have committed an atrocity like that then it proves I made the right decision in finishing work. I don't want my son anywhere near them.'

Keris shakes her head. 'Lottie, they're bound to suspect

something if you do that. It would blow our cover almost immediately!'

'I can't let Albie spend any more time with them. I can't.' My voice emerges high and strained.

'Do you believe he's in danger? Neil's always up there with him, isn't he?'

'That's not the point. If we're right about those two and they've got their "missing" daughter imprisoned, they could be capable of almost anything.' I feel breathless with the thought of sending my son up there like a lamb to the slaughter.

'I beg you, Lottie. If you want to find out the truth, you have to let things run a little longer. It's vital they don't suspect anything.'

Up until we've had this conversation, I've had nobody to share my worries with. Sure, I've mentioned various things to Keris about strange goings-on at Seaspray House before I knew who she was, but she didn't know about my own past at that point, so we were both guarded.

I still feel guilty for keeping the events of the past from my husband, but this is my only chance to finally lift the rock and see what horrors lie under there.

'OK, I won't say anything to Neil,' I say, the fight momentarily knocked out of me. 'For now.'

FORTY-TWO

Charlie sat moodily in the corner of the lounge watching as her mum rushed around to get ready to go over to the Fullers' house yet again.

'Have you seen Claire's school reading book?' She looked around the room frantically. 'I brought it home with me by mistake and she'll get in trouble at school if she doesn't have it. I could swear I put it here on the sideboard but it's not here.'

'Haven't seen it, sorry,' Charlie said laconically. She'd hidden the book under the sofa last night before bed. It would do Miss Smarty-pants good to get a detention instead of the never-ending 'good girl' praise Yasmin and Charlie's own mum gave her on a daily basis.

It's true their lives had improved a hundred-fold since they'd moved into this flat, but it was equally accurate to say there was one area for Charlie that had got much worse. She barely saw her mum now, particularly in the school holidays when Yasmin's demands on her time increased dramatically.

'Can I come to the seaside today with you?' Charlie would plead in the warmer months as Kay packed towels for the beach. 'I won't get in your way; you won't even know I'm there.'

'No. Yasmin won't allow it; she still hasn't forgiven you for bullying poor Claire and neither have I.'

'That was ages ago.' Charlie scowled. 'It's not fair! You're my mum but I never get to see you.'

But Kay was always unmoved. 'You'll have to find something to do to keep yourself busy until I'm back. You can tidy up that mess of a bedroom of yours for starters. Yasmin will evict you if she sees it.'

Charlie watched now as her mother became more and more agitated, pacing back and forth, returning every time to the sideboard as though the book might magically appear there.

Kay had started drinking again a couple of months ago. She was being careful, but Charlie knew the signs. Drinking mainly vodka diluted with water, just drip-feeding herself the alcohol so she existed in a sort of dazed bubble. She'd also started buying multi-packs of cheap mints.

Kay was terrified of Yasmin Fuller finding out, that much was certain. She was still sober enough to know they'd end up in a mouldy old hovel on the wrong side of town again. They would lose everything.

But Charlie was now old enough to understand that despite Yasmin swooping in like Superwoman and transforming their lives on the outside, it wasn't enough to change things for very long because her mum was an alcoholic. This flat, her mum's new job working for the Fullers... it was nothing more than a coat of paint on rotten wood. The drinking was always going to break through again after a bit of wear and tear because, as they'd learned at school, it was a *disease*.

Although it was true that Duncan had been an aggressive drunk and deserved to be sent to prison, her mum had conveniently blamed him for every last thing that had gone wrong in her life.

In fact, Charlie knew only too well her mum was a drunk way before Duncan came onto the scene. Kay was more than capable of messing up her own life without him and it looked to Charlie like she'd already made an impressive start.

FORTY-THREE

LOTTIE

TUESDAY

My phone rings and Keris's name flashes up. 'Can you be free tomorrow afternoon? Mary and Tom Gooding are going to meet us halfway. They're living in Leicester now, so it's a ninety-minute drive for both sides.'

I'm not working for the next two days, but...

'It's just... Albie will need to go to Seaspray straight from school then and... I really don't want that.'

'I get it, Lottie. But the only way we're going to bring this stuff to an end is to get some answers, right?'

Reluctantly, I grunt my agreement.

'Edie is at hockey practice until five-thirty, so I have to be back by then anyway. It won't be for long and then you can come back and pick him up.'

'Fine,' I say. I know she's right. We've got to make some progress and I did ask her to arrange for me to speak to the Goodings.

· · ·

Later, when Neil gets home from work, he looks tired and drawn. I'm not sure where all his bouncing energy and enthusiasm disappeared to. 'Chicken salad tonight,' I say, pretending I haven't noticed his obvious exhaustion. 'That OK for you?'

He looks cautiously my way, sensing the edge to my voice. I'm going to have to do a better job if I want to stop him getting suspicious.

'Chicken salad is fine, thanks,' he says with little zeal.

I start washing the lettuce leaves at the sink. 'Work have asked me to go in tomorrow afternoon, so I thought I would for the extra cash. I'll text Neeta and ask if it's OK for Albie to go up there after school.'

I turn around when he doesn't answer and then he nods vacantly and I'm not sure he's registered what I've said. I put the washed lettuce in a colander.

'Looks like your eczema is up again.' His forearms are patterned with dark, dry patches and angry red tracks where he's scratched himself. I haven't seen his skin like that since his recovery after the accident. He keeps telling me he loves his job, but these signs are telling me differently.

The next day Keris comes up to the cottage and we set off to the meeting place. On the drive there, she asks me a question.

'Have you thought about what you'll do if this is resolved, Lottie? I mean, the Williamses could go to prison and that means Neil won't have a job and you'll have to let the cottage go.'

It has crossed my mind but I've done a good job of pushing it away so far. 'I don't know what we'll do,' I say simply. 'But it can't be any worse than the path we're currently on.'

'Not knowing if they have Claire in that house, you mean?'

'Honestly, it sounds dramatic but sometimes, if nothing

changes, I feel like I'm going to lose both my husband and my son to them. The chance of finding out what happened back then and finally clearing my mum's name is worth the risk.'

We travel to meet the Goodings at a quiet service station just off the M1.

'I said we'd meet them inside,' Keris says, unclipping her seatbelt. 'I just need to warn you again that Mary isn't in a good place right now. Tom told me the unpleasantness with the Williamses has had a big effect on her mental health.'

Understandable. These new revelations have had a big effect on my own wellbeing, too. I feel so unsafe, so jumpy all the time.

We walk inside and she waves to an older couple sitting at a table in the Costa Coffee outlet near the entrance. 'It's them,' she says and we walk over there. Keris makes the introductions.

'Lottie, this is Mary and Tom Gooding.' She smiles at them. 'As I was telling you, Lottie and her husband, Neil, and also their young son have moved into the cottage at Seaspray.' Keris glances at the counter. 'There's no queue so I'll just grab us all a coffee. Everyone OK with a latte?'

We all agree and Keris moves away. I pull out a chair and sit down, smiling at them both in turn. Tom is a small, balding, wiry man who's not holding any weight. Mary is plump but has a kind face and twinkly blue eyes that look troubled. She has on a lightweight pink jacket and a pretty lilac floral scarf tied loosely around her neck. I instantly warm to her.

'Thanks so much for agreeing to meet up today,' I say.

Tom speaks up first. 'Hello, Lottie. We jumped at the chance of meeting you when Keris told us your husband was working for Ted and Neeta. We know how the bay works and we can imagine the gossip going around there about why we left so suddenly.'

Mary looks down at her hands. Her fingers are continuously

twisting a corner of the scarf. 'We want you to know we were happy for many years at Seaspray,' she says. 'But then Ted's health took a bit of a downturn and that's when things started to go awry.'

It's the first I've heard of Ted being unwell. 'We've noticed him coughing,' I say. 'But Neil says he always insists he's fine.'

Tom shrugs. 'Maybe he is, but before we left I felt like change was in the air up there. Something that's worked OK so far, but is now going wrong.'

Keris returns with the coffees. I thank her and take mine before addressing the older couple again.

'Do you believe they're holding someone in that house?' I say bluntly. 'What did you see? Nobody knows I'm here but Keris. I won't repeat anything you tell me.'

Tom and Mary exchange a glance and then he says, 'I thought I saw someone upstairs in their bedroom when they were out. I also saw a child's toy in the sun room as I walked past. When I returned thirty minutes later, it had gone and I swear I heard someone wailing and crying through the open window. Supposedly there was nobody at home. That's how the disagreement started.'

'I spoke to both Neeta and Ted about what I saw. Mary had also seen a shadowy figure moving around upstairs but she'd been... well, I didn't want to mention that.'

'I used to watch the house from the spare bedroom window in the cottage,' Mary said sheepishly. 'It's the one place you can see the house.'

'I found that out,' I say. 'I've been doing the same thing. Tom, I heard that... you attacked Neeta.'

Mary scowls, her fingers tapping on the edge of the table. 'Have you seen that woman? She's like an Amazon warrior next to my Tom.'

'I didn't assault her,' Tom says quickly. 'I told them I

thought there was someone in the house. I insisted I came inside to have a look around – for their own safety! I laid my hands on Neeta's shoulders to try and move her gently aside and that's when Ted grabbed hold of me and told me to leave before he called the police!'

'Obviously he'd be bluffing about that,' Keris scoffs.

'Maybe so. You never quite know whose pockets those two are lining, though. Ted knew some pretty influential people,' Tom says doubtfully. 'But anyway, I didn't need asking twice. Me and Mary had been talking for months about the best time to tell Ted I was finishing the job.'

'He was finding the work hard, particularly as Ted was holding back and putting more work on him,' Mary adds.

'So, can you categorically say there was someone in the house?' I ask.

'I'm ninety per cent sure.' Tom nods. 'It wasn't the first time I'd seen a shadow, or heard someone crying. I'd often go up to my shed to potter around after work hours if Mary had her sister round. That's when I'd sometimes hear odd things, see movement upstairs when I knew for a fact Neeta and Ted were downstairs.'

'We knew something wasn't right for a long time,' Mary agrees. 'But it was obvious the Williamses didn't want to talk about it.'

'I've seen some strange things, too,' I say. 'Similar to what you've just described. Shadowy figures, Neeta talking to someone when Ted isn't in the house. Children's toys when they have no kids. Where I'm struggling is: if someone else is living in the house, then where are they?'

'The obvious place is a basement,' Keris says. 'But I've thoroughly checked the plans Ted submitted back when he built Seaspray House. There is no basement or concealed rooms detailed on there.'

Tom looks at me and gives a wry smile. 'Keris told me you found an old photo upstairs in the cottage, of the original house that used to stand on the hill.'

'I did. Together with a partially written letter I think you might have written, Mary.'

Mary picks up her coffee and I see her hand is shaking slightly. 'I wrote that in a low moment, after... when they'd threatened Tom he'd better leave, or else. I got frightened and... I should have just thrown it away, but I forgot it was there.'

'Well, I kept that photograph for a reason,' Tom says firmly. 'I used to know an old fella, lived down in the bay. He's gone now, God rest his soul. But he told me that during World War II they dug out a big bunker right next to the house to use as an air raid shelter. There weren't many people left around here who could remember that. I've always had an interest in the war and I found the air raid shelter story fascinating, so I found a photo online of the house and got it printed. When Ted saw it, he got angry, ripped it into shreds. I knew then there was something in it.'

'He ordered another one the next day, didn't you, Tom?' Mary says proudly. 'My husband won't be put down.'

The old photograph of the original house flashes into my mind. That white sheeting at the side of it.

Keris takes a sharp breath in. 'If it was never filled in and Seaspray has subsumed that bunker...'

'Could it still be there, under the house?' I say.

Keris looks at Tom. 'In your opinion, could Ted have finished it off like a proper room when he built the house?'

There was no hesitation from Tom. 'Oh, without doubt. They did things properly in those days. That was a hole and a half they'd have dug out. Enough for two rooms, Lottie... maybe even three,' he says gravely. 'Maybe your husband can do a bit of detective work and find out if there's a basement down there?'

Keris frowns and I know she's thinking we can't involve Neil in our investigations. Then she turns to me. 'Better still, is there any way you can get inside Seaspray House and have a look around yourself, Lottie?'

FORTY-FOUR

NEIL

Neil enters Seaspray House, closing the door quietly behind him.

What the hell has he got himself into here? In no time at all, he's in too deep. And it already feels far too deep to do anything about it. He's trapped in no-man's land between telling Lottie the truth and keeping Neeta sweet and on-side.

Neeta has him just where she wants him and she knows it. Right on cue, she appears from a doorway. She's wearing a glamorous kaftan, completely open at the front, revealing a short, clingy vest top and shorts. His heart rate speeds up a notch as she nudges the kaftan off her shoulders and allows the floaty fabric to fall to the floor in a soft pool.

'I've been waiting for you, Neil,' she says in that husky voice of hers. 'Come through and we can get started.'

Thirty minutes later, Neil emerges from the side room and walks back into the cavernous hallway in his socked feet. His T-shirt is sticking to his damp skin. He's hot and bothered and looking forward to a shower when he finishes work. He touches his face with the back of a hand. His cheeks feel hot and flushed. No wonder. Being in that room with Neeta Williams for the last half an hour is enough to make any man overheat, but he's got much more on his mind than that.

At the bottom of the staircase, he looks up at the perfect blue sky through the atrium. This place. It's like nothing he's ever seen before. It triggers something inside him and suddenly he yearns for a part of it. The luxury, the wealth.

When Neil handed Ted the photograph of the old house Lottie had found upstairs in the cottage, Ted had told him how he'd built Seaspray from the ground up.

He'd looked at the photograph with a thoughtful expression. 'Hard to believe this old pile ever existed now. Fifteen years ago we bought it for a good price, demolished it and then I designed and built this place.' They'd been standing at the top of the estate and Ted had looked at the building as he'd spoken, proudly appraising his handiwork.

'Where did you live before?' Neil had asked.

'Not far from York. We had a nice big house back then, but obviously nothing like this,' he'd said easily, surveying the grounds. 'Neeta had tired of life there and wanted a fresh start by the sea. We came into some money and bought the old house, stayed put in York until I got this place finished.'

'Did you get any resistance from the locals?'

Ted pulled a face. 'It's fair to say a few of the locals weren't too happy, but only the same old shower of stalwarts who buck against change of any sort. Most people had already grown tired of the old house. Watching the storm-whipped stone crumbling a little more every year. The younger people seemed to welcome the twist the modern, new building brought to the old fishing village.'

'I'm surprised the local council approved the plans, though,' Neil had remarked. 'You know, with Seaspray looking so different to the rest of the village and also the sheer size of the place.'

Ted had grinned. 'Well, between you and me, I had the help of a good contact in the planning department. He put the right people on the job. Let's just say, when they send out planning officers who've just tipped out of university, they don't look further than the end of their nose. Still wet behind the ears, if you get my drift.' He'd winked at Neil. 'I handpicked a small, trusted team of men who'd worked for me for years and I paid them very well. Well enough they forgot a lot of stuff they saw, *comprendi*? You'd be surprised at what you could get away with back then. Wouldn't be so easy now, of course.'

A shadow had fallen across his face at that point and, just for a few brief seconds, he'd looked incredibly troubled.

Neil walks to the entrance now and puts his boots back on. He's just laced them and stood up straight when the door opens and Ted comes inside.

Neil's heart starts racing, but Ted winks at him. 'Been to see Neeta?'

Neil nods and looks away, but Ted laughs at his expression. 'Don't worry, your secret's safe with me. I know exactly how persuasive my wife can be, believe me. Won't take no for an answer, eh? Maybe she knows what's best for you, buddy. You need to give your future some thought. We all do.'

Neil makes a small sound in his throat. This situation is so messed up.

Then he remembers something. 'Hey, Ted. Lottie is convinced she saw someone creeping around outside in the early hours the other morning. Just thought I'd give you the heads-up.'

He fully expects Ted to laugh and wave him away, but the other man stiffens and the grin slides from his face. 'What exactly happened?'

'She couldn't sleep so went downstairs to get a glass of water. She reckons she saw someone on the hillside between the cottage and Seaspray. But she can get carried away with her imag—'

'Did she describe the person?'

Is it Neil's imagination or has Ted's face turned pale? His hacking cough seems to be getting worse and on occasion, Neil has walked around a corner to find him leaning against a wall as if he's trying to get his breath back.

'She saw a figure, saw movement, but it was really dark out there. So she couldn't see any detail.'

Ted nods. Oddly, Neil thinks, he almost looks relieved. 'Thanks for letting me know. Maybe it's time we got some security up here.'

Neil steps outside and stands for a few moments, enjoying the warmth of the sun on his face. He drags in a long breath as he looks up to the sky. This bright, new shiny life had seemed so amazing at first, but now he's ruined everything. He's been weak and betrayed the woman who's stood by him through everything.

Neil has managed to get himself into an impossible nightmare scenario in record time. Now, he finds himself in the worst dilemma possible and Neeta still hasn't told him exactly what she wants from him.

Does he carry on until he's eventually found out, in what could be weeks or months? Or does he break Lottie's heart by telling her the truth right now? He starts the meandering walk through the immaculate gardens, down to his garden office, scratching at the patches of eczema that have made an unwelcome return. The early feel-good vibes of being here have long gone now and all he's left with is an empty void.

He can't shake the growing sense of doom that the time of reckoning is coming and soon, if he doesn't decide for himself, he's going to be forced to make a choice one way or another.

FORTY-FIVE

LOTTIE

When I dropped Keris off from our meeting with the Goodings, I come back to the cottage. It did me good to meet Tom and Mary and hear what they had to say. I now feel vindicated about my own suspicions that Neil tries so hard to derail every time I share my concerns about his employers.

I also saw the state of poor Mary's nerves and it's made me determined not to end up the same way. I can only do that by staying strong and keeping my mind on what we want to achieve.

It's not long before Albie comes back home with his dad and sets up his homework at the kitchen table. Neil is carrying out a repair on our gate, so I walk down to him at the end of the path.

I freeze when I get close. He has a smear of red lipstick on his cheek. It's very bright and I've seen that colour before... on Neeta Williams.

When he sees me, he smiles but then takes in my expression. 'Hi, love. Is everything OK?' He's guarded, suspicious something's wrong.

I feel shell-shocked and yet I knew it. Deep down, I sensed

something was very wrong... I suspected he was having an affair. Him cosying up to Neeta at the restaurant, working late and coming home smelling of alcohol after Neeta had texted him about some fictitious delivery, no doubt. Also, the way he's consistently turning a blind eye to all the strange happenings I'm trying to talk to him about. The only thing he seems to care about is staying in the job.

'You have something on your cheek,' I say, staring at the obscene mark. I can't tear my eyes away from it.

He frowns, his hand flying up to the wrong side of his face.

'The other side. Here, let me.' I pull a tissue out of my sleeve and rub lightly over his skin. Then I show him the lurid red colour. 'You had lipstick on your cheek. The exact shade Neeta wears.'

His face is tanned but it still pales as his eyes widen.

'It... it's... not what you think, Lottie,' he stammers.

'Don't try and talk me out of it like you do everything else. Don't try and make me think I'm going mad. You had Neeta's lipstick all over your face. Fact.'

He looks at me and he says nothing.

'Aren't you going to tell me I'm imagining it? That's your reaction every time I say something you don't want to hear.'

When he begins to walk away, I chase him down the path.

'At least have the guts to admit it... are you having an affair with her?'

He stands still, but doesn't answer, I pull at the sleeve of his T-shirt, my eyes welling up. 'Why don't you go back? Back to Seaspray to be with her?'

He's going to leave me. For her. What do I care? I want him to leave! The cheating, lying swine. But... I'm also desperate for him to stay. Desperate to keep our family together for Albie's sake.

A muscle in his jaw twitches, but generally his expression is like stone. I think about Albie in the cottage and I stop shouting and goading Neil. I just stand there before saying, 'I knew this place was bad for us. All this time I've tried to tell you something is wrong.' I wipe away the tears rolling down my cheeks and stand there, trying to steel myself to go back inside and face my son. Then something shocks me. Something I didn't expect to see.

A single tear, rolling down Neil's cheek.

'Lottie, I'm sorry. I'm so sorry,' he says and the tears start rolling freely.

I can count the number of times I've seen my husband cry on one hand. He cried tears of joy when Albie was born. He cried with frustration when the doctors told him he might never walk again. He cried tears of gratitude when he felt sensation in his legs again. And now, he's crying because... he's having an affair with Neeta Williams? I feel sick. I don't want to know. I want to pretend none of this is happening.

'I can't carry on like this any more.' He sniffs, wiping his face with the back of a hand. 'If you decide to leave me, I can't blame you. But I have to tell you something, Lottie. Something that's been weighing heavily on my mind for so long.'

I stare at him, terrified what he's about to say. Terrified to hear the words, *I want to be with Neeta*. Even though part of me hates him right now, the old, needy instincts to cling on are still strong.

He pauses, seemingly to gather his strength. When he speaks, his voice sounds raw and hoarse. 'I've betrayed you in the worst way possible. I've lied to you for a long time... and you haven't deserved it. You've only ever supported and wanted to help me.'

The way he's talking, it sounds like he's been having an affair with her for months, not just the few weeks we've been living in the bay.

'Just tell me.' My voice sounds so much colder than I feel

inside. I don't want to hear the words, but I have to. I have to hear him tell me what he's been up to with that conniving bitch.

'The day I had the accident... well, it wasn't an accident.'

'What?' My blood runs cold; every inch of my body freezes.

'I was attacked at work that day, Lottie. The injuries I suffered were from being hit repeatedly on my body with an iron bar, not from a falling statue.'

I look at him. I can't make sense of what he's saying to me. 'You were *attacked*?' I repeat faintly.

'Yes. By two men.'

'But... why didn't you tell the police? I mean, why did you lie to me when it wasn't your fault?'

He sighs. 'That's just it. It was my fault. I knew one of the attackers. He was... my dealer.'

'Your *dealer*?'

'Remember back when I suffered with my back, I went to the doctor and he gave me some pain relief?'

It was about eighteen months before the accident. He had to work so many hours and couldn't afford extra labour at the beginning, so he did the management and the hard graft. Some mornings, he could hardly get out of bed and then, after a visit to the doctor to get medication and, he said, a few chiropractor sessions, the problem just went away.

'The painkillers were a lifesaver but the doctor's supply soon ran out because I doubled the dose and he refused to prescribe more.'

'Because they could be addictive when taken for long periods,' I remark and he nods.

'A guy on site, he saw me suffering one day and took me aside, gave me a couple of opioids and the number of a guy who could supply me for a price, no questions asked.'

Neil and... prescription drug addiction? That is a pairing that never entered my mind. It doesn't sound right at all.

'Anyway, I got behind with my tab. Couldn't pay on time and they decided to teach me a lesson.'

'Those two years of hell... that was down to drug debts?' I whisper.

He nods, avoiding my stare. 'After the accident, the hospital doctors prescribed me opioid painkillers again.'

I think about his insistence of the terrible pain in his legs. The way he fought to carry on with the tablets.

'I did manage to kick the painkillers during my recovery. But... somehow Neeta and Ted, they know about it. They know I lied to you about what happened.'

I don't know how to respond. It doesn't seem real.

He looks at me, his forehead lined and heavy. 'I'm so sorry, Lottie. I've betrayed your trust and I want to put it right. I swear I do.'

I hold on to the fence, feeling dazed and confused. 'But... how do Neeta and Ted know what happened? They didn't even know you back then.'

When he speaks, his voice sounds brittle and forced. 'That's just it. They know everything about me... about us. I don't know how, or why they're so interested in our past! They're black-mailing me, Lottie. Threatening to tell you everything unless I do what they want.'

A high-pitched buzzing sounds in my ears. I hear myself say, 'And what do they want?'

'I don't know yet.' Neil looks down, fresh tears squeezing from his eyes. 'They're keeping me hanging until I get you on side.'

FORTY-SIX

MAY, EIGHTEEN YEARS EARLIER

Yasmin Fuller folded her arms and waited for an answer from Kay Price.

She'd been good enough to rescue this woman and her daughter from their tawdry, miserable life and this was the thanks she'd got. Infuriatingly, Kay remained silent.

'I'll ask you again,' Yasmin said, keeping her voice level but firm. 'Have you been drinking on duty?'

Kay took a deep breath. 'I haven't, Mrs Fuller, no. I swear on my daughter's life I haven't touched a drop. Here... smell my breath.'

Yasmin jumped back as the woman exhaled into her face. 'For God's sake, there's no need for that!'

Kay had become increasingly distracted and vacant over the last few weeks. Yasmin had spoken to her on several occasions and she'd either not answered, or had used the wrong words or phrasing in her reply. This morning, Yasmin felt sure Kay had slurred a couple of times when speaking.

It was becoming clear she'd made a big error in believing the cheap childcare arrangement could work. Graham had said they had to tighten their belts a bit because the building contract situation had slowed.

'No more getting expensive nannies from that posh agency,' he'd mumbled, tapping at his calculator amongst a sea of financial spreadsheets. 'You'll have to somehow manage to look after her yourself, Yasmin. Like all the other mums do around here.'

Having a child was exhausting and help after school and in the holidays certainly eased the burden. That's why she'd come up with the plan to bring Kay in. They'd got a spare flat going and rentals were notoriously slow in the area. She thought she'd come up with the perfect solution, but Kay had let her down.

'You're distracted and acting strangely,' Yasmin said curtly. 'There's something wrong with you, I'm certain of it.'

'Yes, if truth be told, I've been feeling a bit off, a bit out of it. I – I've made an appointment at the doctor's next week,' Kay babbled. 'Perhaps it's my time of life, who knows. I'm going to discuss it with him. It'll be fine, honestly, Mrs Fuller.'

Out of it and so often in the sole care of Claire. Yasmin knew that Kay, who was in her mid-fifties, had been suffering with back ache and other menopausal symptoms and, recently, it had got much worse. But allowing her to look after Claire any longer wouldn't do. It wouldn't do at all until she got some help. Yasmin had observed a decline in attention span with Kay. She'd be trying to sort out the next week's rota of school pick-ups for Claire and Kay's eyes would suddenly turn vacant.

'I'm sorry, Kay. I know you're experiencing some health issues, but I'm afraid the time has come when I'm going to have to make other arrangements for Claire's after-school care. I can't—'

'Oh no, please don't say that, Mrs Fuller. I love looking after Claire; she's such a good girl. I'm asking you... begging you, to please give me another chance. I'll be extra careful to keep more alert until I've seen the doctor, how's that?'

Yasmin knew it would hit Kay financially if she were to stop her services. Plus she'd have to vacate the flat. The older single mum had fallen pregnant at the age of forty-one and her second husband had left her when she'd insisted she wanted to keep the child. She'd intimated money was tight many times but Yasmin saved a ton of money this way, instead of having to employ a qualified nanny with a contract and legal rights.

'I'm sorry, Kay. I've given this a lot of thought and discussed it at length with Graham and we've decided. Sadly, we won't require your services after this weekend, but I'll pay you a month's notice and give you two months to find somewhere else to live. I think that's fair.'

'Oh, you've a heart of gold, Mrs Fuller,' Kay said, her grey eyes glinting with what Yasmin suspected may be poorly concealed malice. Maybe it wasn't a good idea to leave Claire in her care this weekend after all. But what else would she do? Graham was taking some of his most important clients and their families for a weekend at an exclusive adults-only spa hotel. It was a very expensive gamble that he was praying would work: a corporate get-away where clients would be wined and dined and much-needed deals would be made on the golf club and in the spa over a glass of champagne. She couldn't get out of going and, frankly, she could do with the break.

'I need your word that you won't be drinking while I'm away, Kay. Otherwise I won't be able to pay you for this weekend, or the month's notice.'

'You have my word,' Kay said, her voice dull and flat. 'You seem to have blown this up out of all context, Mrs Fuller, because I'm far from out of it. I'm fully capable of taking care of Claire and my own daughter, too, this weekend.'

Yasmin remained unconvinced over her long-term suitability, but she felt confident she'd do as she promised and keep on the straight and narrow over the weekend.

'OK,' Yasmin said reluctantly. 'Just make sure Claire is back home for ten o'clock on Saturday morning.'

FORTY-SEVEN

LOTTIE

After his devastating revelation about the accident that turned out wasn't an accident at all, I piece together the few shreds of dignity I have left and quietly ask Neil to leave the house.

'I'll take Albie to the beach for a couple of hours,' he says, hanging his head. 'I don't know how I'm ever going to make this up to you both, but I will. I swear to God, Lottie, I will.'

I can't speak, can't even tell him that he can never make up for the two years of hell we went through as a family.

'Neeta isn't the person you think she is,' Neil had said before I asked him to give me some time alone. For a moment, I thought he knew the truth of who she really is, but then he continued. 'She's a tortured soul underneath. She's unwell a lot, too. In fact she took a sleeping pill when I left. Ted said it will knock her out for hours.'

No wonder Neeta is tortured, if she's done what Keris believes and faked the disappearance of her daughter. What will Neil do when he finds out the extent of their duplicity? I'm not ready to tell him the truth yet. Once the facts are revealed, I'll have no chance of getting any more information. But what does Neeta want of him?

They're keeping me hanging until I get you on side. Him telling me I'm imagining stuff, telling me I don't know what I'm dealing with... is that Neil trying to get me on side?

When they've left for the beach, I sit quietly on the sofa, taking a little time to reflect.

When we first arrived here at the cottage, I felt so excited about the place, thinking how cosy this room would be in the colder months. I'd imagined the three of us nestled here at night, drinking hot chocolate by the crackling fire and in the glow of candles. Now the room seems cold and impersonal. The log burner is dead, the glass dull and blackened and my visions of our happy little family lying like ashes at my feet.

'Try not to make a mess of your life like I have,' Mum had told me once, pouring herself another drink. 'Your friend Claire has a wonderful future ahead of her, but you... you'll always have to fight for the good things. They won't just land in your lap. Remember that.'

At the time I dismissed her brusque comment as just another criticism, another sign she didn't care about me. But now, as a parent myself, I realise her barbed comments were probably the only way she could express herself. In her own way, she'd always wanted better for me than she'd had. She just expressed it badly.

I think about Ted and Neeta, knowing all about Neil's 'accident' and subsequent lies, and Keris's recent words ring in my ears. *'That kind of coincidence leaves a nasty taste in my mouth... How exactly did Neil hear about the job?'*

Would they really go to so much trouble to get us here? Now I have a chance to find out the extent of their deception. Should I take it and risk everything to find out the truth? Or slink quietly away with my son to lick my wounds and try to piece together some sort of existence on our own, without Neil?

In refusing to face the past, it's become obvious to me I've inadvertently trapped part of myself back there. Ted and

Neeta Williams have shaped my life in ways I probably don't even know yet and although there are still so many unknowns, I'm absolutely certain of one thing: it's now time to face them head on and find out just what the hell the two of them are hiding. And more importantly, what they want of us.

I haven't got much time, but I don't need long. Just enough to get inside the house while Neeta is sleeping and Ted is out.

When I get over to the gate, which is now locked, I punch in Neil's access number into the keypad. It's not fully dark yet but with my dark-grey trackie bottoms and hoodie, I'm blending nicely with the gloomy shadows thrown by the wall surrounding the Seaspray estate.

The gate clicks open and the gardens spread out wide and far. The quickest way to the house and the open windows is straight across the sprawling lawn. But that option leaves me too exposed and I decide I can't risk it. Instead, I hug in close to the bushes and borders and move quickly around the longer route. I approach the side of the house, the one with the bedroom balcony I can see from our spare room window.

This side of the house is in shadow and I see the French doors are still ajar. From the cottage, I'm used to seeing the whole place lit up like a Christmas tree but obviously, with Neeta feeling unwell, she's probably just forgotten to close these doors.

This is a rare opportunity with Neil and Albie being out and Neil mentioning that Ted was at a landscaping exhibition in Leicester. This is the best chance I've had to get close to the property.

I traverse the final border of bushes and then I'm there, at the corner of the house. I'm just about to run across the path to the edge of the first window when I freeze. I can hear music playing... like a lullaby and faint, as if it's coming from a long way away. I cup my ear in an effort to hear better.

'*Hush little baby, Don't say a word...*'

It's the exact lullaby I used to sing to Albie as a baby any time I wanted to relax him or lull him to sleep. Seems a strange song to sing if you haven't got a small child, but perhaps it's just a nostalgia thing.

After checking around the garden, I dash across the path and stand directly under the open window. It's louder now and definitely a lullaby playing on loop, again and again.

'*Hush little baby, Don't you cry...*'

Where is the song coming from? I can see the sun room is completely empty and yet it's definitely coming from this area of the house. Then I see the teddy bear and dolls scattered across the floor.

The hairs on my arms prickle. It's so odd. I try the French doors and, incredibly, one opens. My legs feel shaky but I can't give up now. If Neeta comes in, I'll have to think of an excuse... I'll say I was coming to see if she was OK and I heard the music.

Inside the room, the music is a little louder but infuriatingly far away, like it's been muted somehow. I walk across the sun room, the light fading fast now outside. I grip the gold handle on the door leading further into the house and push it down slowly, trying to avoid any loud clicks. It opens smoothly and I step into a light airy hallway with a glass staircase and a beautiful atrium that sits above it all like a glass canopy.

I pull the sun room door towards me to close it and that's when I realise. The music has faded a little, like I'm leaving it behind. How can that be when it wasn't in the room in the first place? I was expecting it to grow louder as I travelled further into the property.

I spot a doll sitting on the end of a bookcase in the hallway and I freeze. I'm sure I remember seeing this distinctive toy before. Lullabies and dolls are usually for babies but... Claire would be nearly thirty years old now if they'd kept their daughter a prisoner for all this time.

I look inside a couple more rooms but there's no place here where someone could be hidden. The sun room is where the music is and it fades when I move away... that should tell me something. I think about Tom Gooding's remark about the war bunker... could it be under my feet?

I look around. There's not much in here. Just a cluster of wide-weave wicker furniture that glows pale with matching tables and quality cushions. All the walls are plain with no art prints, apart from the far wall that's lined with bookshelves. I creep over and see the shelving is fairly sparse, in keeping with the rest of the interior. The doll perched on the end catches my eye. Close up, she has delicate porcelain features complete with rosebud lips and disconcertingly lifelike eyes with black lashes.

An ache starts in my belly. I can't seem to tear my eyes away from her and then it hits me like a bolt of lightning.

I've seen this doll before. In Claire Fuller's bedroom.

I reach out my hand to touch her antique lace dress when a book tips over and falls to the floor. I freeze and wait. I'm just about to reach for the doll again when a thud sounds directly above my head. I stand stock still and listen and there it is again... thud, thud... like footsteps. Neeta must be awake and out of bed.

I turn and rush to the French doors, slipping out and leaving them slightly ajar as I'd found them. I run down the side of the house and crouch behind a couple of large bushes.

After a minute or so, Neeta appears at the French doors. She's wearing a white robe and peers out, looking around. She has the book in her hand that I knocked off the shelf. I stay very still and watch as she closes the doors and then tries the handles to make sure they're locked.

She moves away from the doors, and I see a light turn on in

the entrance hall, meaning I'm safe. She's moved out of the room altogether. My hands start to tingle and I wiggle my fingers to release tension from my close escape. I've an overwhelming urge to run out of here before Ted gets back but I force myself to keep calm and move swiftly down the edge of the garden, ensuring I keep close to the shrubbery.

I look back one last time and freeze as I process what I've just witnessed. Neeta walking in front of the window upstairs in her bedroom and a glimpse of a shadowy figure moving quickly across the sun room.

I hesitate, torn between running back to the doors shouting Claire's name and hammering at the glass, or returning to the cottage to plan my next move before Albie and Neil return from the beach.

I stare through the glass and the room is still. No shadows, no figure, no movement at all. I turn and continue my exit from the grounds.

When I get back to the cottage, Albie and Neil are still out. When I've calmed down, I call Keris and tell her what I've seen.

'Did you get a good look at the person in the sun room?' she asks.

'No. It was movement, shadows but... definitely a person.'

She falls silent for a moment and then begins to murmur as if she is thinking out loud. 'Why, though? Why would you fake your daughter's disappearance and then keep her in the house, an effective prisoner for nearly twenty years?'

'If that's Claire I've seen in the house, she would have every opportunity to bang on the windows, run out of the house... but she doesn't.'

'It doesn't make sense.' Keris blows out air in frustration. 'Just keep doing what you're doing, Lottie. Try and watch the house as much as possible. You're bound to get a clearer sighting soon.'

When Albie and Neil return, we speak to each other civilly until Albie goes to bed and then Neil and I hardly say another word to each other. He sleeps on the small sofa without me having to ask him to.

We feel further apart than we've ever been in the whole of our marriage.

FORTY-EIGHT

THURSDAY

I'm not at work today, so after taking Albie to school, I come straight back home and take a coffee and slice of toast up to the spare room. Around mid-morning, I watch Neeta open her boot and take a large, bulging bag for life out from the house. I can't see what's in it but it's obvious she's going somewhere.

Whatever was wrong with her yesterday, she seems to be fully recovered now.

I'm ready to go from the school run so I slip on some flat shoes and run out to the car. A few minutes later, Neeta's silver Porsche Boxster crawls past the cottage. I start the engine and then wait a further minute before driving out onto the track. I see her car at the bottom of the hill just turning left. By the time I get down there, there are three vehicles between us. Once we get out of Whitsend Bay, we join the A169, which is the main road out of here. It's also the road that leads to the moors near Pocklington.

There's plenty of traffic on the road and I'm easily able to remain a few vehicles behind Neeta's car. After around an hour, she turns off for the moors.

There is less traffic now and I'm forced to lag quite a way behind, but I know this area and so I anticipate correctly she's heading for a large car park frequented by hikers and dog walkers. I park the other end and watch while Neeta gets out of the car, stretches her arms above her head and then gets a pair of walking boots from the car. She sits in the driver's seat with her legs out and puts them on.

My heart drops a little. She's only doing what lots of people do around here: parking up and going for a walk on the moors. Nothing unusual about that. It's quite a drive from Whitsend Bay, but now it makes more sense because I know this area must hold a lot of memories for Neeta.

I expect her to lock the car and walk away but, first, she takes the large bag from the boot before setting off. I lace my own sturdy walking boots and, after a minute or two, follow at a distance.

Between Neeta and me is a small group of walkers and a couple of dogs. I'm wearing a baseball cap, the peak pulled down low over my face. After about twenty minutes, Neeta veers off at a tangent, away from the path. I let her go and then run quickly to crouch behind a couple of large hawthorn bushes.

The ground is wide open in front of me and I can observe her comfortably from here. Suddenly Neeta stops walking and places the bag down beside her. She sits then in what looks like quiet contemplation for about ten minutes before retrieving a bunch of flowers from the bag and something small and pink. She dabs at her eyes with a tissue, sitting hunched over the flowers that she has arranged simply on the grass.

Slowly, she gets to her feet and I lower my head. As she moves in a wide arc around the cluster of bushes, I'm able to crawl in the opposite direction and remain out of her view. I'm not sure she'd notice me anyway: her face is set and staring, as if she's in another place altogether. She has folded the bag under her arm, the contents left behind where she sat.

I wait for a good five minutes this time until she's away off, heading back towards the car park. Then I stand up and walk over to the spot where the flowers and pink object are. I look down in surprise. A small heart-shaped stone is laid flush in the ground. It's been kept clean and free of earth and I can easily read the lettering.

To our beautiful angel. Forever loved, forever missed.

Stunned, I look at the flowers... daisies and poppies tied with a red ribbon. The small pink item I spotted at a distance is a little furry bear with a red heart on its tummy.

I look around but I can only see walkers at a distance. It's not unusual to see a makeshift grave or tribute here, but I've never seen an engraved stone like this. Most people stick to the formal paths, so would never know it's here.

Still, it's a shock to have witnessed this. If Keris is right and the Williamses faked their daughter's abduction and at the same time are mourning her death... how screwed up is that?

None of it makes any sense.

FORTY-NINE

NEIL

Neeta has been out this morning, so he waits until he sees her car back on the drive before taking a late lunch break.

He walks up to the house and crosses the entrance hallway, muddy footprints from his work boots spoiling the shine on the pristine tiles. Shafts of light descend from the atrium, falling onto the stairs and performing dazzling reflections from the mirrored sections of the steps.

He rubs a hand across his forehead, feeling the slick dampness on his fingers. He's already thrown up twice this morning and he's been unable to complete some urgent orders because his hands are shaking too badly to use the computer in his garden office.

He can't get Lottie's face out of his head. The disappointment etched around her mouth, her dull, vacant eyes. Something very bad is happening in this house, maybe even worse than he's imagined.

Neeta appears in a doorway. 'Sorry I was late back, I thought you weren't going to – gosh, you look awful. Come in.'

He walks into the cool space and feels grateful for the air-conditioning.

He stands in the middle of the large sun room. Out to sea he can see the long shape of what looks like a cruise liner on the horizon. The sky is azure blue and the sea is calm, tiny peaks of white froth dotted here and there. 'I don't want any more nonsense about what you know about me. Just tell me what you want me to do.'

'Come.' He follows her into the room where they sit on chairs facing the view. Neeta fills two glasses from a jug filled with iced water on the wicker and glass table. She hands him one and he drinks greedily. 'Talk to me,' she says.

'I should never have betrayed Lottie about my injuries. Yesterday when I got home, she saw your lipstick on my cheek and she...' His voice fades to nothing.

'She what?'

'She thought we were having an affair. I've had to tell her the truth about what really happened that day.'

Neil drains the glass and puts it down on the table. 'I've come up today to tell you I'm done. I'm not interested in whatever it is you've got in mind, the offer of money. I have to do it for the sake of my marriage.'

'Not so fast, Neil. Ted and I would like to speak to you. Now that you've told Lottie about the accident, the time's come that you both need to know everything.'

'Everything about what?' He's sweating now. His face, the back of his neck, under his arms. He turns at a sound in the doorway behind him. Ted is standing there.

'Everything about what you'll both need to do if you want to have a good life,' Ted says carefully. He walks across the room and pulls up a chair. 'There's no easy way to tell you all this, Neil, so I'm just going to come out and say it.'

'Say what?' Neil feels increasingly queasy. He looks down at the immaculate floor and imagines a pool of his vomit there.

'Let me get you another glass of water,' Neeta says, eyeing his expression. There's something very weird happening between these two and yet he can't put a name to it. He thinks about Lottie's outlandish claims and, suddenly, they don't seem as crazy.

'I'll start at the beginning. You think you found this job yourself but that was an illusion.'

'No, an agency contacted me about it,' Neil says defensively.

Ted gives him a tight smile. 'Actually, Neil, I know a lot of influential people all over the country. It didn't take me too long to find out what really happened on the day of your "accident". As you know, I have a wide range of contacts and I was able to discern through casual enquiries that it wasn't an accident after all but the consequence of you failing to pay some pretty dodgy characters. We waited until you were fit for work again and then we placed the job at Seaspray in your hands.'

Neil picks up the glass of iced water and drains it in one go. 'I haven't a clue what you're talking about.' His voice sounds steady but his stomach is swirling dangerously.

'We're not here to argue, Neil. You need to button it and listen up.' Neeta glares at Ted. 'Just tell him, for God's sake. Tell him everything now.'

'Why don't *you* tell him if you know it all?'

Neil looks from one to the other. His head is pounding and he feels so hot. Lottie was right all along. These people are stone-cold crazy.

'Fine.' Neeta throws her husband a filthy look and then trains her stare to Neil. 'We got you here under false pretences, OK? We know you didn't have an accident, Neil. We know you owed a lot of money to your dealer, the guy who supplied you with illegal painkillers.'

Neil's face drains of colour in an instant. 'But why would you do that, give me the job?'

'It gave us the perfect backdrop to get you both here.'

'But... why? Why are you so interested in me?'

Neeta smiles disingenuously. 'It's not just about you. It's about Lottie, too and, most of all, it's about us.'

Neil looks at her, dumbstruck. The inside of his mouth is prickling with saliva.

'We knew Lottie when she was a child,' Ted says matter-of-factly. 'She doesn't remember us. We're different people on every level, now. But our daughter, Claire, was your wife's friend at school.'

They knew Lottie? How could that be? 'Your daughter? I thought you said you had no children.'

'Our daughter went missing,' Neeta says icily. 'We believe her childminder abducted her. That childminder's name was Kay Price.'

They both watch him steadily. *Kay Price?* Isn't that the name of Lottie's mum? The woman who had abandoned Lottie when she was only thirteen?

'I can see you've made the connection. Lottie's mum disappeared with our daughter.' Neeta watches him.

He knows about her mum taking off one day and never coming back... but abducting a kid? Lottie has never told him anything like that.

Saliva rushes into his mouth. He stands up and Neeta takes one look at his face and realises what's about to happen. 'In there!' She pushes him forward and points to a door.'

Neil staggers into the small cloakroom and vomits into the toilet. He can hear Neeta and Ted bickering outside. He flushes and splashes cold water onto his face before returning to the sun room.

He glances out of the tall windows, out over the gardens to the trees that he knows conceal Lottie's vantage point from the spare room. Is she watching the house now? All that stuff she's said about the Williamses and he accused her of paranoia. Why didn't he listen? And Lottie *knew* their missing daughter? Why on earth has she never shared that with him about her mum?

'You'll have a thousand questions, we know that. This will be a shock, but you need to see everything before you can make sense of it,' Neeta says, almost regretfully.

'There's one more thing you need to do before we tell you everything. Call Lottie and get her up here,' Ted adds. 'Now Lottie knows about the accident, you both need to see this.'

The way they're both looking at him... it makes his flesh crawl. A rush of regret pours through him. He thinks about Lottie and Albie and everything he's taken for granted in his life.

What the hell are these two about to do? Fear trickles through his body like ice-cold poison.

He takes his phone out of his pocket and he calls Lottie.

FIFTY

LOTTIE

I'm still upstairs in the spare bedroom when Neil rings. I'm in no mood for his urgent demand.

'Lottie? I need you to come up to Seaspray House immediately.'

I give a bitter laugh. 'I want you back here to pack a bag. I don't want you anywhere near me or our son.'

All he's said, his promises, his claims to make amends to us both... it's all shot to pieces now.

'Listen to me.' The urgency of his tone takes me back. 'Neeta told me about your school friend going missing, your mum's involvement. They want to talk to us both.'

My heart lurches inside my chest. The Williamses have wrong-footed me, told Neil before I had the chance to explain my own omissions. 'I'm on my way,' I say.

Before I leave the cottage, I quickly text Keris.

Neeta and Ted want to speak to me and Neil up at Seaspray. Think everything might be coming to a head. Please pick up Albie from school if I'm not there.

.   .   .

Neil meets me at the door of Seaspray House. 'I'm sorry I doubted you, Lottie,' he leans in and whispers. 'You were right about them. They're deranged.'

He leads me through the enormous glass entrance hall. I turn my head towards the sun room. The door is closed and I can't hear any singing or crying from in there.

I perch on the end seat of one of the sofas in the palatial lounge. Neeta and Ted are nowhere to be seen. I've wanted to get inside this house for so long, kept thinking what a dream it must be to live somewhere like this. But now, my flesh is crawling and I can't wait to get out of here. But first, I need to hear what they have got to say that's so important and confidential they've summoned us both here.

I glance over at Neil, who sits across from me, his head hanging. Periodically he looks up and I feel his eyes willing me to respond, but I refuse to. I've no interest in interacting with him at the moment. I don't even feel like I know him any longer.

Ted walks in without looking at us and sits in an elaborate French-inspired armchair with its raspberry velvet padded seat cushion and golden scrolls for armrests and decoration behind the head. The house is so clinical and modern-looking, the statement piece of furniture looks out of place. A softness in a place with nothing but hard surfaces.

Neeta enters the room, seeming to glide across it, looking effortlessly elegant in that way she has. I watch her: her features, her mannerisms. I still can't see Yasmin Fuller in there behind the façade. She seems calm and collected and is clearly in control. Now I realise that although Ted has always seemed to be his own man with Neeta often claiming she defers to him, in actual fact, I'd now bet my bottom dollar that Neeta is the one in their relationship who pulls the strings.

Neeta sits down next to Neil and I feel a twinge of jealousy and fury that despite everything, they're so brazen. She takes a breath, glances at Ted and says, 'Lottie, Neil, thank you for agreeing to speak with us. Frankly, the last few days have been extremely stressful – for all of us, I think. It's a relief to speak freely today and get this sorted out. We hope you will feel you can speak freely, too.'

'About the fact you've been lying through your teeth to us all this time?' I snap. It's a relief to speak my mind at last.

'I really hope we can keep this conversation civil,' Neeta replies tightly. Ted starts coughing and reaches for his glass of water. Neeta watches him and waits until he's taken a sip and settles again. 'This will be like no conversation you've ever had or will ever have again, so we all need to just take a breath and put animosity behind us. Focus on the facts... at least at this point in time.'

Everything has always got to be on her terms. She has told so many lies, worn a mask for years and took us for fools from the moment we got to Whitsend Bay. Now she's ready to remove the mask, does she really think we can forget about all that's gone before? Well, fat chance. I've no intention of stopping my sniping and unhelpful comments.

She looks at Ted and he begins to speak. 'A year ago, I was diagnosed with chronic obstructive pulmonary disease. That's COPD for short. You may have heard of the condition?'

Grudgingly, Neil says, 'My dad was a face worker in the coal mines. He died of COPD fifteen years ago.'

Ted nods. 'A lot of miners contracted the disease through exposure to extreme levels of coal dust.'

Neil's father died before we even met, but he told me once how terrible it was watching his dad die, gasping for breath. Near the end, he'd been forced to always keep an oxygen tank by his side. Was this to be Ted's fate?

'For me, it was caused by exposure to asbestos years ago,'

Ted continues. 'I contracted asbestosis and the COPD developed as a complication of that.'

'You've always looked so healthy,' I say guardedly, reminding myself I can't trust a thing they say.

'That may be so, but the last few months it's been harder to hide my symptoms, Lottie. I'm deteriorating rapidly. Even the medication has stopped working as well recently.'

'I've noticed you've had trouble with your breath, and you've needed to rest more during the working day,' Neil remarks.

Ted nods. 'And it's getting worse. That's why we need your help.'

I look quizzically at Neil before I can stop myself. What are they going to ask us to do?

'Ted and I are married only in name,' Neeta says matter-of-factly. 'We would have split up years ago if it hadn't been for... our unsolvable problem.'

'My life expectancy is reduced by the COPD and further complicated by other issues I won't go into at this point in time,' Ted says. 'But the upshot is that doctors have told me my life expectancy might not exceed another five to seven years.'

'Look, we want to change our lives,' Neeta says suddenly. She's fidgeting, chewing the inside of her cheek, the serene image slipping. 'But we can only do that if you agree to our proposal. If you do, your lives will change for the better, too.'

'Are you going to tell us what you want from us, or have we got to guess?' I snap. 'You talked about us being straight with each other – well, I'll kick off. I know you used to be Yasmin and Graham Fuller. I know your daughter, Claire, was supposedly abducted twenty years ago.'

Neeta's face reddens but she doesn't try and deny anything.

'We wondered when you were going to tell us.' She smiles. 'We just discovered your friend Keris Travers was playing a double game and in league with Tom and Mary Gooding.'

I'm emboldened and annoyed by her casual response. The way they have feelers out in everyone else's lives. 'For what it's worth, I think you have someone else living in this house,' I say, looking around the walls. 'And I think that person is your "missing" daughter, Claire.'

Ted rubs his forehead. 'Christ.'

I'm encouraged by his reaction even though Neeta remains stony-faced. Neil regards me with amazement. It's fairly obvious I just hit the bullseye.

'You sound confident, Lottie,' Neeta says. 'Or should I say *Charlie*? So can I ask, if you're so certain of your theory, why you haven't gone to the police?'

FIFTY-ONE

'You knew the girl who went missing, knew she was Ted and Neeta's daughter but you never told me.' Neil looks at me aghast.

'That makes two of us that kept things to ourselves then,' I shoot back, sounding more confident than I feel. 'I was thirteen years old when Mum left and these two fraudsters weren't Ted and Neeta back then. I didn't recognise either of them when we moved here.' I regard them both. 'They look very, very different to how I remember.'

'We're all very different now to the people we were twenty years ago.' Neeta looks at me. 'You're a completely different person, *Lottie*. You've reinvented yourself, too.'

I blank her. I won't let her intimidate me. I was just a kid back then.

Neil is staring at me with an expression I recognise. He's thinking, *Who is this person I thought I knew?* Well, now he knows how it feels. I don't care what he thinks any more. But it does feel right we get all this out in the open now.

'I told you Mum left, but... she left under a shadow.' I address Neil and block the Williamses out. 'She was accused of having something to do with Claire's disappearance. These two made her life a living hell with the media and the local community and now—' I glare at Neeta '—you've virtually confirmed my suspicions are correct and therefore Tom and Mary Gooding are right, too. It seems Mum was innocent after all. Because Claire wasn't abducted.'

Neil looks shell-shocked.

'Too many lies, secrets and old grievances,' Neeta mumbles almost to herself. Then she stands up unexpectedly. 'It's been interesting to hear your theories, but enough is enough. It's time for the truth. Follow me.'

Ted's face looks grey. He stands up and follows his wife out of the room. Neil and I are led into the sun room. My heartbeat is throbbing in my throat. The crying, the lullaby, the shadowy figure I've seen in here... I haven't seen Claire for nearly twenty years.

Neeta walks across the room to the bookshelves I stood in front of yesterday. Ted pushes the rattan furniture aside before Neeta places her hands on the antique doll on the end of the shelf and makes a quick, strange manoeuvre. A low, mechanical hum begins. She presses a button and a large square of floor opens up. She steps down onto something solid and the hum increases as she is lowered down before the floor slides back into place.

The floor is solid again and, if Ted were to push the furniture back into place, nothing would look amiss in the room. Neeta has disappeared into thin air and the humming sound has stopped.

'What the hell...' Neil murmurs.

'You have her,' I whisper to Ted. 'You actually have your daughter imprisoned down there.' I've known it, suspected it all this time but seeing *this*... this trick with my own eyes is still shocking.

The quiet whirring begins again. Ted covers his face with

his hands as if that might block out what's happening. The tops of two heads appear as the platform travels up to ground level until the two women are revealed.

And suddenly, there she is in front of my very eyes. And the world stops turning.

FIFTY-TWO

MAY, EIGHTEEN YEARS EARLIER

On Sunday morning, the Fullers arrived back after their corporate weekend away. Yasmin had spoken to Kay several times over the day and night they'd been absent and she'd also spoken to Claire before bed last night.

Her daughter had been in good spirits and was looking forward to takeaway pizza and a movie with Kay.

Yasmin didn't panic at first. Kay was thirty minutes late dropping Claire back home, which was unusual, but then she didn't usually keep Claire overnight. Kay's bad back was probably grumbling and there would be Claire's overnight bag to pack before bringing her back home at the agreed time of ten-thirty.

When it got to eleven-fifteen, Yasmin had unpacked, made a coffee and then she called Kay. The call went straight to answerphone. She rang her landline, which rang out. At twelve noon, she and Graham got in the car and drove over to Kay's house. There was nobody home. The neighbour came out and said she'd seen Kay and Claire getting into the car and said they were going for a walk before she dropped Claire back at home.

'I've got a horrible feeling about this,' Yasmin told Graham as he reversed off the driveway. 'I think I made a bad mistake. I should never have left Claire in that woman's care. What if she's been drinking and driving?'

'Don't be silly. She's a registered childminder,' Graham reasoned. 'And she's looked after Claire for a while now. You're just panicking.'

Claire had told Yasmin on many occasions that Kay liked to walk on the moors. 'It's boring, Mum,' she'd said. 'There are no swings or slide and Kay goes on and on about the colour of the heather, or which birds nest there. Charlie gets out of it because you've told her she's not allowed to play with me.'

Yasmin had laughed. 'I know Kay is a firm believer that children need fresh air and, let's be honest, Claire, you don't get much. You'd rather watch *Tracy Beaker* than go out walking.'

Claire had scowled. 'Maybe it's because *Tracy Beaker* is actually *interesting*.'

'We've got another mile and a half on this road, then turn right,' she told her husband. Yasmin thought how grown-up Claire was getting. Sure, she had a bit of attitude at times, but she was generally quite funny and Yasmin loved spending time with her. It was just handy to have Kay's services for when it all got a bit much for her.

Graham spotted the car as they drove around the isolated roads. 'That's Kay's blue Nissan.' He pointed. 'I wonder if they've got lost or something. Let's climb that little incline and we should be able to spot them easily.

They climbed up and looked around. It was early afternoon and the light was good. 'Bloody nothing,' Yasmin cursed in frustration. 'I should have never trusted that woman.'

'Don't panic,' Graham said. 'They're probably around here somewhere but in a – wait. Is that them?'

A single arm, waving. The person was lying down. 'That's them,' Yasmin said breathlessly, taking off running. 'We saw Kay's car so this must be her. She must have hurt her back and had to lie flat.'

'But... where's Claire?' Graham said, looking around. 'I hope she hasn't left her alone so she can get help.'

'God, don't say that, Graham.' She narrowed her eyes and shouted. 'Claire?'

Kay began waving harder and yelling. 'I think we need to get over there right away,' Graham said.

When they reached Kay, she was wailing and groaning so much Yasmin couldn't tell a word she was saying. When she looked around and there was no sign of her daughter, the panic rose up inside her like a tidal wave.

'Where's Claire? Where is she?'

Graham ran away from them, shouting out Claire's name.

Yasmin reached down and grabbed Kay's arm, causing her to yelp out in pain. 'Shut the hell up and tell me... where's my daughter?' she yelled.

But Kay did not stop wailing. She raised her other hand and pointed to the direction Graham was running in.

'She... I told her... oh God, no! I told her not to run... to be careful...'

Yasmin pulled roughly again on the childminder's arm and Kay screamed out. 'My back... stop! I think I've slipped some discs. That's why I couldn't go after her. That's why—'

'For God's sake, you're not making any sense,' Yasmin screeched. 'Where's my daughter? Just tell me!'

As suddenly as she'd started, Kay stopped wailing and fell silent. Then she pointed again to a crop of rocks very close to where Graham now stood shouting Claire's name.

'She's over there,' Kay said in a hoarse whisper.

. . .

Graham climbed back up the bank and held Yasmin tightly, his hand covering her eyes in an effort to stop her seeing the broken body of their daughter.

'She's gone, Yasmin,' he sobbed. 'There's no pulse.'

She felt completely empty inside. Quiet and numb. She'd left her daughter in the care of that... that incapable woman, helped her get away from her deadbeat life against her better judgement and now... now she'd lost everything worth living for.

Graham released Yasmin and cursed. 'Not a wisp of a signal to be had up here. Let's get you back to the car and I'll drive until we can call the police.'

Yasmin thought about Kay's back problems, the fact she'd had a hard life and could pass this off as an accident. If she hadn't been drinking it would be just a sad accident...

'No. She's not getting away with this.' Shaking, Yasmin turned from her daughter's lifeless body and looked tearfully at her husband. 'We'll take them both home with us and then decide what to do.'

FIFTY-THREE

LOTTIE

Neeta leads the wretched figure, the person who used to be my friend, Claire, across the room. She still has her head down and her shoulders stooped, preventing me from seeing her features. Claire will be nearly thirty years old now, but she walks like a much older woman.

She stops moving suddenly, as if she's only just become aware there are other people in the room. She lifts her head and looks around and my breath catches in my throat. Her face, worn and wrinkled, her pale eyes meet mine and then I see it. I know in an instant the whole story.

A strangled noise fills the air and I realise it's coming from me.

'Mum?' I whisper. Then louder, 'Mum? Is it... is it really you? It's me... it's Charlie.'

Everyone is looking at me. Neil stands frozen.

I rush forward, my arms outstretched and then stop just inches away from her. She's hunched over, but at the sound of my voice, she looks up at me like a frightened animal and huddles into Neeta's side.

Our eyes lock together. We have the same dark-blue eyes. Both filled with tears of disbelief and horror.

'Mum?' Gently, slowly, I try to fold my arms around her bony form. She inches closer still to Neeta, rigid and weak. 'It's me, Charlie. Oh Mum, oh God...'

Why is she turning away from me and to the monster who's kept her a prisoner all this time? That can't be right.

I feel Neil's hand on my shoulder. I haven't got the strength to shrug him off but I don't want him near me. I just want to hold my mum... and more than anything, I want her to hold me, too.

She's in her mid-seventies now but she could be in her late eighties. It's clear she can't fully straighten her back and her baggy brown skirt and cream T-shirt hang from her bony frame. She looks so frail... this small shadow of a person I've been watching from the bedroom window.

Neeta's hand tentatively pats Mum's back as she continues to try and nestle closer to her. Neeta's expression tells the story of a person who is just tolerating the moment but can't wait until this embarrassing inconvenience has passed. Mum shifts her head slightly until she can see me.

In that moment, I realise that all the hurt that has damaged Mum over the last twenty years has ensured that she can never be the same. I will never get the mum I used to know back again. The chance of ever making things right between us has been taken from me by what they've done to her.

I take my hands from Mum and turn, slowly, to face Neeta Williams. She's not cowering, doesn't look away from my intense stare.

'You...' I fly at Neeta, fingers bent like claws. I'm moving fast, like lightning. My features are pulled tight into a scream. I can hear myself, feel the momentum running powerfully through me. I have only one thought in my head. *Make her pay.*

Neil wraps his arms around me from behind like a bear hug. 'Let me go!' I yell and struggle.

'Calm down, Lottie,' he hisses in my ear. 'Calm down. Think of your mum. We need to get her out of here.'

'Yes, calm down Lottie,' Neeta says. 'You don't know everything yet. You don't know why I've organised this little reunion or why we brought you and Neil to Seaspray House in the first place. It's time for us to tell you a little story.'

FIFTY-FOUR

'About four months ago, Duncan, your mum's old friend, turned up at the front door,' Ted says.

My breath catches in my throat and I can't speak for a moment. Memories of creepy Duncan, the threats he'd make when Mum was working, the way he'd assault me if I came out of my bedroom.

'He'd been looking for us for years, apparently. Bent on revenge because we whisked you and your mum away to a better life away from him,' Ted continues. 'He'd finally managed to get himself clean through some kind of NHS rehab facility. Although he'd stopped drinking, the rehab didn't improve who he was as a person. He was here for one reason... money.'

'He'd been skulking around watching the house,' Neeta adds, shuddering. 'Seen things he shouldn't at the windows. Seen *people* he shouldn't.'

'He saw Mum?' I say faintly.

Neeta nods. 'He told us, if we didn't pay him off, he'd go straight to the police and to the papers, too.'

Ted sighs. 'Fool that I am, I did give him money. A

substantial amount of money. I thought that had done the trick because he disappeared and we didn't hear anything else.'

Neeta rubs her forehead. 'Still, we knew something had to change or we were going to be in big, big trouble. Ted's health was failing and we knew that before long, Duncan would probably start telling anyone who would listen that he'd seen your mum in here.'

'Then you mentioned the sighting of someone skulking around in the early hours to Neil. That could only be one person.'

'Duncan?' I whisper.

Ted nods. 'We knew we had to act fast but we didn't panic too much, not at first. I'd designed the subterranean annexe well enough that I felt confident nobody would find it on a routine inspection. So even if the police came here, we weren't in any immediate danger.'

But if it was Duncan I'd seen sneaking around in the middle of the night then he is back on the scene. 'Is Duncan blackmailing you again?'

A strange smile passes across Ted's lips. 'No. Duncan is no longer a threat, thankfully.'

I frown, not understanding. 'Have you paid him off again?'

'No, no. Sadly, we heard Duncan was killed two days ago in a hit and run accident,' Neeta says simply.

I gasp. 'And you two are behind his death?'

'Absolutely not!' Ted scowls. 'Seems he's been using our money to rekindle his longstanding relationship with the demon drink and staggered into the road back in Pocklington. A car hit him but didn't stop. So, happily, Duncan is no longer a problem to us.'

'Poetic justice,' Neeta simpers, oblivious to the irony of her own despicable behaviour.

Ted coughs. 'Still, all this was a big wake-up call. We knew the time had come to move on with our lives and that left one very big problem... what to do with Kay.'

'Whatever you might think of us, we're not murderers,' Neeta says defensively.

But I still have so many unanswered questions.

'The day you found Claire's body, why didn't you just go to the police and let them deal with Mum, decide if she was guilty of your daughter's death in some way?'

'Let her give them some sob story about fainting and it being an accident and have them let her go free? Never! Once we knew we'd lost Claire, the only thing left for us to give us any chance of peace was to punish Kay. It just took us a few days to work out how to do it. That meant we had to bury our beloved daughter and keep it to ourselves.'

The grave on the moors I saw her visit...

'What started out as a revenge – our conviction that Claire had died at the hands of your mum, so why should she have her freedom – morphed into something else very quickly.'

'We realised we couldn't just release Kay, or we'd go to prison. Months passed; years rolled by. Kay became... I don't know, *dependent* on us. This sounds hard to believe but she doesn't want to escape. Look at her... she's dependent on us. She's become family.'

'Don't you dare presume that. You kept her here against her will. All these years I've been tortured, wondering what happened. Mum never left me. It was all your doing.'

'Maybe so... at first. But over time she stopped being a prisoner and accepted her situation. She was afraid of the outside world and that's why she stuck to the shadows. That's why we kept the house closed down to visitors, so Kay had some freedom within these walls.'

'Stockholm syndrome,' Neil murmurs.

'There's an element of that, I'm sure. But to this day, Kay completely blames herself for Claire's death and wants to make amends. Her annexe is filled with Claire's things. She sings songs our daughter loved and cries for hours on end,' Ted says. 'Her mental health has deteriorated to the point where she believes Claire is alive and a baby again.'

The lullaby I heard...

'She clearly needs medical help and you failed to provide that,' I say from behind gritted teeth. 'It's a complete tissue of lies to tell yourself she's wanted to be here, stuck in an underground hellhole for almost two decades.'

Neeta is undaunted. 'Your mum has formed a bond with us to the extent we've been able to allow her regular time outside her annexe for years.'

'Her prison, you mean,' I snap. 'You never let her out in the sun, in the garden. You've never sought help for her.'

'Don't you see, we couldn't do that!' Neeta cries out. 'We'd have gone to prison. You must see that. We were in a catch-22 position.'

'We've spent hours, days, trying to think around the problem. Then Neeta came up with the idea of getting you two here under the guise of a job.' Ted starts to cough.

Neeta hands him a glass of water and we wait until he can continue. 'Ted had kept an eye on you for years. So it wasn't that hard to set things up.'

Ted starts to talk about how he set the estate manager position up to tempt Neil to apply. I hear words like 'CV', 'agency' and 'interview', but I can't focus on his words because I'm watching Mum.

She's moved slightly away from Neeta now and she stands looking down at her clasped hands in front of her. The hands that held me and nursed me as a young child, the hands that sometimes slapped me away in frustration as I got older in her many episodes of drunken frustration.

Neil's affronted by what Ted is saying. I'm vaguely aware of him asking questions, demanding answers. I sidestep away from them all and move closer to Mum.

She looks up from her hands, her eyes flicker onto my face and she quickly looks down again. I stand still and calm in front of her. I don't move any closer. She looks up again then looks away. Looks again… and this time, our eyes lock together for a couple of seconds.

'I'm Charlie, your daughter,' I whisper. 'I've missed you so much, Mum.'

Her face remains frozen like a mask, but I think there's the slightest flicker behind her eyes. I can sense her there, taking it all in.

'Do you recognise me, Mum?' I feel sick with desperation to hold her, to wrap my arms around her but I know that will be too much for her.

She's looking at me for longer now, before looking away. But she still doesn't speak. She hasn't said a single word yet.

My heart squeezes in on itself as I realise the cold, hard truth. I might as well be a stranger standing here for all Mum remembers me.

FIFTY-FIVE

'Lottie?' Neil waves a hand in front of my face and I focus on his pale, drawn features. 'Come on, we're taking your mum to the cottage. Let's get her out of here.'

Neil carries Mum down to the cottage, accompanied by Ted. I thank my lucky stars Albie is with Keris. I don't know how we're going to explain all this to him. He's going to feel like the ground is shifting beneath his feet. Just like I do.

It's a priority I let Keris know what's happening, the crazy developments that have been made since my last text to her. But I can't do that now. We have to sort Mum out first.

We get her comfortable in the living room to start with... as comfortable as we can. Mum sits in the chair with her arms wrapped around herself, rocking back and forth. She reminds me of a wild animal that's just been contained. Her head is turning, her eyes searching the walls, the floor, the ceiling. She doesn't feel safe.

If Albie comes home to this he's going to be traumatised. We have to do what's best for Mum, but we have to think of Albie's wellbeing, too.

'She's completely self-sufficient,' Neeta is saying like we're discussing the needs of a rescue dog. 'She can carry out her own self-care: shower, dress, use the bathroom. You can make her meals but her appetite is very small.'

I look at this thin, broken woman. She's not the mum I used to know, will never be so again. Between them, Ted and Neeta Williams have destroyed her. Suddenly Neeta's casual words and instructions fill me with fury.

'You bitch. You cruel, heartless cow.' I turn on her. 'What happened to Claire was an accident. The punishment you've meted out to my mum does not fit the crime.'

'An accident caused by Kay's drinking and neglect, no doubt,' Neeta says crisply, not an ounce of emotion in her voice.

'You had no right. Mum had a disease. She was an alcoholic. You must have known that but you still employed her to look after Claire. To save money because Ted's business was in trouble.'

Ted speaks up. 'Of course you're angry, Lottie, I can understand that. But you must realise we never expected it to go on so long. We didn't think it through. We were just crippled by grief and the need to avenge Claire's death.'

'Why should Kay continue to be a mother to you when she'd robbed me of my daughter?' Neeta spits. 'It was natural justice, despite what the law said.'

'There's nothing you can do now to stop me calling the police,' I say calmly. 'All your efforts have been for nothing. You've just delayed the point where you go to prison.'

'That's as may be,' Ted says, giving me a sad smile. 'But if you go to the authorities, they won't let you keep your mum. Surely, you know that? She'll have to be investigated for her part in Claire's death too. She'll have to go through psychological evaluations before they decide she's unfit to stand trial and that can take months and months... maybe longer. Then there's the press interest. The media storm would be crazy; it would invade every area of your life. Unearth all your own secrets.'

Neil's so-called accident, his addiction, Mum's alcoholism...

'The press blamed her for Claire's disappearance back then and they'd do the same now. Look at her, Lottie. You can't do that to her; it will finish her off.'

My eyes flick to Mum, sitting completely still with her hands neatly folded in her lap, staring at the wall. Her skin is grey, her eyes faded and dull. She is a mere husk of the woman she used to be.

An unbidden question presents itself. *Was I better off before I found Mum again?* At least my feelings of abandonment were familiar, like a recurring ache that's hard to bear... but that I knew would go away again soon. I don't know where to start with the tidal wave of emotion that's coming for me now.

Mum didn't leave me; she was taken. Now I've found her... and she doesn't want me all over again.

'How long has she got to live? How long do you have with her, for her to get to know her grandson and hopefully enjoy what life she has left? We'll give you enough money you need never worry again,' Ted says smoothly. 'Alternatively, if you want her to spend her last few years in an institution, then so be it. Go ahead and call the police.'

Neeta steps forward and holds out her hands, imploring me. 'Do the right thing for all of us, Lottie. That is, give your mum a happy life and yourselves, too.'

I look away from her in disgust. 'What about Keris? What about Tom and Mary Gooding? These people all know what you're up to, can blow your cover at any time. Are you going to pay them off, too?'

'They *suspect*, but they know nothing for certain,' Ted says firmly. 'They've seen shadows; they have never seen enough of Kay to identify her. They think our behaviour has been odd, but being odd is not a crime. Only the people standing here, right now in this room, know the facts of the matter. But time is of the essence. We must all move fast.'

Neeta continues. 'We'll be gone in a few weeks and nobody will ever find us. Ted has sorted out new passports, identities for us. You will have the financial means to start a new life anywhere you choose and, if you wish, Ted can help you with that too.'

'A narrow window of opportunity has opened for us all to start again,' Ted adds. 'But it won't be there for long.' He looks at both of us in turn. 'The decision, the fate of us all lies in your hands now.'

Neil reaches for my hand and turns to them. 'Go now. Leave us. We can talk again in the morning.'

FIFTY-SIX

The weekend that the Fullers were away had gone well. Kay had kept her promise to Mrs Fuller: she had stayed well away from the drink and had felt better for it.

There had been times, over the past couple of days, she'd have dearly loved a couple of gins to help ease her back pain, but she hadn't given in. She'd taken a couple of painkillers that had helped take the edge off, but that was it.

The weekend had been hard work, but Kay hoped that when Mrs Fuller returned, she'd realise Kay could be trusted to do a good job after all and scrap her plan to fire her and evict them from the flat. Even Charlie had been better behaved than usual. She could easily get jealous of Claire getting all the attention and that in turn could make her peevish and mean. Kay loved her daughter dearly, but Charlie would have a very different life to the over-protected Claire Fuller and that coloured Kay's treatment of her.

The hard knocks of life would not get anywhere near Claire Fuller in the cosseted world she was being raised in. But Charlie... well, her Charlie was a different story. The only gift Kay could give her daughter – at least the only one that would do her any good – was the gift of resilience. Kay herself had enjoyed a gentle upbringing and really, what good had it done her? The brutality and deprivation of adult life had shaken her to the core. She wanted Charlie to grow up prepared for what life could, and no doubt would, throw at her. *Tough love.* That's what they called it. Kay was raising Charlie with plenty of tough love and she felt certain her daughter would understand and undoubtedly thank her for it when she got older.

It was with this attitude in mind that Kay reacted when Charlie whinged and whined to go to the moors with them on the Saturday morning the Fullers were returning. The answer had been a resounding *no*. Kay was still angry with Charlie for bullying Claire. When Yasmin Fuller had turned up at the front door, Kay had wanted the ground to open up and swallow her. When she told Kay what Charlie had been doing, she'd had to grovel and apologise and that was going to take lots of time and lots of chores for Charlie to make up.

'I'd rather stay in and watch television with Charlie,' Claire said in a petulant voice when Kay told her to get ready. 'The moors are boring and it might be muddy there.'

Kay rolled her eyes. She was such a prissy little thing. 'Stop fussing. There hasn't been enough rain to make it muddy! Come on, get your boots on. I don't want your mum thinking I've just plonked you in front of the box all weekend. Fresh air's what you need to put some colour in those pale cheeks before we get you back home.'

Claire's temper worsened shortly after they set off in the car when Kay revealed she'd left Claire's water bottle in the kitchen. 'I'm thirsty,' she whined. 'I won't be able to walk far at all, now.'

Kay was fast losing patience. She felt tired because her back had been hurting her all night long. Driving was only making it worse so she felt relieved when they reached the moors. She left her phone in the vehicle because she knew, from her many trips up here, there was no phone signal at all once you left the car park.

Claire was evidently still in a mood and set off well in front of Kay, her feet stomping the ground unnecessarily hard. Kay found she couldn't keep up.

'Slow down, Claire. My back is hurting me this morning, you know that.'

Kay's words fell on deaf ears. Claire had slipped into full-on spoilt brat mode and all Kay could do was wait for her to stomp her way out of it. But that didn't quite go to plan.

Over the next few minutes, Claire purposely sped up, looking back and smirking as Kay lagged even further behind. Once they'd got beyond the car park, they hadn't seen another soul and Kay worried that Claire could get lost if she persisted in racing ahead.

Finally, the childminder's patience snapped. 'That's enough, young lady. Stop this silliness right now. Stop walking!'

A peal of laughter and then Claire called, 'Catch me if you can!' And took off, running off in the direction of a dangerous area Kay happened to know featured a hidden, sharp drop.

'Wait! Claire, please,' Kay called but her charge was picking up the pace. The bottom of her back cramped in protest. 'We're not going that way... stop!'

Gasping and holding her back as she struggled on, Kay was relieved to look up and see Claire had finally stopped running. She'd sat down and appeared to be waiting for Kay. She breathed a sigh of relief and eased off slightly, but as she drew closer, the girl sprang up again and started off.

'Claire, stop! Don't run here, you're too close to the edge.'

The wind picked up and took Kay's words along with it. Claire was full of mischief, running and looking behind her in delight at Kay's vain attempt to catch up.

Kay pushed against the pain to speed up and then cried out as a tremendous jolt shot up her leg, into her hip and she fell forward, twisting her spine as she tried to right herself. White light flashed before her eyes as her back spasmed and suddenly, she was looking up at the blue sky and white clouds and she could not move an inch.

After a few seconds, and realising she must stay completely still until help came, Kay was able to process what had happened. She'd stepped into a hole, lost her balance and was now marooned on her back in absolute agony.

'Claire,' she called, hardly making a sound at all. 'Claire, wait... be careful.' She needed Claire to come back and to raise the alarm back at the car park.

There was no response and then Kay heard Claire cry out and scream and then... well, then there was nothing at all.

FIFTY-SEVEN

MARY

When Ted and Neeta return home, Mary Gooding stands outside the open doors of the sun room, in the gardens of Seaspray House, and watches as they pour drinks and congratulate themselves.

'We did it.' Ted holds up his glass. 'I think we've bloody well pulled it off!'

Neeta bites her bottom lip. 'Although they haven't actually agreed to it yet, don't forget.'

'It's a done deal.' Ted puffs out his chest and takes a deep breath in without coughing. 'There's no way they'll turn down our offer. They'll ruin their own lives as well as ours if they go to the police.'

'That thing about you only having a short time to live was genius, I'll give you that,' Neeta adds.

They chuckle softly and take a sip of their drinks.

A sharp pain shoots through Mary's skull and she squeezes her eyes shut and presses hard on her temples with both hands until it abates. This couple, they specialise in ruining the lives of the people around them. The very people who have shown them unerring loyalty and commitment.

She steps inside the sun room and the door creaks as she closes it behind her, causing the couple to turn round sharply.

'*Mary?*' Neeta lets out a startled noise. 'What the hell are you doing here?'

'Get out of this house now!' Ted storms forward, still holding his drink. His face turns puce as he raises his other hand as if to strike her. He thinks her so pathetic and weak he can fend her off with one hand. Well, she'll show him.

His face falls when she raises her arm and he sees she is clutching a large ball pein hammer. The crack of his skull is loud and clear like a whip. It splits the air around them as well as Ted's bone. The blood spatters everywhere on those beautiful white tiles and he seems, to her, to fall in slow motion, the heavy cut-glass tumbler slipping from his hand and shattering into a thousand pieces like the crystals on those beautiful chandeliers.

Mary smiles down at Ted's lifeless body, his staring, sightless eyes. Turns out he's not such a tough guy after all.

Neeta's blood-curdling screams fill the room. She drops her own glass and starts to run. But it's too late. Mary is already on her, bashing with the hammer on Neeta's shoulder, her arm and a good hard blow to the side of her head that sends her staggering back.

Somehow, Neeta manages to recover and she's off up the stairs like a slippery, deadly serpent under all those fancy clothes and finery.

But Neeta is injured and slow and Mary easily catches up with her before she reaches the bedroom.

'Too late to lock the door,' she sings softly as Neeta begins to beg, blood pouring from her head wound. Mary tips her head to the side as she regards her previous employer curiously. 'What's that phrase you used a little while ago? *Poetic justice*, that was it! Well, now it's time to pay for what you've done, for ruining all our lives.'

'Mary, please. Don't! Please don't hurt me,' Neeta sobs. 'It was Ted that insisted on getting rid of Tom from the cottage. I tried to change his mind; I swear I did. I always liked you both and—'

Mary frowns and narrows her eyes. 'My Tom had a heart attack yesterday. Did you know that?' she says quietly in her strange sing-song manner. 'They tried their best to save him but he died in the ambulance.'

'Oh Mary, no. I'm so sorry. I am.'

'He never got over the shame and the embarrassment of the lies you told about him assaulting you. The community he grew up in and loved, they turned against him, against us. And it broke his heart, do you know that?' Mary raises the hammer.

'I can give you money, lots of money,' Neeta shrieks, her wild eyes pinned to Mary's hand. 'You can buy a house, start again somewhere new and—'

Just before Mary begins to rain blows down on Neeta's head, she smiles and says calmly through the screaming, 'This is the only thing I want. I want it more than anything in the world.'

Afterwards, when the deed is done, Mary goes back downstairs to find the cleaning equipment.

She hums happily as she begins to scrub away the unsightly stains. Mary has always been good at cleaning and this is a beautiful house that deserves to sparkle again. The pain in her head has gone now. She's felt so much better since she stopped taking all that unnecessary medication the hospital gave her.

It's true, she's always known something was wrong, here at Seaspray House. She'd known, almost from the very moment they'd arrived, that the day would come when everyone finally saw the truth. Despite everyone telling her she was imagining things, Mary had felt the pressure building like a knotted rope slowly tightening around her neck. So in some ways, it was no surprise to see that poor, wretched woman paraded in front of Lottie and Neil.

But never, not in a million years, had she expected it all to end like this. To hear them say they'd buried their own child in an unmarked grave and concealed her death. It was a travesty, a terrible crime.

Still, Mary thinks, taking a moment to enjoy the wonderful view of the ocean and the sunshine streaming in at the windows, the Williamses were big on people getting what they deserved.

Mary has certainly seen justice done today. Her Tom would have been so proud.

EPILOGUE

LOTTIE

THREE MONTHS LATER

Keris volunteers to pick up Mrs Cornell and bring her back to our house. We're enjoying glorious weather for September and Mum is sitting in the garden with Albie so I'm just putting together a few small plates of snacks for us to nibble on as we all catch up over a few cups of tea. I've made a Victoria sponge for dessert. I remember it was always Mum's favourite.

I'm looking forward to seeing Mrs Cornell again; it's going to be good for us all to get together again. Mum's regular visits to the hospital and her need for a stable, uneventful life mean she's not able to travel long distances, but doctors say a friendly face from the past will do her the world of good.

We're renting a pleasant three-bedroomed house with a good-sized garden in Whitby, which is only about eight minutes away from Seaspray in the car. It means Albie can stay at the same school, then, next September, he'll start at secondary school with Edie, which is even closer.

Neil has got a job at a landscaping company also in the area and I've just been promoted at JLG Sports so I'm now Mel's assistant manager.

What happened at Seaspray House all seems like a long time ago now and yet, sometimes, in the middle of the night when I wake to check Mum's OK, I see the dark square of window next to my bed and for a split second, I think I'm back there.

The day Mary Gooding came back to Seaspray, I forgot to text Keris when we took Mum back down to the cottage. She'd already tried my phone and couldn't get an answer, so Keris took a gamble and called the police. By this time, the Williamses had left the cottage and returned to Seaspray when Neil told them we'd think about their offer.

'I didn't know what had happened, but I had this really bad feeling,' Keris told me. 'I didn't want to come up there with the kids but I knew it had to stop. Knew it was time to get the police involved. I'd just heard that Tom Gooding had died of a heart attack and I thought, enough is enough.'

Unbeknown to us, from the garden, Mary had witnessed the whole thing with us finding Mum up at Seaspray. When they returned from the cottage, she attacked the Williamses. When the police arrived, Mary was in the process of trying to clean the place of their blood. The detective inspector told us she thought the house was pristine, but she'd barely scratched the surface. Keris visits Mary, who is currently in a clinic recovering from a breakdown before evaluations will take place on her mental health. She's a kind, good woman who the Williamses pushed too far. When she lost her beloved Tom, she lost control of everything.

We don't know what will happen to Seaspray Estate yet. The Williamses died intestate, so there's a lot of legal wrangling to be done, of which we'll thankfully have no part.

Neil and I are receiving couples' counselling. We've decided we want to try and iron out some of our problems.

We've both lied to each other; both of us have regrets. But one thing we agree on is that we do love each other and we want to try and keep our family together for ourselves and for Albie.

Claire Fuller's body has been exhumed from the moors and she was given a funeral and official burial locally. Sometimes I take flowers to the churchyard where she's been laid to rest and talk to her about the old days. I wasn't such a great friend, but I've forgiven myself for that. I tried my best under difficult circumstances and I was just a kid.

I walk outside now to check on Mum and Albie. She's holding a tiny bouquet of daisies and buttercups he's picked for her. Mum still doesn't say much but she's responding a lot more, smiling and nodding and she does say the odd thing.

But last night was a milestone. I made her a cup of tea in bed, plumped up her pillows and brushed her hair gently off her face. I put on her favourite, André Rieu, and made sure the volume wasn't too loud and that the remote control was in her reach.

'I'll pop back in a little while to get you comfortable before you sleep, Mum,' I said before kissing her on her forehead. Then, as I did every night, I whispered, 'I love you so much, Mum.'

She sort of croaked, a strange sound I hadn't heard before. I turned around and then I heard her broken, cracked voice. 'Love you, Charlie,' she said softly and then, 'I never left you.'

I rushed back to the bed and reached for her hand. 'I know that now, Mum. I know.'

When I stepped outside the room, I could barely breathe for the tears of happiness that coursed down my cheeks.

When I see Mum and Albie are OK, I go back inside. Walking up the garden, I look at the house next door. We don't know them very well, have only said hello a few times.

They're quite strange. She hardly goes out of the house and he seems to spend his time tinkering around in the shed at the bottom of the garden. One thing I've learned is that it takes all sorts and you're never quite sure what people get up to behind closed doors.

Still, I've promised Neil I'm keeping well away from the spare room window.

For now at least.

A LETTER FROM K.L. SLATER

Thank you so much for reading *The Bedroom Window* and I really hope you enjoyed the book. If you did and would like to keep up to date with all my latest releases, just sign up at the following link. Your email address will never be shared and you can unsubscribe at any time.

www.bookouture.com/kl-slater

The witness protection programme has always fascinated me: how, with the help of police specialists, people change their names, appearances and personal history and manage to live their lives with the people around them being none the wiser. In *The Bedroom Window*, I sort of flipped that idea around, so a couple who appear, to all intents and purposes, to be one thing, when secretly they are disguising and building falsehoods to hoodwink others and avoid detection for a heinous crime.

As always, I was interested in writing the book about how past events shape us in different ways and to explore the conundrum of whether we can truly escape our past until we face it head-on.

I love a nice juicy plot as much as the next reader, but what I find more fascinating are the relationships – good and bad – between people. The suspicions, the undercurrents and tensions... I hope I have managed to capture a little of this in *The Bedroom Window*.

This book is set largely in North Yorkshire, the coastline of which my husband and I visit often. I love the Yorkshire people, the food and the landscape and I am lucky to regard it as a second home. Readers should be aware I'm a devil for often taking the liberty of changing street names or geographical details to suit the story.

I do hope you enjoyed reading *The Bedroom Window* and getting to know the characters. If so, I would be very grateful if you could take a few minutes to write a review. I'd love to hear what you think, and it makes such a difference helping new readers to discover one of my books for the first time.

I love hearing from my readers – you can get in touch on my Facebook page, through Twitter, Goodreads or my website.

Thank you to all my wonderful readers... until next time,

Kim x

https://klslaterauthor.com

facebook.com/KimLSlaterAuthor
twitter.com/KimLSlater

ACKNOWLEDGEMENTS

Writing is a solitary business but there are so many people that have my back!

Huge thanks to my editor at Bookouture, Lydia Vassar-Smith, for her expert insight and editorial support.

Thanks to ALL the Bookouture team for everything they do – which is so much more than I can document here. I'm so grateful for all the people from all departments who work like a well-oiled machine to get my books out there to my wonderful readers.

Thanks, as always, to my wonderful literary agent, Camilla Bolton, who is always there with expert advice and unwavering support at the end of a text, an email, a phone call. Thanks also to Camilla's assistant, the wonderful Jade Kavanagh, who works so hard on my behalf. Thanks also to the rest of the hard-working team at Darley Anderson Literary, TV and Film Agency.

I am very grateful to copyeditor Donna Hillyer and proof-reader Becca Allen, who have both cast their eagle eyes over the story and made it the best it can be.

Thanks as always to my writing buddy, Angela Marsons, who continues to be a brilliant support and inspiration to me in my writing career.

Massive thanks as always go to my family, especially to my husband and daughter, who are always so understanding and willing to put outings on hold and to rearrange to suit writing deadlines.

Special thanks to Henry Steadman, who has worked so hard to pull another amazing cover out of the bag.

Thank you to the bloggers and reviewers who do so much to support authors and thank you to everyone who has taken the time to post a positive review online or has taken part in my blog tour. It is always noticed and much appreciated.

Last but not least, thank you SO much to my wonderful readers. I love receiving all your wonderful comments and messages and I am truly grateful for the support from each and every one of you.